Praise for *A Most Uncommon Degree of Popularity*

"Expertly blend[s] the nuances of the mother-daughter dance into a narrative . . . Astute and absorbing."
—*Library Journal*

"Jane Austen lives! Kathleen Gilles Seidel's wit, social insight, and wry, compassionate view sound like no one else."
—Mary Jo Putney, *New York Times* bestselling author of *The Marriage Spell*

"Absolutely the most fascinating writer. She turns an insightful and entertaining eye on the elite world of private school teenage girls and the moms who care . . . maybe too much?"
—Susan Elizabeth Phillips, *New York Times* bestselling author of *Natural Born Charmer*

"Tellingly—and often poignantly—pinpoints the deep and unexpected feelings as a mother and daughter negotiate the tricky, often fraught, transition from child to teenager."
—Elizabeth Buchan, *New York Times* bestselling author of *Wives Behaving Badly*

"A piercing tale of a perfect mother caught between her desires for her children and the realities of their lives . . . a page-turning, irresistible read."
—Amy Scheibe, author of *What Do You Do All Day?*

"Heart-wrenching, funny, and insightful . . . I gobbled this delicious novel up in one weekend."
—Karen Quinn, author of *Wife in the Fast Lane*

"A gripping and very adult tale, and above all, entertaining."
—Laurie Gwen Shapiro, author of *Brand X: The Boyfriend Account*

a most

uncommon

degree

of popularity

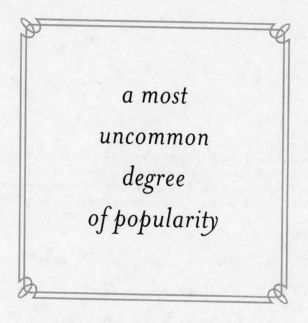

a most
uncommon
degree
of popularity

Kathleen Gilles Seidel

St. Martin's Griffin
New York

www.stmartins.com

Book design by Irene Vallye

Library of Congress Cataloging-in-Publication Data

Seidel, Kathleen Gilles.
   A most uncommon degree of popularity / Kathleen Gilles Seidel.
      p. cm.
   ISBN-13: 978-0-312-33327-0
   ISBN-10: 0-312-33327-7
   1. Girls—Fiction. 2. Popularity—Fiction. 3. Female friendship—Fiction.
4. Mothers and daughters—Fiction. 5. Rejection (Psychology)—Fiction.
6. Washington (D.C.)—Fiction. I. Title.

PS3569.E5136M64 2006
813'.54—dc22

                                                        2005052042

First St. Martin's Griffin Edition: February 2007

10 9 8 7 6 5 4 3 2 1

For Candy Fowler,

a fellow traveler

Her daughter enjoyed a most uncommon degree of popularity . . .

—Jane Austen, *Emma*

a most

uncommon

degree

of popularity

Our darling little babies turned into teenagers overnight.

It happened Labor Day weekend, right before the kids started sixth grade. One of the families with a swimming pool was having a party, and I was expecting the sort of event that this family had hosted a number of times before—invite the whole grade and let the kids splash around like happy little unisex puppies. Then my daughter, Erin, changed clothes three times, dashed across the street to lend her friend a shirt, and got six phone calls in thirty minutes.

She now stood at the railing of our wide front porch waiting for her ride. I had never imagined that my sweet child could look so ultrateen. Her dELiA's denim miniskirt rode low on her narrow hips, her tangerine Old Navy flip-flops showed off brightly polished toenails, and her white Express tank top emphasized the glow of her summer tan and the swell of her new, little breasts. She looked healthy, confident, and even—oh, lord—a little sexy.

I had one consolation. I knew that underneath this studied, teenaged ensemble she had on little-girl Limited Too underpants, which were waist-high white cotton and decorated with pink flying pigs. At least we weren't shopping for underwear at Victoria's Secret.

The midafternoon sun was still above the trees. When Erin's ride arrived, she launched herself down the front steps and across the yard. Her flip-flops slapped against her feet as she ran, and her shadow, slanting long across the grass, danced as she waved to her friends in the car.

My name is Lydia Meadows. I'm married with two kids, and we live in Washington, D.C., in a neighborhood with beautiful trees and three too many embassies, so that just when you are dashing madly to get home to pick up a forgotten pair of soccer cleats, one of the embassies is giving a party. This means you run into clogged streets, orange traffic cones, and hired parking valets who want you either to leave your car with them or to turn around and get back on the main road, which you don't want to do because you and the soccer cleats don't live on the main road, but on one of the neighborhood streets beyond the embassy.

My three closest friends have daughters who are my daughter's three closest friends. We live in the same neighborhood, and our kids go to the same school. Because we are always running into people we know while shopping in little stores with wrought-iron bistro tables on the sidewalks, our lives have a pleasant small-town feel. It is a completely bogus feeling—what small town has a dELiA's, an Old Navy, an Express, and a Limited Too, to say nothing (and, indeed, our kids do say nothing) of Congress and the White House? Our neighborhood is a theme-park version of a small town, but having grown up in an actual small town, I like the theme park better.

My daughter's new teenaged thing continued through the rest of Labor Day weekend; the phone rang continually. On Monday, in hopes of making my five-foot-three self look taller, I put on a cotton sweater that was the same shade of bottle green as my twill slacks. Since my eyes are greenish and I had used freckle-avoidance sunscreen faithfully this summer, I thought I looked pretty good. Erin, however, took one look at me and moaned, "Oh, Mom, you *match*," as if that were some kind of biblical sin. An hour later she asked if she could get her hair highlighted.

She is eleven years old. She isn't getting her hair highlighted.

She and her friends go to the Alden School, a small academically oriented private school with a specialty in music. It used to be a prim all-girls school—it was founded at the turn of the previous century under the delicious name of "Miss Alden's School"—and in those days the students wore uniforms. About fifteen years ago financial woes forced the school to become coed, and the uniforms have been replaced by a dress code that is Byzantine in its complexity. Students may not wear blue denim, but black denim is acceptable. Open-toed shoes may be worn as long as the shoe has a strap wrapping around the back of the ankle. Shirts must have a collar, but girls may wear jewel-necked shirts as long as the neck edge is finished with a contrasting trim or a faggoting or other decorative stitch. "Faggoting or other decorative stitch" is actually a phrase in the official dress code. Fortunately my husband and I are both lawyers, and so with our combined legal training and my knowledge of garment construction techniques—I sew and so unlike most people I do know what a faggoting stitch is—we are able to keep our children in compliance with the dress code. I can't imagine how other families do it.

Erin's first-day-of-school outfit Tuesday morning didn't comply with the spirit of the dress code, but when she came down the back stairs into the kitchen, I could spot no technical violations. She was wearing a little cotton-fleece drawstring skirt and a white collared blouse that was suitably tucked into the skirt's waistband. But the blouse was unbuttoned and beneath it she was wearing a turquoise tank top. The principal of the middle school was not going to like the extent to which the skirt resembled athletic wear, but fortunately we had a new headmaster this year, and I felt sure he would not form a committee for the purpose of adding to the dress code a prohibition against cotton-fleece drawstring skirts.

Private schools can be spectacularly absurd in their attention to detail.

The school is housed on the grounds of an old estate near Sibley Hospital. The high school and the administrative offices are in the seedily grand white mansion, which faces a broad, green lawn that we have not yet turned into a soccer field. Sloping behind the mansion are wooded grounds whose trees soften the lines of the two modern buildings that house the lower school and the middle school.

Normally my friends and I carpool to the kids' many activities with a schedule that makes both the school's dress and the nation's tax codes look straightforward, but on the first day of school each family takes and picks up its own children. So in the afternoon I parked on a neighborhood street—rules governing the formation and behavior of automobiles in the carpool line take up two and a half pages of the school handbook—followed a well-worn path through the trees, and emerged into the rear parking lot that was between the lower- and the middle-school buildings.

In good weather the students wait for their rides outside, and I could see my seven-year-old son on the lower-school playground in the midst of some sort of controlled seven-year-old rowdiness. I waved to him and then turned to the middle school to look for Erin.

Although this was not specified in the handbook, the eighth graders always wait for their rides near the big oak tree, the seventh graders take over the steps, and the sixth graders are on the blacktop. I didn't see Erin at first, but as I moved closer to the blacktop, I spotted her in the middle of a group of sixth-grade girls.

Indeed she and her three closest friends—the daughters of my three closest friends—were right in the middle of the group, and they were dressed virtually identically in these sweatpants-like skirts, unbuttoned but tucked-in white blouses, and vividly colored tanks. The other girls, none of whom had on this precise combination of garments, were hovering around the four of them. The farther a girl was standing from our four, the less animated she was.

If I hadn't known better, I would have said that my daughter and her friends were the popular girls.

Erin? Popular?

I had been a smart girl in the middle of Indiana. There was no way that I had been popular. I had had my place, I hadn't been a complete outcast, but on a normal day I had felt that every other girl in the school—at least among those worth thinking about—was prettier and better dressed. So I certainly wanted my daughter to feel better about her clothes and her friends than I had. I didn't want her to feel as if she didn't belong. I didn't want her to be the one standing at the edge of a group, not knowing whom to talk to. I didn't want her to feel left out, but I had never expected her to be *popular*.

Popular girls were manipulative little blond bitch-goddesses. Erin's hair was an unhighlighted brown.

I saw my friend Mimi coming across the parking lot. Her daughter, Rachel, was also wearing the drawstring skirt, white blouse, and bright tank.

I met her halfway and asked, "Were you popular in school?"

"Are you kidding?" She gestured toward herself. She was short, Jewish, and overweight. She did a great job of putting herself together; her dark hair was short and spiky, and she was not afraid to use her breadth as a canvas. Some days she was a walking art gallery. Today her jacket was hand-painted silk, with cascades of vermilion lilies and lime accents. Her jewelry was richly colored fused-glass pieces from the artists at the Glen Echo studios. She had perfect skin: flawlessly smooth without a single freckle or acne scar. I like thinking about texture, and so I had encouraged her to emphasize the loveliness of her skin by wearing smooth, finely woven fabrics. She had taken my advice and so her clothes and scarves floated around her with a wonderful liquidness. You would no more ask whether she looked fat than you would ask that about the Capitol. But she couldn't have had such confidence in her teen years.

I pointed toward the girls, wondering if she saw what I did.

She did. "Holy crap." Mimi shook her head, looked at me, her dark eyebrows arched in surprise, and then looked back at the girls. "I would have never expected this."

"Me neither."

"This explains why Rachel won't talk to me anymore. The popular girls never talked to *me*."

In the seventy-two hours since discovering that my daughter was a teenager, I had read about forty thousand books on parenting teenaged girls. I wasn't sure how much they were going to help. One had suggested that if my daughter became pregnant, we should first decide who had ownership of the issue. I have no idea what I would do in such a situation—Erin hadn't started menstruating yet—but a calm discussion of who "owned" the issue probably wouldn't happen right off. Another book had warned me to be aware of the "dark side" of raising a child in an affluent home; apparently extreme anxiety about being thrown in the poorhouse builds character.

If you believe these books, teenaged girls are confused, anxious, depressed, and destructive. We need to teach our daughters how to identify their pain, the source of which is skinny fashion models, high-achieving parents, and above all else, popular girls.

Popular girls shatter the self-esteem of other girls; they persecute outsiders, they torment, tease, bully, exclude, and scapegoat. The books were full of advice on how to arm your child against these Queen Bees, but none of the books, not a one, said what you should do if your own child was popular.

Erin looked pretty and happy as she stood in that crowd of girls, and frankly, that made me feel good. I was glad that she was happy. I had worked hard to have her be happy. Chattering away, she was gesturing with her arms, her body moving freely. If her back was turned toward one child, a moment later she was facing that child with her back to someone else. She didn't seem to be torturing anyone to establish her own status.

Of course, her status had been securely established in the first five minutes of the school day. She was one of the four girls wearing exactly the right clothes.

"Did you know that they were going to dress alike?" I asked Mimi.

Mimi shook her head. "No. Rachel did ask me to get her that skirt last week, but it was very cheap and she had found it on the Internet. I didn't have to go to the mall."

That was exactly what had happened in our house, too. The girls had obviously been smarter than sixth-grade kids ought to be. If they had chosen an expensive, logo-studded, designer skirt, chances were that at least one of us moms would have refused to buy it. In fact, I hope that we all would have. But this skirt was completely unobjectionable; the price was reasonable, the design modest. There was nothing at all special about it . . . until four girls, all of them friends, had worn it on the first day of middle school.

Later that afternoon Chloe Zimmerman's mother called me, and Alexis Fairling's and Ariel Sommers's mothers e-mailed me, asking where we had gotten the skirt. Their daughters wanted one, too.

My husband, Jamie, is a litigator, and he is preparing for a huge, messy case that will go to trial in Texas in January. It's pretty clear that the only way I am going to be able to get his attention until the case is over is to talk about the kids.

So after dinner I told him about what I had seen on the blacktop. "I think Erin is popular."

Jamie is a low-key guy with auburn hair, a dry wit, and a second baseman's agile build. On the surface at least, he is not your usual prima-donna trial attorney. He deliberately makes a neutral first impression and then gradually allows people to re-alize how much they like him. This is an asset during long tri-als. He has done well on several cases because after the first day and a half the jury decides that he is the only lawyer on either side that they can stand.

"That's good, isn't it?" he replied to my remark about Erin. "Aren't we glad that she has friends?"

I waved my hand. "We know that she has friends. Being

popular isn't about having friends. It's about having power. It's about being the Pol Pot of the sixth grade."

"So are we really concerned about our eleven-year-old child turning into a genocidal Cambodian dictator?"

I made a face at him.

"Seriously, Lydia, aren't you making too much of this? So Erin called her friends to see what they were going to wear on the first day of school. That's what girls do, isn't it?"

Of course, they did, and, of course, I was making too much of this. But that didn't mean that there was no issue.

I probably feel a little guilty because two years ago I quit work. I no longer draw a paycheck; I no longer have my day controlled by the demands of a job. When Jamie is extremely busy, I therefore feel that I have to justify demanding his attention, and so I tend to exaggerate things. *You need to listen to this because it is really, really important.* Then he reacts to my exaggeration, not to the thing itself.

Ah, marriage.

He and I met in law school and as stressed first-year law students, we were equals. We did everything together; we studied together, made course outlines together, and were generally exhausted together. Then, after we were married and both working at law firms, we continued on these parallel tracks, working at jobs that seemed equally important.

We continued to do everything together. We talked about our cases and edited each other's writing. We grocery-shopped together, we cooked together. We even set aside Thursday evenings to watch TV and fold laundry together. He was my friend, my companion, my colleague, my pal.

But I was the one who had the uterus. I loved Erin when she was no bigger than the vitamin pills I was taking on her behalf. After she was born, I downshifted careerwise and took a job at the Environmental Protection Agency. I believed in environmental causes, but it turned out that I didn't find them that interesting. I had liked law when it was about people, people trying to live with other people. At EPA, my work was about companies trying to live with government regulations. I didn't want to come home and talk about what I had done during the day.

Jamie became a partner with associates to manage, and he talked to them about his cases, not to me. We talked about Erin and later Thomas. Our lives became more and more traditional. Even though I was still working, I was in charge of hiring and managing whoever was taking care of the kids and the house. Any laundry that that lady didn't fold I did, and Jamie became not my friend, companion, and pal, but my husband.

As he took on more and more challenging cases, I started spending more time with the other moms whom I met on Saturday afternoons at the playground or the park. When Jamie was going to be out of town for a long stretch, I hired a babysitter one night a week and took photography classes at the Corcoran, an art museum with an extensive adult arts-education program. Whenever I was in a boring meeting, I would imagine taking pictures of the participants, mentally arranging the light and cropping the shot so that the portrait would be as unflattering as possible.

Like so many working mothers, I had assumed that things would become easier when the kids started school. Instead life became more difficult. The kids started having activities—activities that I had to sign them up for, activities that I had to get them to, activities that I also had to get myself to. Having a child in the first grade is a full-time job. No one tells you that, but it is true. Schools love to use Ivy League–educated lawyers and tenured college professors as classroom aides and temporary clerical support, and the lawyers cut out alphabet letters and the professors stuff envelopes because they desperately want the teachers to think that they are really good parents. The whole time I was growing up my primary goal had been to please and impress my teachers. I wasn't about to let go of that objective just because the teachers were now my kids' teachers.

I was always rushing. I liked to cook, but it seemed as if there was never anything in the house to make, and so either I stopped at the Safeway on the way home from work or I made pasta. Or both—stopped at the Safeway and bought pasta because I was too tired to think of anything else that everyone would eat. We live in an old house, and yes, it is grand and gorgeous with twelve-foot ceilings, leaded-glass windows, and two staircases, but the stupid thing is always falling apart. We had a nanny-housekeeper, but she was not going to call the plumber and negotiate with the electrician, and even though she kept the house cleaner than it ever would be under my care, she didn't deal with the mounds of mail that arrived every day. So there was mail everywhere in our house. Every available surface had mail on it.

How could I work when we got so much mail?

I hated feeling that I never had time for anything. I was always having to leave one place early to get to another place late. There were so many things that I liked to do that I never could do. I liked to sew. I liked to futz around home-decorating stores. I wanted to take actual photographs instead of just imagined ones.

Quitting work had felt like a hard decision, the hardest decision that any woman on the face of the earth ever had to make . . . which was demented. Quitting work is a hard decision if it means that you have to move from a house with a yard into a terrace apartment with a little patio. It's hard if it means that the kids would have to give up music lessons and summer camp. But when the worst consequence of quitting work is that when people at parties ask "What do you do?"—which is the only thing anyone ever asks at Washington parties—and you have to say "Nothing," that's not really hard; that's what Jamie calls "white suffering," the agonies of the affluent.

But the message I had always received was that a woman has to have a career, that work is her identity, not her relationships, not her children, not her home or her hobbies, but her work. If a woman doesn't work, she is nothing. My mother hadn't had a career, and she had become frustrated and angry, unwilling to engage in anything that she considered beneath her intelligence, but unable to find any volunteer or housewife activities that weren't.

I was afraid I would disappear if I quit work. I was afraid people would stop seeing me.

I finally made the decision standing in the pediatrician's

office. My son Thomas had an ear infection. I had soccer car-pool duty that day, and I wanted to get his prescription filled before I picked the girls up. So I hurried him out of the exam-ining room, went to the front desk, and presented his fee slip and our fifteen-dollar co-pay to the receptionist. All she needed to do was take the slip, pick up her pen, write "$15" in a little box, rip off my pink copy, and hand that back to me. But she had a long-sleeved shirt underneath her smock, and apparently there was something deeply troubling about the cuff of this shirt. She needed to twitch it into place before she took the paperwork from me. So she twitched her cuff, took the fee slip, looked at it, and picked up her pen. Then I heard someone ask what time she was leaving and before she an-swered, *she laid her pen down.* I wanted to choke her. Surely she accepted payments and separated fee slips a hundred times a day. Surely she could do this while she said what time she was leaving, surely a little multitasking here wasn't too much to ask, but no, she had to say "five-fifteen" empty-handed. And then, just as I knew she would do, she adjusted her cuff before picking up her pen again. Do you know how long it takes to adjust a cuff?

I was truly, truly ready to kill her, and I was even more ready to murder the kind of person that I had become, because it really does only take one point five seconds to adjust a cuff. I was every bit as angry and bitchy as my unfulfilled, nonwork-ing mother had ever been. If that was going to happen anyway, I might as well do it while having fun in the home-dec stores.

So I quit, and I loved it. I loved the freedom and the flexi-bility. I loved having some order and serenity in our family's life. I loved not having to go to the office on beautiful autumn days. I loved not having to go on cold, rainy ones.

I'd always been active in the kids' classrooms, but when I was working, I had never done anything for the school as a whole. Now I had time for that. Last year I had been on the curriculum committee. My friend Blair and I had agreed to chair the Spring Fair, and I would probably run for the board of trustees the following year.

I'm not a perfectionist, so there is still clutter in the house, but it's no longer hopeless clutter. In three hours, with a little help from the kids, I can make the first floor look as if some magazine-type family lived in it, and since we have a one-day-a-week cleaning lady, we aren't going to be shut down by the health department.

It's a very nice way to live, it really is. I have *time*. I can finish reading the books for my book club. I can stand in a parking lot after a school function and talk to my friends for forty-five minutes. I don't want to kill Erin when she feels that she has to try on seventeen million versions of the same pair of pants. The expiration of my driver's license does not cause a crisis.

But Jamie and I have become completely traditional in our marriage. He makes the money, and I take care of the house and the kids. He has absolutely no idea what I do all day. He likes the fact that our lives run smoothly; he's very proud of the kids and recognizes that that is, in some measure, to my credit. But he never thinks about what it takes to achieve this, and he would have no clue how much of it involves relationships—relationships with the kids' teachers, relationships with their doctors, relationships with the soccer coaches, relationships with the plumber and the electrician, relationships with my friends. Not only do I have to tend to my relationships, I have to monitor the kids' relationships, how they are getting along with their teachers, coaches, and friends.

I negotiate, I schmooze, I placate. Isn't that what lawyers do?

At the end of the first week of school, Erin and her three friends decided to have a sleepover at our house on Friday night. This was quite routine. The four of them were at one house or another at least once every weekend. Around seven o'clock she told me that three of the "guys"—apparently they were no longer "boys"—were coming over to watch a movie. While this was not routine, it seemed like no big deal. She had named the boys, and they were all kids we had known forever.

When the boys arrived, there were five of them, not three, but the two additional ones were also familiar faces, so I thought that, too, was no big deal. We keep plenty of sodas in the basement refrigerator, so whether we have four, seven, or nine kids staring at a TV screen doesn't make much difference, just an extra couple bags of microwave popcorn.

Oh, silly me.

2

The Alden School is a divided community. The largest segment of the school population comes from families like ours. As different as the four of us friends and our husbands are as individuals, we have a lot in common as a sociological phenomenon. We are "meritocrats." Aristocrats are born into their privileges; we meritocrats have earned ours, or at least that's what we believe about ourselves.

None of us grew up in D.C. or Boston or New York or whatever cities we have landed in. We got here because we had had great SAT scores.

We benefited from the decision of many private colleges and universities that they would no longer educate only the trust fund–cushioned offspring of the Protestant establishment. So those colleges went looking for socioeconomically ordinary kids with great SAT scores, and they found us in places such as Indianapolis, Missoula, and Arkansas City. Smart, ambitious, and goal-oriented, we spent the next four to eight years getting extraordinary educations, and at the end we married one another and didn't go home. We moved to the cities and went to work.

Men and women alike, we became lawyers and consultants. We worked in communications and information. We made money and we had power, and we felt that we had earned our place through intelligence, educational credentials, and hard work. Family, breeding, and manners have had nothing to do with our success, and we are simultaneously proud and defensive about that. Commentators who think that we are providing insufficient moral leadership use the term *meritocrats* disparagingly, but none of us can figure out how it can be an insult. We are proud that we have earned what we have.

We aren't social climbers. We aren't pretending to be of aristocratic summer-in-Bar-Harbor lineage even though we are now the ones who can afford second homes in Maine. We are too well-educated to crave the flashy tastelessness of the nouveau-riche land developers even though our money is every bit as new as theirs. Our middle-American backgrounds show in how informal our lives are. Everyone always answers her own door and serves at her own table. None of us have breast implants, and we wear comfortable shoes. My friends and I are middle-class soccer moms.

With upper-crust incomes.

The other families at Alden are the alumnae families in

which the mothers and the grandmothers went to Alden themselves. They do represent the aristocrats, the summer-in-Bar-Harbor old-line money, the Wasp establishment, the traditionally privileged, the people who would have had their heads cut off if we'd had a revolution in 1950.

As individuals the alumnae mothers are as different from one another as we are. Some of the women are delicately feminine; others are jolly hockey-sticks athletic. Some are conscientious and reliable; some whine. Some are intelligent and belong to interesting book clubs; others shop a lot.

But you can always tell them from us. They are mothers; we are moms. Their hair is light and smooth, their cheekbones are good, and their figures are trim. They always put their best foot forward and are much more disciplined about their grooming than we are. There is a confidence to them, an ease and poise that is gradually giving way to bewilderment.

They are bewildered because we have taken their place, a place that they didn't even know they'd had until they lost it. Sometimes that "place" is literal. Blair and her family live in a house that one of the alumnae moms had grown up in. More often we seem to be living the lives that their parents grew up in. We have money; they don't anymore. We have jobs with influence; they are realtors. We've stayed married; they haven't.

They have assumed too much. Their parents had always enough money; they assumed that they would as well. When they were girls, they had always been in the right dance classes; they had always been invited to the right birthday parties. As a result, they assumed that those opportunities would come to their children as a matter of course.

But now they are living side by side with us, and we never assume that anything will ever happen as a matter of course. We believe that you have to work for everything. Just as we once studied and studied to be sure that we passed the bar exam on our first try, we now program the speed dials on our phones on the first day that a preschool day camp releases its registration forms. We use our BlackBerries and our fax machines to get our kids on a soccer team with their friends. Our kids don't just get invited to the right birthday parties; we compete madly to be sure that our kids *host* the right birthday parties.

We are probably very annoying.

Several times during the year the school sponsors grade-level coffees, giving the parents (i.e., the mothers) an opportunity to network (i.e., gossip). We "new" families attend faithfully because the coffees are another chance to show the school what really great parents we are. Even the mothers who work show up on their way to the office.

Although the alumnae mothers are very active in the school's many fund-raising activities, they come only to the first of these coffees. Then their attendance drops off. Either they don't need to have the staff think that they are really great parents or our obsessive interest in our children's lives drives them nuts.

The first sixth-grade parents' coffee was Tuesday morning

of the second week of school. It was held in the multipurpose room of the middle school. The tables had been pushed against the wall, and the chairs were arranged in a rough circle.

I knew that Mimi Gold would not be there. Although she is just as obsessed as the rest of us, Mimi always has to miss the first coffee. She runs a nanny-placement service, and the first two weeks of September are always devoted to working out problems arising from new placements.

But my other two close friends, Blair Branson and Annelise Rosen, had already arrived. Annelise had her purse on the chair next to her. She was saving a seat for me. We always did that sort of thing for one another.

Of the four of us, Annelise and I met first. The girls were babies, and we were two attorneys desperate to talk about infant poo and sleep schedules. We were also both midwesterners. I am from Indiana, and Annelise is from Wisconsin; she and I are friendly, open, and pride ourselves on our unpretentiousness.

People often mistake one of us for the other. We both are small with boyish builds. We both have our hair cut in short feathery layers, and both of us would be dishwater blondes if we didn't spend a lot of money on highlights.

But her features are broad and Dutch while mine are narrow and Irish. My eyes are greenish blue while hers are an unusual dramatically dark brown. We also don't carry ourselves the same way. She is gentler than I am, more diffident, more vulnerable. Her husband, Joel, is pretty critical of her. I don't know why she puts up with it, but she does.

Our fourth friend, Blair Branson, is from South Carolina,

and people who don't know better assume that she must be a debutante from a gracious old Southern family. She is the most conventionally attractive of the four of us—she has shoulder-length black hair and very fair skin—and she dresses almost as well as our daughters do, wearing clothes of a classic, conservative cut, but in colors that are boldly feminine—aqua, periwinkle, persimmon, and lime.

If she were the old-line aristocrat that she looks like, she would still be in South Carolina, divorced and wondering why someone like me was living in her grandmother's beautiful house.

Blair's father was a pharmacist, and her mother spent all her time working in his store, never going to white-glove luncheons with the other ladies. Blair had been like me, the smartest girl in the grade, the outsider. Being the outsider was what she knew, what she was comfortable with. When she went to college at Penn, she realized that what made her an outsider there was not being smart and ambitious—everyone was smart and ambitious—but being a Southerner. So she became more Southern.

She is the most guarded of the four of us, the one who has been the hardest to get to know. But if Annelise and I are the most alike in personality and appearance, then Blair and I have the most abilities and interests in common. We had both been art history majors in college and we each have a good eye and a strong design sense. When I set out to waste time in a home-dec shop, I always call Blair to come with me.

Of the nearly twenty-five people who had come to this parents' coffee, I knew everyone there except for one woman. I nudged Annelise and Blair. They shook their heads. Neither of them knew her, either. She looked slender and fit, and her hair was chin-length and light. Wearing nicely fitting pleated khaki trousers, a sleeveless black silk shirt, and narrow black loafers, she was well-groomed in the understated way that the alumnae mothers have. I would have introduced myself to her, but it was clear that the women who had stopped in on their way to work were eager to get the meeting started so I stayed in my seat.

Eight minutes after the coffee was supposed to begin—which wasn't bad—the principal of the middle school, Martha Shot, began speaking. Mrs. Shot herself was a graduate of the school, and her manner and dress were a bit too prim for our tastes, but she was the principal and we listened to school principals.

According to her, our darling children were going to start being significantly less darling. That they hated the way we dressed would be the least of it. "They will look you right in the eye and lie to you," Mrs. Shot said. "If they call you from their cell phone and say they are at Susie's house and Susie's mother is there, tell them that you are going to call Susie's landline and ask to speak to her mother. The story may suddenly change."

My child would never do that. Every mother in the circle must have been thinking that. I certainly was, but we were probably all fooling ourselves.

"You aren't going to be seeing too much of this in the sixth grade," she said. "What we face in sixth grade are social issues. Friendships realign, and some of the kids are going to feel excluded. What most of them want, at this age, is to be exactly like all the other kids."

I understood that. My mother had wanted my brother and me to be smart. We had the *Encyclopedia Britannica* and subscribed to the Sunday *New York Times*, even though it arrived in Indiana on the following Wednesday. If she had ever thought about it, Mother would have been proud that I didn't dress like the other girls. Somehow that proved I was smart.

What I had wanted was to be smart *and* exactly like everyone else.

"The children," Mrs. Shot continued, "especially the girls, become very cliquish. There is a clear hierarchy, and each child knows her own place even if her parents do not. Unfortunately the system is always in motion, and the individual child can feel deeply hurt."

She paused, waiting for someone to speak. No one did. I'm a good sport at moments like this, always willing to jump in with a vague, conciliatory remark.

So I said, "Is being eleven as awful as we remember it?"

There was a sudden stirring in the room. At least half of the women were glaring resentfully at me.

What was going on? Why were they looking at me this way? What had I done wrong? The whole point of vague, conciliatory remarks is that they are never wrong.

It was those skirts, those four stupid, cotton-fleece drawstring skirts, four scraps of fabric declaring which girls were in and which were out.

I wasn't a too-smart-to-be-popular junior-high semi-misfit

anymore. I was now the mother of a popular girl, and the other mothers were going to make me pay for that.

I know how your daughter feels, I wanted to hop up on my chair and shriek. *I used to be one of those girls who didn't know where to stand, didn't know whom to talk to.*

But no one cared about what I knew or understood. They only cared about their own daughters.

"Children are very vulnerable at this age," Fran Zimmerman, Chloe's mom, said finally. Although Chloe played on Erin's soccer team, they weren't particularly close. In fact, I didn't think that Erin had ever been to the Zimmermans' house. Chloe had been to ours, of course, but that was because I was nutty enough to let Erin invite fifty million squealing piglets in for slumber parties. "Exclusionary behavior is never acceptable."

Fran Zimmerman was angry. Her shoulders were back, her jaw was forward. "Some children exclude other children just to show that they can do it."

She had better not be talking about *my* kid. Every time Erin had more than three or four girls to something, she included Chloe.

"Cliques are very dangerous," Ariel Sommers's mother said. "They can be very destructive."

I felt Annelise and Blair shifting uneasily beside me. Were these other women calling our four girls a clique?

It's just a matter of seat belts, I wanted to explain. *Blair and Annelise drive sedans with only five seat belts so we have to limit our car pools to four girls. The girls aren't a clique; they are a car pool.*

Of course the car pool had a uniform—cotton-fleece draw-string skirts. That might sound a bit like a clique.

I felt sick.

The new headmaster, Chris Goddard, had come in after the meeting had started. He was standing, leaning against one of the counters, his arms folded. I could look at him by shifting my eyes slightly. He was a lean man with close-cropped hair and wire-rimmed glasses. He had a thoughtful look about him, but the lines on his face were deeper than you would expect from a man in his forties. He straightened and spoke. "Exclusion is going to happen. Kids do have friends, and sometimes it is hard to distinguish between appropriate acts of friendships and inappropriate exclusion."

"No, it is not hard to make that distinction," Fran Zimmerman insisted. "And it is very, very painful for a child to be left out of something, particularly when the other children insist on flaunting it."

"But some things are just unforgivable, whether they are repeated or not," Alexis Fairling's mom said. "This school year has gotten off to an awful start."

Now Linda Fairling had no business complaining about her child being left out of things. It wasn't Alexis who got left out of things, it was Linda herself. She was forever trying to maneuver her way into one of our car pools, but she was always late, always, always, always. I'll drive a car pool with Genghis Khan if he—or rather his wife—is going to show up on time. With Linda Fairling I won't.

"I have to agree," Diane Sommers said. "Some of the girls have been devastated at the level of rejection."

Blair couldn't help herself. Her black hair brushed against the yoke of her lemon-colored shirt as she turned to look at Diane. "The level of rejection? What are you talking about?"

"First there was Adam's party"—that was the swimming pool party the Saturday before Labor Day—"and then there was Erin's party, and—"

"What?" I interrupted. "Erin's party? Erin didn't have a party."

Now that was exactly the wrong thing to say. "You weren't there?" Fran Zimmerman almost sounded happy that I was so utterly in the wrong. "You didn't know your daughter was having a party Friday night? A failure to provide adequate supervision is a cause for grave concern."

"Of course, I provided adequate supervision," I snapped, wondering if I had. "It wasn't a party, just a bunch of kids watching a movie."

"How many were there?" she demanded.

"Nine."

The room was quiet.

Okay, that didn't sound so great. To many people nine kids was a lot, nine kids was a party. But our house is big, and my housekeeping standards are cheerful. The furniture in our sun-room is indestructible, the carpet is the color of spilled Coke, and there is always some kind of salty, greasy junk food in the cabinet next to the refrigerator with the sodas. I had not had to do a thing in order to have nine kids over.

But some of the women in this circle had houses every bit as big as mine. Why did my kid have to invite their kids over when they didn't invite her? I had read Jane Austen. There were some situations in which dinner invitations didn't have to be reciprocated; if you were too la-di-da to slum it in your guests' home, then they didn't have to invite you back or something like that. But surely that didn't apply here.

Or did it? Had Erin's cotton-fleece drawstring skirt turned her into Lady Catherine de Bourgh?

"As Mr. Goddard said," I replied, cowardly invoking our new headmaster's authority, "these kids are her friends. She needs to be able to invite her friends over to her house for casual get-togethers without worrying that it is going to hurt other kids' feelings."

"What we parents have to worry about," preached Diane Sommers, "is the children who *like* to hurt other children's feelings." Then she turned to me with a simpering, wildly insincere smile. "Not that that applies in your daughter's case, of course."

That did it. I'm going to go to heaven, there can be no question about it. My slate has been forever wiped clean by the fact that I didn't haul off and slug Diane Sommers. Talk about white suffering. These women were hurt because their daughters had been excluded. The girls might be over it by now, but the mothers weren't. They felt bad and so they were trying to punish me by making me feel as bad as they did. I felt Annelise press her arm against mine in support.

Some of the alumnae mothers were slipping out of the room. You couldn't blame them. To endure this conversation, your goal in life had to be keeping your child from ever feeling bad for one single minute of his or her—mostly her—entire life. Boys' mothers seem a little saner than girls' mothers, probably because girls' mothers relive through their daughters every injury ever done to them when they were growing up.

Linda Fairling chimed in. "The books also caution against mothers duplicating the children's social patterns. One of them calls it the 'Mothers' Mafia,' women who collude or are complicitous in their daughters' exclusionary actions."

Collude or are complicitous in . . . I hadn't heard talk like that since I quit practicing law. She made it sound as if we could be prosecuted under the RICO Act when all we wanted to do was get our kids to places on time, which meant not driving with her. No wonder the alumnae mothers thought we were deranged. We were.

But Annelise, lovely, gentle, brown-eyed, please-don't-criticize-me Annelise, had put her purse on an empty chair to save it for me. Did that make her a blond bitch-goddess mom?

Chris Goddard stepped forward again. "There's no way that the school—or any other institution or person—can keep a child from occasionally feeling rejected or having hurt feelings. And, to be honest, the school's efforts are going to be focused on identifying kids, whether bullies or victims, who are at significant emotional risk."

That was, thank God, a conversation stopper. People were willing to criticize my child endlessly, but no one wanted to identify her own daughter as being at "significant emotional risk."

"And," he continued, "the fifth-grade teachers probably would have already spotted the hard-core bullies, but they report that this class is one of the nicest that they have seen."

I appreciated that. It seemed as if he were standing up for

me and my daughter. He wasn't going to say flat-out that these other mothers were overreacting, but he was coming pretty close.

It was a good note to end on. Mrs. Shot stood back up and reminded us how to log on to the school's Web site, and the meeting was over.

Fran Zimmerman, Diane Sommers, and Linda Fairling left the room quickly. They didn't want to talk to us even though Diane Sommers needed to; she had e-mailed me yesterday about wanting to borrow my coffee urns. But Candace Singer was waiting by the water fountain when Blair, Annelise, and I came out of the multipurpose room.

Candace was a gray-eyed, medium-framed woman who wore a lot of navy. She was on the silent auction committee for this year's Spring Fair. Blair and I were chairing the whole fair, but the auction committee was the most important committee.

I hoped that she wanted to talk to us about the silent auction, but her intent mom-with-a-mission look suggested that we weren't going to be that lucky. She spoke to Blair. "I didn't want to say anything at the meeting, but I thought you would want to know—"

My experience is that when people tell you things that they "think you want to know," the issue at hand is usually something that *they* want you to know, but that you could have been just peachy without ever having heard word one.

"—that Brittany was rather rude to my Suzanne the other day."

Brittany is Blair's older daughter. She and her husband Bruce had given both their girls names that start with *B*.

"I'm sorry to hear that," Blair said. "I shall certainly speak to her about it."

"Oh, no, don't—at least don't say anything specific. Suzanne would die if she thought that I was interfering. But surely you will want to discuss the general need for politeness with her."

Semifaux Southerner that she is, Blair did not like being lectured about the importance of good manners. "You will need to be a little more specific."

Candace glanced up and down the hall as if there was something intensely secret in what she was about to say. "At lunch yesterday Suzanne was talking about a new dress that we got her, and apparently Brittany completely snubbed her and didn't say one word about it. Brittany was sitting right in the middle of the table and refused to participate in the conversation. Just refused. Didn't say a word. She made it very clear that she didn't like the dress, and now Suzanne thinks that we should return it."

I stared at her. This kid got a new dress. She liked her dress. But Brittany Branson did not say anything about the dress when it was described to her so Suzanne didn't like the dress anymore.

"Yesterday?" Blair sounded relieved. "That explains it. Brittany had a headache yesterday. No wonder she wasn't very chatty. She felt terrible. I had to pick her up early."

"But is that an excuse for spoiling another child's pleasure in a new dress?"

"I'm sure she didn't mean to," Blair apologized. "When she gets one of those headaches, it's all that she can do to hold herself together."

That explanation wasn't good enough for Candace Singer. She had come into this conversation with a story—her daughter had been the victim; popular-girl Brittany had been the tormentor. Candace didn't want a rational explanation for Brittany's behavior; she wanted to make Brittany's mother squirm.

Blair wasn't squirming. She was furious. "I would suppose," she said, her voice very slow, very Southern, "that—"

I didn't think any of us needed to hear what Blair was supposing. Like me, Blair used to practice law, and she knew how to fight dirty. I upended my purse, letting its contents scatter across Blair's feet.

"Oh, Lydia, you klutz," Annelise said brightly. She, too, was an ex-lawyer and had clearly understood the intention behind my maneuver. She took Candace by the arm and started down the hall. "Tell me, Candace, where did you buy this dress? I never know where to take Elise anymore."

Blair knelt down to help me gather up what had been in my purse. "Brittany had a migraine," she whispered angrily. "She wasn't rude. She was sick."

I winced as I saw my cell phone on the floor next to the zippered pouch in which I carry Band-Aids and safety pins. Why hadn't I thought about my poor phone before I started throwing stuff? I picked it up tenderly and was relieved to see that its little green window was still glowing.

"Apparently popular girls aren't allowed to be sick," I said, standing back up. It was so strange to talk about Erin and her friends this way. "Everything they do will be interpreted as a criticism of the less-confident kids."

"Because their mothers are telling them to interpret it that way," Blair snapped as she handed me my car keys.

All of this was ironic because Blair had had her own bad experiences with popular girls. On her first day of junior high, the girls she had eaten lunch with all through elementary school had pretended that there was no room for her at their lunch table. "Those little bitches wouldn't even look at me," she had reported.

And now someone was thinking of her daughter as one of the little bitches. Things do look different when your own child has a seat at the table.

Annelise was waiting for us at the door, and the three of us started walking toward the parking lot.

"Do our girls really have that much power?" Annelise asked. "Where do they get it from?"

"Maybe it's our fault," I said. "Is there a feminine for mafiosos? Mafiosas? Because apparently that's what we are, the Mothers' Mafia." I also had seen this in one of the books on raising teenagers. "Conspiring to keep unworthy children from being included in birthday parties, play dates, and Scout troops."

"That's definitely me." Annelise was rarely sarcastic, but she was now. "Trying to keep kids out of the Scout troop."

Annelise had been the girls' Brownie leader, and she had wanted to keep the troop together, but Girl Scouts seemed so uncool that at the end of Brownies it had fizzled. Keeping kids *out* of the troop had not been her problem.

We were heading toward her car. She had borrowed my 178-inch tablecloth last week. On her way to school this morning, she had picked it up from the dry cleaner's, and it was in her car now.

"What happened to the whole 'it takes a village to raise a child' thing?" she continued. "Why does working together turn us into organized criminals?"

"Because the mothers of popular girls are supposed to be even worse than the popular girls themselves," I said.

"I don't know how you can say that." Blair sniffed. "I thought we were a whole lot nicer to Candace Singer than she deserved."

"That's only because Lydia dumped her purse on your feet," Annelise pointed out. "If we had let you, you would have confirmed every awful stereotype about mean, bitchy popular girls."

"She criticized my daughter," Blair defended herself. "What was I supposed to do?"

"Be glad that you have friends who dump their purses on your feet," I said. I took my tablecloth from Annelise. "Do you think there's any chance that our girls are as nasty as we always thought the popular girls were?"

"I just can't believe that," Annelise said. "Not about our girls."

Our girls weren't mean. They were lively and good-tempered, they were generous and confident, secure in their relationships with one another. That's why other kids liked them. That's why other kids noticed what they wore and wanted to be invited to our homes.

And that's why the mothers of those other kids were accusing them of inappropriately exclusionary behavior.

The three of us were perfectly capable of standing here for another half an hour, saying the same things over and over, but coming toward us across the parking lot was Pam Ruby, one of the few boys' mothers present at the coffee. She was accompanied by the new blond woman whom Pam introduced as Mary Paige Caudwell.

"Mary Paige and her daughter, Faith, just moved back to town from Texas," Pam said, "but she went to school here. Her grandmother was Florence Paige, Mrs. Chester T. Paige."

It took me a minute to place the name. The Alden School's dreary and inadequate gym was named the "Mrs. Chester T. Paige Gymnasium." So Mary Paige Caudwell wasn't just an alumna; she was an alumna from a family with "a history of giving." Having a history of giving scored a lot of points with the school's development office.

Blair and Annelise shook hands with Mrs. Chester T. Paige's granddaughter. My arms were linked under the folds of the plastic-swaddled tablecloth so I had to make do with a nod. I tried to make it an incredibly friendly nod; I didn't want anyone thinking me the stuck-up mother of a bitchy popular girl.

We chatted about nothing for a moment, and then Mary Paige asked about getting her daughter—Mrs. Chester T.'s great-granddaughter—onto the soccer team.

"Oh, goodness," Blair answered. "I hate to say this in light of that meeting, but the team's been full for years."

For all that we are supposed to be meritocrats, the soccer team that our girls play on is as closed and restricted as a debutante ball. Our kids "earned" their place on the team not because of their talent, but because we, their parents, had been good with speed dials and fax machines back when they were five.

The weekend soccer teams are organized not by the school, but by the city. A parent-coach assembles a bunch of five-year-olds who spend at least one season swarming randomly around the ball as if they were a little pack of honeybees. Then if the kids—and more important, the parents—get along, they pretty much stay together for years. Because the league wants the kids to be playing, not sitting on the bench, there is a limit to how many can be on a team. Until a player leaves, the coach can't add additional players just because the potential new player is an exceptionally talented athlete or, as happens more often on the girls' teams, is everyone's best friend. Otherwise the cool teams would have forty girls on them, and the players would be better prepared for beauty college—as they would spend their time playing with one another's hair—than for an athletic competition.

"There are other teams with vacancies," Annelise said.

"But this is the team that she wants to be on," Mary Paige said. "Don't you think that the league would understand the difficulties associated with moving into the area?"

"They may understand," I said. The tablecloth was getting heavy, and my arms were starting to sweat against the plastic. "But they won't do anything. Every year someone tries to get them to change their mind, and it never works. We've had some of the city's finest legal talent threatening to sue to get their kids on a particular team, and it doesn't work."

"It can't hurt to make the call, can it? Perhaps asking nicely will be more effective than threatening to sue."

There was a little edge to her voice. I hadn't intended to be flip, although it was true about parents threatening to sue, but apparently my new self—stuck-up bitch-goddess mom— had shone through.

"At least the sixth-grade girls' ensemble has fall auditions," Mary Paige continued. "When I was a student, they were done in the spring of the fifth grade, and a new girl didn't have any chance at all."

"Does your daughter sing?" This was from Blair.

"She has a nice little voice," Mary Paige said with a tone that indicated that we were supposed to acknowledge this as false modesty.

I could sense Annelise and Blair exchanging glances.

Alden's particular strength as a school is music. All the little kids sing in the lower-school choruses, but in middle school the students with the best voices start getting more opportunities. The sixth-grade girls' ensemble consists of ten girls in white dresses and violet sashes, and every year they sing at a White House tea. It is quite a big deal.

The girls have to audition, and ten are selected. My kids aren't musical and so I didn't have a horse in this race, but I knew that people had expended a lot of energy last spring counting to ten. The conclusion seemed to be that for this grade it would be pretty easy to predict which ten girls would be chosen, and all three of Erin's friends were on every list.

But Mrs. Barton, the music director of the middle school, while not an alumna herself, had been at the school for almost thirty years, and she had liked the place better before it went coed and all of us motley new people had shown up. To the extent that she could, she ran the sixth-grade ensemble like a debutante ball. If the last spot came down to a choice between an alumnae daughter, as Faith Caudwell was, and another girl, Mrs. Barton would find a reason to give the spot to a girl whose mother had been in the ensemble.

If Faith Caudwell really did have a "nice little voice," then counting to ten had suddenly gotten a whole lot harder.

3

There are, no doubt, children who lovingly confide in their mothers, sharing their secrets, sorrows, and dreams. The rest of us have to rely on the car pools. You sit in the driver's seat and never say a word. After a while, if you are lucky, the kids forget that you are there and they start talking.

All four of us listened intently for any indications of major bitch-goddess behavior. The girls weren't angels, but they didn't seem to be criticizing the other girls endlessly. And at home Erin seemed happy. She was being nice to her little brother. Whenever trouble is brewing in our family, the first sign of it is usually Erin tormenting Thomas.

So maybe the books were wrong. Maybe you could have at the center of a middle-school class a group of friendly, happy, healthy girls who, while a definite group, weren't predators, who didn't realize how much power they had, girls whose excellent childhood nutrition had somehow resulted in perfect saintliness.

But what else would you expect the mother of a popular girl to think?

The school's Spring Fair was one of its major fund-raising activities. During the day there were pony rides, a moon bounce, a crafts sale, a plant sale, and tons of games. In the evening there was a barbecue with silent and live auctions. Blair and I were chairing the fair this year; it was the first time that non-alums had run it.

Although we were determined not to let planning the fair take over our lives for the next seven months, we sat down to start going over the material from the previous years on Thursday of the second week of school. The auditions for the sixth-grade girls' ensemble had been on Wednesday, and the results were going to be announced on Friday.

"We've got to do something on Thursday," Blair had said. "Otherwise I am going to spend the whole day fretting. Brittany is going to die if she is girl number eleven."

The important information about the fair had been put in binders instead of files, and I laid the notebooks out on the kitchen table, wondering which of the previous chairpersons had been loopy enough to cover six three-ring binders with cobalt-and-lemon Provençal fabric. It is true that one day toward the end of my kitchen renovation, Blair and I—who liked art projects as much as our kids did—had covered a pencil cup, a letter box, and a couple of in-out trays with the room's black-and-white toile fabric, but we knew that we were wasting time, and somehow that made it okay.

That she and I had both gone to law school was a sign of the feminist movement's growing pains. Like Annelise we had gone to law school because we knew that we "had" to have careers, and it seemed as if going to law school would keep our options open longer. Since we were hard-working and determined, we had done well in law school, and since we were thorough and organized, we were perfectly adequate lawyers.

But we were more suited to girly work, the kind that "hear me roar" women weren't supposed to do. We could sew and we liked looking at wallpaper books. We were each slowly establishing second careers for ourselves. Blair had taken a number of classes in landscape design and was now working with a few clients on their yards. Enough people had raved about the pictures I had taken of my kids and their friends that I was now photographing children professionally.

Neither of us, however, thought of ourselves as "working." If we had to join one team or the other, we would join Annelise, who was definitely not working, rather than Mimi, who was running a successful business.

We examined the workmanship on the notebook covers. Blair thought that we could have done a better job, and I said that yes, we could have, but I hoped that we wouldn't have done it in the first place, much less have done it better. Once we stopped looking at the notebooks' pretty clothes and started looking at the information enclosed, we realized that it wasn't organized usefully.

"Wouldn't it make more sense," I said, "to have all the financial information in one, all the food contracts in another, and so on?"

Blair agreed. "Otherwise we are going to be flipping through six notebooks."

We started opening the binders' rings and lifting the pages out. My kitchen table was a refectory one so it was easy to pull out an extra leaf so that we could make many different piles.

I loved my kitchen. I survived my last year at EPA by going to work and thinking about the remodeling plans. The kitchen extended across the entire width of the house, and we had gained yet more space by taking out the separate butler's pantry. My kitchen was now only slightly smaller than an F-14 fighter jet and had about the same amount of technology.

The walls and cabinetry were a butter yellow, and the granite countertops were charcoal. On the walls were oversized black-and-white pictures that I had taken of the children. A big reading chair was upholstered in the black-and-white toile, and the toile was repeated in the roman shades at the windows. The table nestled into the bay window, and a padded bench— my son, Thomas, was incapable of sitting still in a regular chair—curved along the wall underneath the window. A narrow shelf near the table held the pencil cups and storage boxes that Blair and I had covered, as I had assumed that the kids would do their homework at the kitchen table.

They didn't. They did their homework on the kitchen floor. And not on the open carpeted space in front of the television. No, they stretched out on the slate between the island and the sink so that I had to step over them, their binders, and their backpacks if I was doing something as silly as trying to make dinner. And despite the enormity of this kitchen, they invariably managed to position themselves so that they got not only in my way, but in each other's, thus giving themselves something else to fight about. *He kicked me, Mom. He did it on purpose. . . . Yeah, but she looked at me funny.*

During the daytime, the side door to the kitchen was never locked when we were at home, and everyone knew that. So if my station wagon was in the driveway, close friends came around and let themselves in just as if we all lived in Mayberry or on Walton's Mountain. Back when a more elegant family had lived here, this door was probably the "tradesmen's entrance" to the house, but it was now the door all our friends used. In fact, the only people who came to my front door were the actual tradesmen—the delivery guys and the repairmen.

Once Blair and I got the papers reorganized, I opened my laptop, and we started entering numbers in a spreadsheet—the previous chairs had been too ladylike to know how to use Microsoft Excel—when we heard the door open.

It was Mimi. She was flushed and her lips were narrow. "I can't believe it; I've never been so angry in my life."

With her short, spiky haircut Mimi always looked a little aggressive. Now she was on whatever the Jewish equivalent of a warpath is. I got up, moving toward the door. "What's wrong? What happened?"

Behind me, Blair rose more slowly. "Is it the ensemble?"

"It sure is. Brittany and Elise are in. Rachel is not."

So Blair's and Annelise's daughters had made it into the ensemble. Mimi's had not.

I looked back over my shoulder at Blair. Her shirt was ultramarine, and she was wearing a thin silver necklace. Normally the most poised of us, she looked startled now, uncertain how to react. This was good news for her family, but still. . . .

You weren't supposed to find out from someone else that your daughter was in the ensemble. She was supposed to rush in from school and tell you herself. It was her news. You weren't supposed to find out about it as a sidebar to someone else's drama.

I took over. "How do you know? I thought they weren't going to announce it until tomorrow."

"They called me in special. And it wasn't just Mrs. Barton." She was the director of the ensemble. "The fifth-grade music teachers were there, too. They wanted to *explain*." Mimi was sarcastic. "They said they wanted me to *understand*."

This seemed odd, but maybe this was always done with the close calls and we hadn't known about it. "What did they say? What were you supposed to understand?"

"That she doesn't have an ensemble voice. That she sings as well as the other girls, but she is a soloist."

Now I didn't know enough about singing to know if, at age eleven, one can be typed as having an ensemble or a soloist voice—it certainly sounded odd—but I did know that Rachel Gold didn't have an ensemble personality. Brittany whined a bit too much, Elise was too much of a follower, my Erin could be a martyr, but Mimi's Rachel needed to be in charge. I had helped Annelise with the Brownie troop back when the girls were in Scouts, and Rachel always wanted to be at the center of things. She had to be patrol leader, she had to sell the most cookies, she had to have every decision go her way. She was as hard-working and energetic as her mother, but she could be tiresome.

The fifth-grade chorus had had one behavior problem after another last year, and Rachel had been somewhere between a ringleader and a scapegoat.

"It's that the teachers don't like her," Mimi said. "That's all it is. They don't like her. I admit that she has trouble with authority figures that she doesn't respect. And if that's what Alden wants, blind, unthinking obedience, then it is not the school we think it is."

As Rachel's former assistant Scout leader, I did not appreciate the remark about unworthy authority figures, but I was sure that was the last thing on Mimi's mind.

"I know she could have behaved better last year," Mimi continued. "They all could have. But who would have thought that it would have this effect?"

"Then don't you think this will be a good lesson for her?" I said. "Kids have to understand that being disruptive has consequences." This far in her young life Rachel Gold had learned that the consequence of being disruptive was that you got your own way.

"Of course, they need to learn that. But not on something as important as this. Have them stay after school; have them write 'I will not talk in chorus' a jillion times, but don't keep them out of the ensemble. I'm going to fix this, and I'm going straight to Chris Goddard because you know this is just about the Caudwell girl being from an alumnae family."

I did not know any such thing. "Don't you think you should go to Martha Shot first?" She was the middle-school principal.

"People have been going to Martha Shot for years about the ensemble. She and Grace Barton are great pals. She'll never interfere."

She had a point there.

"I've got to go," she continued, turning toward the door. "I just wanted to come here first and calm down."

I was about to say that she might not be completely calm yet and that maybe she should sit down and have a cup of coffee, but before I could figure out how to say tactfully something so obvious, she was gone.

Blair and I looked at each other. "She's going to try to get them to change the results, isn't she?" I asked.

Blair nodded.

"That's not right," I said. "Why do we try to fix everything in our kids' lives? Why can't we ever let them take their lumps? Our parents didn't act this way. They just told us to deal with things."

Blair nodded again.

"You have not," I pointed out, "said one thing since Mimi walked in here. What are you thinking?"

Blair sat back down at the table. As she moved, her black

hair swung and I could see that she was wearing silver earrings that matched her necklace. My kitchen didn't get direct light until the afternoon, so the silver of her jewelry had no sparkle or depth. She carefully closed and straightened a notebook. "I'm wondering why my daughter might have to learn how to deal with rejection just so Mimi's daughter doesn't have to."

I sat down, too.

Blair went on. "Mimi is so angry that she is just thinking about this as a simple switch between Rachel and the new girl, but the new girl—Faith—may be in there for good."

"Leaving someone else to get axed," I finished. "Do you think it might be Brittany?"

"Actually it's more likely to be Elise since Mrs. Barton might not like how short Elise is, which just makes me angrier because Annelise will turn into a major doormat if this happens."

How unlike her to call Annelise a "doormat." God knows it was true enough, but that wasn't the sort of thing that we ever said about one another. That was one of the "rules" of our friendship—that among the four of us we did not talk behind one another's backs.

But if Blair and I were breaking that rule, Mimi was breaking a more important one. We had never spelled it out, but didn't we have a pact that we were all working together, all pulling in the same direction? That one of us would not sabotage the others? That no one would be unusually permissive, providing extra treats so that her house would be more fun than the others?

47

Mimi was violating the pact, declaring that what happened to her child was so much more important than what happened to anyone else's.

This was how a diva-cheerleader mom would behave, and I didn't find the thought very funny.

Blair flipped open the notebook that she had just closed, making it clear that she was done talking about this, even though it was still clearly on her mind. We worked the rest of the morning with grim efficiency, stopping only when Bruce, Blair's husband, called her on her cell phone, saying that he couldn't find his American Express card and could she go home and look for it.

I had some clients that afternoon. It was a pair of siblings, a baby and a toddler, and it was clear within five minutes that the shoot was going to be a disaster. The baby was cutting a tooth and would not be consoled. This upset the mother, which in turn upset the toddler, and I wasn't bringing much serenity to the table myself. So I quickly offered to reschedule, saying that, of course, there would be no additional sitting fee or charge for the film I had already used. That's what I always did in cases like this. I got as many clients from being nice as I did from the quality of my work. But as I was helping the other woman gather her things, I felt as if I were standing a distance from myself, hearing myself being nice.

I couldn't stop thinking about what Mimi was doing.

Despite how soft and slow Blair's accent is, despite how perfect her manners are, there are some hard edges to her. If her own daughter was not in the ensemble, Blair would put the best face on it, setting an example for Brittany about being gracious and forgiving in defeat. But unbeknownst to the girls, she would draw a line and have as little as possible to do with Mimi.

A few years ago ago the husband of a teacher in the lower school had died suddenly. The funeral was going to be enormous, but there was no money for caterers. Someone had called me, her voice hurried. "Could the four of you"—she hadn't needed to name who she was talking about—"handle the fruit and cheese platters for the reception?"

"Of course, we can." My kitchen had been in renovation hell at the moment, but that didn't matter. I knew where my friends kept their knives. I could cut up fruit in their houses just as well as I could in my own.

"I don't need to call the others, do I?"

"No. They'll be glad to help."

And, of course, they were glad to help.

I love stuff like that, having other people think of my friends and me as generous and reliable. I like that one of us can speak for the others, that we are a team. These women weren't simply my friends; we were also professional associates, all in the business of raising children and maintaining a community.

Our friendship was like a lighthouse. Each of us was piloting a boat that carried our individual families, our houses, our marriages; steering that boat on its journey was the central mission of each of our lives. But our friendship provided navigational guidance. When I wasn't sure on which side of the rocks to guide my family's craft, talking to my friends gave me a map. And when I thought one of them was headed toward the rocks, I dumped my purse on her feet.

The lighthouse spread out a circle of light because it had four windows, but at the moment Mimi was seeing only the light from one window—her own.

It was my day to pick up the older girls at school and take them to soccer practice. The conversation in the car made it clear that the results from the ensemble auditions hadn't been announced yet.

When I do this half of the soccer drive, Mimi picks up the younger kids—her son and mine, Blair's and Annelise's younger daughters. If Mimi gets back before I do, she holds on to Thomas until I get home.

As I drove down our block, I could see Thomas and Mimi's son, Gideon, playing in the small grassy space in front of the Golds' house. In such cases I usually get out of my car, check our narrow street for traffic, and wave Thomas to come home on his own. Today I crossed the street.

Mimi's house has a covered entry instead of the deep, wide porch that we have. I could see her through her screen door, standing in the front hall, looking through the mail. Her screen door served as a scrim, blurring her outline.

When she saw me, she pushed aside Banjo—her family's big, gloriously stupid dog—and opened the door. "I am a crazy woman; I'm on a mission."

She was vibrating with energy. One of the things that I liked about her was how willing she was to fight the good fight. Confrontation didn't make her sick and miserable; she thrived on it.

Of all of us, she was the only entrepreneur, the only one

who had had the sense not to go to law school. When we had all been working full-time, we had continually been frustrated by how difficult it was to find decent child care. In this nightmare Mimi saw a marketing opportunity. She opened a nanny-placement firm. She specialized in what she correctly assumed would be the truly desperate; she represented only families who had already been through at least two nannies.

One of the keys to her success was her mother, an exuberant but no-nonsense former pediatric nurse from Queens. Bubbe—all of us addressed her by the Yiddish word for grandmother—came in from New York, sat down with the families, and forced them to admit that they were as much of the problem as the nannies. She had worked while raising her children so she was entirely sympathetic to the choices that the families were making, but she could also see that if you lived on a two-acre lot in the far suburbs and you wouldn't let your nanny put the kids in a car, so that she was there for twelve hours a day with a newborn and a two-year-old, she was probably going to quit unless she was such a lousy nanny that she couldn't get another job.

"I would not work for you," Bubbe would tell some of the families. "And, tell me, honestly, would you work for yourselves?"

And if they didn't get it, she told them she didn't want her daughter working with them and that Mimi would be giving them their money back, and they were far too desperate to accept that.

Once Mimi's business got established, she hired two part-time social workers in addition to her mother, and this high-intervention model was changing families who had started out as impossible employers. It didn't work all the time, but often enough that when the older girls started third grade, Mimi was able to put both kids in Alden, and then the following year she and Ben bought the house across the street from us.

In her brisk no-nonsense way she was a very good neighbor. If she had to go out to the grocery store during a thunderstorm or on a Sunday evening, she would check to see if I needed something. I might not cry on her shoulder, but when I was done crying and was ready to start fixing whatever was making me cry, Mimi would be the first I would call, except that I wouldn't need to call her. She would be there.

So although she wasn't going to like me lecturing her, I felt an obligation to warn her on how choppy the waters were going to be.

I glanced over my shoulder to be sure that none of the kids were listening. "Mimi, I'm really afraid that if you succeed in getting Rachel in the ensemble, the repercussions might not be very pleasant."

She had been holding a handful of junk mail that she was obviously getting ready to throw away. She tossed it back down on the hall table. The Talbots catalog slid to the floor. "Oh, God, I know what you are going to say, and you're right. I was so pissed off that I was just thinking about this as being between Rachel and Faith, but Grace Barton disabused me of that right away."

"What did she say?"

"We were walking up to Chris Goddard's office at the high

school. 'And which of your daughter's little friends'"—Mimi mimicked Mrs. Barton with a simpering saccharineness—"'should be expected to step aside? Shall we ask for volunteers?'"

That had to have thrown cold water even on Mimi's anger. "What did you say?"

"Fortunately, I think very well on my feet. I said that I wasn't asking someone to be kicked off for Rachel. I was asking why there had to be ten girls. Why not make the size of the ensemble responsive to the size of the talent pool? Some years there should be nine girls, and some years thirteen. They don't enter competitions; there are no rules governing the size. Why not have eleven girls this year?"

"That does make sense," I admitted.

"I know. It makes me think that if I'm always going to be this brilliant on my feet, I ought to exercise more."

"But Mrs. Barton couldn't have liked that idea. Did her 'we've always done it this way' cut any ice with Chris Goddard?"

"Those words never came out of her mouth," Mimi said. "I'm guessing that the staff has already realized that argument doesn't work with him. She said that the issue was the sashes."

The girls in the ensemble provided their own white dresses and the school lent them violet sashes.

"The sashes? This is about the *sashes?*"

"Yes, darling. That's what Mrs. Barton says. She's lying, of course, but she says the problem is that there are only ten sashes, and how could we ever find exactly the same fabric to make another?"

"You couldn't—why do I feel that sometime in the next

53

month Blair or I am going to be making a whole bunch of new violet sashes?"

She smiled wickedly. "Because I said you would."

We both laughed, and I bent down to help her pick up the mail she had dropped. I felt light and happy. I was relieved. Nothing was going to change among the four of us.

I was glad that Jamie was out of town that evening. Not only could we eat dinner at five-thirty when the kids were actually hungry, but I knew that if he had been in town, I would, in the name of healthy marital communication, have attempted to explain why I had been so upset all day, and he would never, not in a hundred million years, ever have understood.

You felt that your life was falling apart because Mimi Gold was going to talk to the music teachers? What does that have to do with us? Erin didn't try out.

And he would have indeed said *"us."* *"What does that have to do with us?"*

Where was the *"us"*? He was so completely wrapped up in this trial that he had no idea what was going on in this house. My friends knew much more about my life than he did.

4

The sixth-grade girls' ensemble did indeed have eleven voices this year, but the director Grace Barton did a phenomenally bitchy thing when she typed up the list. All of the girls from Brittany Branson and Faith Caudwell to Elise Rosen and Chloe Zimmerman were listed alphabetically, except Rachel Gold. Her name was last.

Ensemble rehearsals started immediately. The girls were going to be rehearsing three times a week right after school. That meant that we had to redo all the carpool schedules. I keep my Monday and Tuesday afternoons clear for clients, so on Thursday and Friday afternoons I went to school and picked up Erin and the little kids—my Thomas, Blair's and Annelise's younger daughters, and Mimi's son. It was unusual for Erin to be the only one of the older girls in the car, and she complained about it. Then on Wednesdays, I had my two kids and Blair's younger daughter because all the Jewish kids—Annelise isn't Jewish, but Joel is, and they are raising their kids Jewish—had to go to Hebrew School and there was another car pool to take care of that. That left Blair without a car pool for Brittany on Wednesday afternoons since Elise and Rachel dashed off to Hebrew School after rehearsal, but in truth, it hardly mattered since we all lived within a few miles of school, and most of the time it took longer to figure out who was going to drive than it did to make the actual drive.

We survived the first week of rehearsals with everyone following the new schedule, but then on Friday of the second week, the last week in September, Annelise called me from her cell phone. She had gotten confused about the schedule and now she was stuck in traffic. She couldn't find Mimi or Blair. Was there any way I could go get the three girls at rehearsal? "It's a special trip for you, I know, I know, but I will never get there."

"It's no problem." I meant that; it really wasn't a problem, and none of us kept score about who was doing how many favors for whom. I hung up the phone, grabbed my purse, and called out to Erin, who was in the sunroom, watching TV. "I've got to go to school and pick up the other girls. Do you want to come?"

It never occurred to me that she would say no, but she did. Surprised, I went through the living room and looked into the sunroom. She was lying on the sofa, watching the Disney

Channel. She had gotten braces in August, and they had changed the shape of the lower part of her face. She was a little squarer, a little swollen. I still wasn't entirely used to it.

"Oh, come on, honey," I said. She was old enough to stay home alone, but this seemed strange. We were picking up her friends. "It's a pretty day, and you aren't doing anything,"

"I said I didn't want to go."

And I probably should have accepted that on the first go-round. "Okay. I should be home soon. If Elise doesn't have a key, I'll bring her here. Her mom's in traffic."

"She has a key," Erin muttered.

The rehearsal was still in progress when I got to the middle-school music room. Chris Goddard, the new headmaster, was standing in the doorway, listening.

Because our music and arts are so strong and our sports facilities so secondary, Alden draws families with unathletic sons. The boys in our high school are remarkable. Misfits at other schools, they flourish here; they are witty, talented, and proud that they can't catch a football. We are one of the few high schools in the country able to stage Shakespeare's history plays. No one else has enough boys willing to wear tights. The talent of these young men is raising the school's profile, taking it far beyond its original image of refined girls singing prettily. They produce graphic novels. They create award-winning Web sites. They make music out of their computers. They get into great colleges. The gratitude of their families is being expressed in significant financial donations.

So when the school had sought a new head, one unstated

assumption was that if it were a man, he should have once been like these guys.

And we found him. Although he now had neat close-cropped hair and well-shaped wire-rimmed glasses, Chris Goddard had, for three years in his youth, been road manager for a rock band, quitting because—at least this was his public explanation—he was tired of being the only person who wore a watch or thought that watches mattered. Since then he had acquired all the appropriate educational credentials. He had finished college, gotten an M.A., taught, been vice principal at one private school and director of academic affairs at another. While alumnae families held the majority on the search committee, the new families made the case that Chris had the demonstrated commitment to music that we wanted and if any person could make the trains run on time, it was the road manager of a rock band.

I approached him and murmured my name. I didn't expect him to recognize me. The school had hundreds of families, and even once people had an approximate read on me, they still often confused me with Annelise.

He smiled. "I know who you are. Erin is in the sixth grade, Thomas is in the second. You're on the curriculum committee, and you're running the Spring Fair."

"You're good," I said.

"No." He shook his head. "Your family is important to the school, and you are the person everyone borrows stuff from."

"My claim to fame," I said with a flick of my hand, and the discouraging thought that what I had said was true.

He was surprisingly well-dressed. He wasn't wearing a tie

and there was nothing flashy to his garb, but the pleats on his trousers hung perfectly, and the legs broke symmetrically over his narrow loafers.

I didn't know much about Chris's personal life, but the people who had interviewed him while on the search committee said that there wasn't a lot to know. He had never been married, but he wasn't gay. It took only a moment in his presence to sense his heterosexual charm. He did have a college-aged son, the result of a brief "on the road" relationship. The boy had been raised by his maternal grandparents, and Chris had not even known of his existence for the first few years of the boy's life. Chris had concealed none of this from the search committee, and because the backyard of a member of the committee butted up to Annelise's backyard, we had gotten all the dirt.

"Your daughter's not in the ensemble, is she?" Chris asked now.

"No, I'm here to pick up her friends."

"Is that an issue for her, that her friends are in the ensemble?"

"Oh, no," I said lightly, "she didn't try out. There was never any question of her being in."

"But does she feel excluded in other ways?"

Suddenly I wasn't sure of the answer to that. Last year Erin would certainly have wanted to come to school with me. She had always grabbed any chance to see her friends. "I don't know," I admitted.

"The one thing that gave me pause about enlarging the ensemble," he said, "was Martha Shot saying that if we had more than ten girls, the ensemble would take over the social life of the sixth grade. The ensemble girls would be on the bus, and the rest wouldn't. It's hard to imagine that one girl would make such a difference, but she said one could."

"I'm sure it depends on the mix of kids." The bond between Erin, Elise, Brittany, and Rachel was so strong, their lives intersected in so many ways with so many shared activities, that I couldn't imagine the ensemble changing their friendship.

He nodded. "Of course. I hope you'll keep me posted if there are problems."

I had assumed that Mimi's ranting and ravings had been the force behind the ensemble increasing in size. Now I wondered. Perhaps it had as much to do with a power struggle between a new headmaster and a teacher with thirty years' tenure. If so, I was a little surprised that the headmaster had won.

Oh, well, we would never know. The faculty and staff do a good job of keeping parents out of their own civil wars, probably because they know the parents would start by filing lawsuits and end up in negotiations with a Third-World nation that had nuclear-weaponry capability.

The rehearsal was ending. The eleven girls had been arranged by voice, but as soon as they were dismissed, they sorted themselves out into smaller groups. Elise, Brittany, and Rachel were together, of course, and as they crossed the music room toward me, they were joined by the girl I now knew to be Faith Caudwell, the alumnae daughter who had moved back from Texas and been given the tenth spot in the ensemble.

The girls hardly reacted to seeing me instead of one of

their own mothers. They were so used to being driven by any of us that they probably didn't even notice that I was there without Erin. Faith Caudwell stuck with us all the way to the car almost as if she were coming along.

"Do you have a ride?" I asked her.

"Oh, yes, but my mom's always late. That's the way she is."

Okay, one more person whom I, intolerant bitch that I am, didn't want to drive a car pool with.

The three girls said good-bye to Faith, they all promised that they would call one another the minute that they got home, and then in the car they talked about her, saying the usual sorts of things that kids said about other kids, that she was really really nice and really really fun and they really really liked her.

Jamie's parents came down from Pittsburgh for the weekend, and we were out and about so much that I didn't think about whether the phone was ringing. Erin always checked the messages as soon as we got in, and so I don't know how many she got.

The following Friday afternoon she was again on the sofa watching the Disney Channel. Earlier in the week she had declared that the Disney Channel was for babies, and since her brother watched it, he must be a baby.

I donned my helpful-mother cap. "Do you want me to call Mrs. Rosen"—that was Annelise—"and have her drop the girls off here after rehearsal? We've got time to get a movie before they would get here, and then we could call for a pizza."

"No." Her tone suggested that my helpful-mother cap was a black ski mask.

"Well, honey, why not?" I chirped. "Isn't that better than just sitting here?"

"They're all going to Faith's after the rehearsal. They're spending the night with her."

"Oh."

I hadn't meant anything by that "oh." I was surprised, that was all, but clearly Erin assumed that I had meant something, and of course, whatever I meant was the Wrong Thing.

"Faith and I don't know each other," she snapped. "We don't have any classes together. Why would she have invited me?"

She was right, of course she was. And Faith's mother probably only had enough seat belts for four girls. Even if she had more, she would have taken other girls from the ensemble, not Erin.

But still Erin had been left out; she had been excluded. Her friends were all at a sleepover to which she had not been invited.

Oh, did I know that feeling, the feeling of having not been invited. That's what my life had been like at her age.

Erin is quiet at school. She is like her dad, reserved and observant. But when she is with her friends, she gets carried away; she squeals and chatters with giddy exuberance. They all do. Their voices are high-pitched, and they talk reallyreally-fast, and their braces slur their speech. Adults can barely understand them, which is fine because they aren't speaking to us.

Today, however, Erin was silent and sullen.

I wanted to know more. Was this just a one-time thing, or

did we have a problem? At lunch who was sitting with whom? And in the halls, who was speaking to whom? But there was no way that she was going to tell me. I could ask pleasantly, I could badger endlessly, I could withhold food, she was not going to tell me. I thought I could help if I knew more, but she didn't think so, and whether or not she had the right to remain silent, she certainly had the power to do so.

I expected one of my friends to say something. We were all at the girls' soccer game the next afternoon, and I waited for one of them to mention the previous evening's activities. *It was so odd not to have Erin in the car this morning. . . . Did Erin mind not being invited? . . . Never occurred to me that Erin wouldn't be there. . . .*

Or even if they didn't express regret at Erin's not being invited, I would have expected whoever had picked up the girls on Saturday morning to have described Mary Paige's house to the rest of us.

But the sleepover at Faith's house seemed to be a taboo subject. That was odd. It was if the lighthouse had suddenly gone dim.

The following Friday Brittany was having a sleepover with the four girls from the ensemble, and this time, of course, Erin was invited—Blair wouldn't have allowed Brittany not to invite Erin. Blair picked up the four ensemble girls after rehearsal, but since she drove a sedan with five seat belts, she didn't have room for Erin. The seat belt that had always been Erin's was now Faith's. Even though the Bransons lived only four blocks from us and so Erin often walked over there, I drove her. I sensed that she felt odd about coming separately from the other girls, and I thought that my magical mother-presence would help her feel better.

If it did, she hid it well.

Jamie thought that he had a good chance of getting some key evidence excluded early and so—fun guy that he was—he worked that Friday evening. One of Thomas's friends came over. Both boys were yummy little things, serious, sweet, and extremely interested in all things violent and destructive.

After Thomas's soccer game Saturday morning I picked up Rachel and Erin at Blair's house. The girls hardly spoke to each other. I couldn't tell if they were fighting or if they just hadn't had enough sleep. Erin spent the rest of the day on the sofa, watching the Disney Channel until it was time for her afternoon soccer game. Thomas got more phone calls than she did.

Faith Caudwell came to the soccer game even though her mother had not been able to get her on the team. She talked with whatever girls weren't on the field. Erin is one of the better players on the team so, as always, she played most of the game, but at halftime it looked as if all the conversation was about the ensemble. Erin stood at the edge of the group without a lot to say.

And the conversation among us mothers was about the ensemble as well. Mimi was outraged that Grace Barton was picking on Rachel. "Chloe asked Rachel what page they were on, Rachel answered, and Rachel got yelled at."

What did you expect? I wanted to say. *We knew that Mrs. Barton was petty. We knew she played favorites. We could have predicted this. And can't any of you see what Erin is going through? Don't you think her suffering is worse?*

The lighthouse was dark indeed.

Back home after the game I carried Thomas's clean laundry upstairs. As I put it away, I found a pair of Jamie's socks mixed in with Thomas's so I headed toward the front of the house where our bedroom is. Erin's door was shut. I paused, listening. She was crying.

I moved close to the door, pulling my shoulders in as if trying to wedge myself into the angle created by the door and the casing trim.

I knocked lightly. "Erin, sweetie . . ."

"Go away, Mom." Her voice was thick and muffled. "Just go away."

My hand dropped to the doorknob. I could go in. The keys necessary for locking the bedroom doors had been lost years ago. I could go in and scoop her up in my arms and hold her and let her cry until everything was all right again.

But her crying in my arms wasn't going to fix this. It would make me feel better, not her.

I was not going to barge in. I knocked once more.

"Leave me alone. Please leave me alone."

So I did. I put Jamie's socks away and went down the front stairs.

Our front hall is painted a pale, cool sage green, and descending the stairway wall is a series of pictures I had taken of Erin and her friends. I had started taking them when the girls were six—the first year I had taken a class at the Corcoran—and have taken one a year since then. Identically framed in silver-toned wood, the pictures were black-and-whites of four barefoot girls in white against a white background. One time they were all dancing. Another time they were perched on a series of black stools. Sometimes they were laughing, sometimes they were sweetly serious. Last year they had rejected the idea of four matching white dresses, so they had worn faded denim jeans and white T-shirts, and they were playing leapfrog. Brittany and Rachel were crouched while the two smaller girls, Erin and Elise, were in midair, their arms down, their legs spread, their hair flying. I had used a wide-angle lens with a two point eight f-stop and a shutter speed of 1/500 seconds on that one. To my eye the early pictures, taken with my old Nikon, were amateurish, but whenever I went to take those first ones down, I would stop seeing them as a photographer, and I would get weepy at how exquisitely textured very young children were, and I would leave the pictures hanging.

Every year these pictures were my holiday gift to my friends, and we all have them hanging in prominent places in our houses.

What kind of picture was I going to be able to take this year?

· · ·

Later in the week I asked Erin if she wanted to have everyone over that Friday evening. "You could certainly have Faith, too. We could pick them all up from the ensemble."

I drive what my son, with his expensive private-school vocabulary, calls "a big-ass station wagon" so I can transport more kids than anyone else.

"No," she said. "They won't want to come."

"Erin! These are your friends. They have been your friends since you were four. Why wouldn't they want to come?"

"They just won't. I don't want to call them."

If Erin was being as prickly with them as she was with me, they might not want to come. Her reaction to being excluded from a few things was probably going to guarantee her being excluded from many more. I had to figure out some way to break the cycle.

"I can call their moms. There's nothing strange about that."

"It won't do any good. Faith set up this schedule. Brittany had everyone last week. This week it's Elise's turn, then Rachel's and then Faith's again."

A schedule? A schedule of "everyone" that did not include Erin? To say nothing of the other seven girls in the ensemble? I could not believe that my friends were going to tolerate that. "Elise invited you to her house, didn't she?"

"Yeah, but I didn't know if you would let me go."

Not let her go? Where had that come from? Why wouldn't I let her go to Annelise and Elise's house? "Of course you can go."

"It doesn't matter." Erin was mumbling, not looking at me. "Faith isn't allowed to come to our house."

I couldn't believe that I had heard her right. "What do you mean, she's not allowed to come to our house?" Why would anyone not be *allowed* to come to our house? There's always a parent here. We don't have guns. The bathrooms and the dishes are clean . . . or clean enough.

"I don't know, that's just what she's telling the others, that she is not allowed to come here."

"She's telling everyone that?" How must that make Erin feel, having some holier-than-thou kid implying that there was something so wrong with our house that she couldn't set foot into it?

"Don't get into it, Mom."

Don't get into it? Fat chance of that.

I called Mary Paige Caudwell that evening and asked her if she would like to get together for coffee one morning after we dropped the kids off at school. Normally I would have asked her to the house, but since she might be afraid of my house cooties, I suggested that we meet at Starbucks.

"I'd love to get together," she trilled, "but wouldn't you rather go out to lunch?"

Going out to lunch is still a symbol to me of women who are at home without enough to do. "Sure, we can do that. Do you want me to come over to Virginia?" A lot of us District residents have a phobia about going into Virginia because it always seems so far away, but Faith and Mary Paige lived right across the Chain Bridge, and Annelise and Blair had exclaimed several times how close their house really was.

"Oh, there's nothing over here." And Mary Paige named a place in Georgetown.

I agreed even though this meeting was now going to be a gigantic pain in the ass. I only live five miles from George-town, but parking is a chore. And the restaurant she named was not one that you went to in your meet-at-Starbucks sweats. So I was going to have to get dressed up, and, since I had initiated the invitation, no doubt pay for a very nice lunch.

That afternoon Pam Ruby stopped by the house to return a stockpot. Pam, an alumna and a mother of sons, was a gossip, but she—unlike my friends and me—was sane enough not to be interested in the social activities of a bunch of eleven-year-olds. She gossiped about the lives of the adults, which meant that she must never talk about me because I clearly have no life.

I asked her about Mary Paige.

"Her sister was my year, but Mary Paige was a couple years ahead of us," Pam answered. "So I didn't really know her that well."

Which was not going to stop Pam from talking. Apparently Mary Paige had spent her married life in Houston, but she and her husband were separated and getting a divorce. "The money part really surprised her," Pam said. "She saw lots of other women stay in their houses and keep their lifestyle after a divorce, but she wasn't going to be able to. I guess the economy of Texas is really in the toilet."

Indeed it was, and my gun-for-hire husband was defending the men who had helped put it there.

"So she came back here and she's just renting that house in Virginia. The other gals say that it's nice, but it is rented. And it is in Virginia. She says she's just there temporarily, but I don't know what her plans are. The judge is saying that she ought to go back to work and she doesn't want to."

"Her not wanting to work may not go very far with a judge."

"Everyone's working these days," Pam agreed. She was a realtor. "But Mary Paige's trying to build this big case that having to drive Faith to and from school all the time keeps her from being able to have a job."

I reminded myself of the source. Pam exaggerated. Surely it wasn't possible that a woman could feel so entitled to being supported that she thought that a judge would award her alimony because she didn't have a good car pool?

Or was it?

"And she was really unhappy about Faith not getting on a certain soccer team," Pam continued. "Your daughter runs around with that bunch, doesn't she? When Mary Paige first got back into town, Kate Collins had a little luncheon for her because they were in the same class, although luck of the draw, all of us with sixth graders had boys. Mary Paige wanted to know who the popular girls were. She really wanted to be sure that Faith got in with that crowd."

How casual she was about calling my daughter "popular."
"She wanted her kid to have designer-label friends?"

Pam laughed. "That's what happens when you move to Texas. You start caring too much about designer labels. That's Texas for you."

Oh, great, here Erin was so unhappy because someone had stuck the label "popular" on her forehead, a label that, in Erin's case, had lasted for all of three weeks.

We all wanted our kids to be happy. I couldn't fault Mary Paige for that. But wanting to be sure that she was "popular"? Did that really arise out of concern for the girl's needs or out of the mother's own image of herself?

Well, look at me. What a hypocrite I was being. I was quick to stereotype Mary Paige as a my-daughter-will-be-popular-at-all-costs mom in exactly the way I did not want people stereotyping me.

But my child had been made so unhappy. I wondered if Mary Paige understood what was happening, that the result of trying to get Faith included was that Erin was being excluded. I was going to give Mary Paige the benefit of the doubt and assume that she hadn't known enough about the kids' relationships to understand.

But her daughter had to know, and her daughter had to like it.

If all these jillions of books about raising teenaged girls knew anything, then girls like Faith Caudwell were the dangerous ones. Faith had lost her father and her home. She had something to prove, and often the only way some teenaged girls know how to build themselves up is to tear someone else down.

Mary Paige Caudwell was one of the Old Guard families who had assumed too much. She had assumed that she could divorce her husband and keep her country-club lifestyle. She had assumed that she could move back to D.C. and that her daughter could slide into the place that she once had. She had assumed that being a descendant of Mrs. Chester T. Paige still meant something.

So I decided that I was not going to fuss about the price of lunch. I certainly minded being maneuvered into something, but the money itself wouldn't mean anything to me, and if Mary Paige felt that the only way she could go out to a nice restaurant was to finagle someone else into paying for it, then I should feel some compassion.

That high-minded generosity disappeared as I sat in the restaurant for twenty-five minutes with only a glass of iced tea for company. I had failed to remember what Faith had said about her mother always being late, and I arrived at the restaurant my usual five minutes early. Twenty minutes after our agreed-upon meeting time, Mary Paige arrived, a sorority-sister type sweater tied gracefully over her shoulders, smiling a little apology. "Parking's just not what it used to be, is it?"

"No. I don't even try to find street parking anymore," I said, sounding extremely pleasant for someone who had spent twenty-five minutes bonding with a glass of iced tea.

She sat down and shook out her napkin with a flourish. "Now shall we have Bloody Marys or were you planning on ordering a bottle of wine?"

I blinked. I wasn't planning on doing either. I gestured at my iced tea. "I'm fine."

"Oh, let's have fun. You aren't in AA, are you?"

Surely there is a middle ground between not drinking in the middle of the day and being engaged in a lifelong struggle with alcoholism, but I already felt like a frump—I didn't have a sorority-sister sweater using me as a coatrack—and I didn't want to compound that by being a goody-goody. So moments later a watery-looking reddish drink appeared before me. One sip told me that it wasn't water making it look watery. If I drank all this, I was going to be one happy girl.

We chatted a bit. How had the school changed since she had been a student? Oh, the facilities were nicer. But it was hard to get used to the boys and the absence of uniforms.

I asked her about her own interests.

She had been an "interior-design professional," but hadn't actually worked since Faith had been born.

"Do you think you might go back to it?" I asked.

"Oh, I still have a hand in it." She spoke as if I had been trying to insult her. "I always have something going on, either in my own home or at friends'. And, of course, every charity wants to put on a house tour or do a designers' showhouse. I've been *very* involved in organizing those."

In my experience people who say they are *very* involved in something—as opposed to the people who actually are and just keep their mouths shut about it—express a lot of opinions without doing much work.

"But you must feel as I do," she continued. "The women who are working have no control over their time. It can be hard to find anyone to have lunch with because everyone's at the office." She drawled out the word "office" as if mocking her friends' self-importance.

I don't like it when people try to divide women into opposing armies of working mothers and nonworking mothers. "But wouldn't interior design give you a lot of flexibility?" I asked.

"Not creatively. I have such a definite vision that compromise is painful."

So she couldn't work with clients. That's what interior designers do—work with clients.

"I'm taking some transition time right now," she continued. "My number one priority has to be Faith and her needs, not my own."

That gave me the opening I needed. "My daughter says that Faith isn't allowed to come to our house."

"Isn't allowed? Oh, no, no, no, *no*," she trilled. "It's not a case of not being allowed. Why on earth would I forbid her to come to your house? I think it's more a case of not wanting to."

And that was supposed to make me feel better? That the kid just didn't *want* to come to our house?

"You see," Mary Paige continued, "my grandparents lived in that house, and I spent a lot of time there growing up since it was so close to the school. I really have so many wonderful memories that I just don't think that I could stand to go inside. I helped my mother clean it out, and it was so horribly sad. I had really hoped that we would keep it in the family, but my uncles insisted on selling it. And then everyone was so disappointed at what it finally sold for. It was so awful to let it go that I just can't imagine going back in and facing all those memories again. I hope that you don't think that I am horribly fragile."

I guess I could respect her feelings, but on the other hand, she had lost her husband, her own home, and apparently all financial security. Surely, having someone else living in her grandparents' house was a minor loss in comparison to those.

And, anyway, what did her wonderful memories have to do with Faith coming? We bought the house when Erin—and therefore Faith—had been three, and it had been sitting on the market for at least six months before that. Faith would have no memories of the place.

"It may feel like an altogether different house," I said. "We have made a lot of changes."

"I had heard that. You got the house for such a good price it's no wonder you felt that you could do a lot." She shook her head as if she couldn't believe how little we had paid for the house. That offended me; we had negotiated a fair price, but we had not done better than that. "My grandmother had such wonderful taste. I think that's why I became interested in interior design, because my grandmother's house was so exquisite. Tell me you didn't strip the dining-room wallpaper, do tell me you didn't do that."

"We did."

She winced. "It was hand-blocked in China; it was more than a hundred years old when my grandmother put it up. It was so valuable. I don't suppose you realized that or you wouldn't have acted so precipitously."

I didn't say anything. Both her grandparents had smoked. From their first potty trip in the morning to turning out the light at night, the pair of them had had cigarettes going. The house sat on the market so long not just because of its absurdly high asking price, but also because it had reeked of tobacco. All the carpets and window treatments had to be ripped out before we moved in. The walls—even the ones that had been papered—had to be coated with a sealant to kill the smell.

"Of course," I said, "I can't insist on Faith coming to our house, but Erin really minds that Faith is telling the other girls that she is not allowed to come."

"Oh, it's just girls." She waved her hand. "They won't pay any attention."

I wondered how I could take a picture of her that would be wildly unflattering. The woman didn't have even a trace of softness under her jaw, but I knew that if I positioned the camera and the light right, I could make her look as if she had a double chin. And there was a streak of makeup caught in the two delicate lines at the outer corner of her eye. The lines were years away from being crow's feet, but I could make them look like the Red River Valley.

"No, Mary Paige." My secret vindictiveness gave me enough serenity to keep my voice calm. "This is really making my daughter uncomfortable."

"Well, if it is that important, of course, I will speak to Faith. But you know, teenaged girls. One word from their mothers and they do the exact opposite. Now tell me about Grandmother's azaleas. I can't wait to see them again this spring, although I suppose they were a little overgrown."

Like everything else in the yard, the azaleas had not been pruned in years. They had been big and showy when they bloomed, but underneath the outer layer of blossoms, they had been full of spindly branches. Blair had finally taken over and pruned them ruthlessly, warning me that it was going to be two years before they would fill out at the appropriate proportion.

Mary Paige thanked me beautifully as I signed the credit card slip, but I knew that talking to her had been a mistake. I could hear what she would go home and tell her daughter.

Mrs. Meadows thinks you aren't being very nice to Erin. She would roll her eyes, making it clear that Erin was too pathetic to worry about. That would only make things worse.

Had I just done exactly what Fran Zimmerman and Candace Singer had done at the beginning of the year? No, I was innocent on that score. I hadn't tried to make Mary Paige feel bad; I was trying to fix this. I was trying to be helpful.

Which was undoubtedly what Fran and Candace would have said that they had been trying to do.

It's all so different when it is your own kid.

5

Chris Goddard asked Blair and me to meet with him about the Spring Fair, but the day we were scheduled to see him, Brittany was having another migraine, and Blair wanted to stay home with her. So I went alone.

Chris's office was in the old Alden family mansion. Miss Alden had first started teaching young ladies piano and voice in her father's music room, and then after her parents died, she turned the whole house into an academic school. Eventually new buildings were built for the lower and middle school, but the high school continued to meet in the mansion.

Chris's office was on the first floor in what had once been the summer parlor. The room projected out from the main body of the house and had tall, white-mullioned windows on three sides. The crooked, spreading branches of a bur oak tree arched over the peaked roof, and its yellowing leaves filtered the thin October sunshine. It seemed almost colder in Chris's office than it was outside, and not surprisingly he was wearing a black cashmere sweater under his taupe suede blazer.

On the credenza behind his desk was a wood-framed photograph of a boy, almost a young man. The photo was in color, and while there was a little too much shadow along the subject's nose, the background was nicely balanced—a yellow brick, white-trimmed building that looked familiar.

Chris was sitting at his desk, flipping through a stack of papers. Each page was a handwritten list entered on a preprinted form. His left hand was holding down the lower corner of the stack, and I noticed his watch. The band was leather; the face was thin and gold.

You don't buy a watch like that on a headmaster's salary—at least not on the Alden School's headmaster salary. Both Chris Goddard's effortless elegance and his son were thanks to his road manager days.

He was shaking his head. "We're going to get hammered on the early decisions," he said.

I had been trying to imagine him with a ponytail and a faded T-shirt so it took me a moment to understand. He was talking about the high-school kids' college applications.

"Half of these lists have no rhyme or reason to them. And they all have the same two safeties, which means neither one is a safety anymore." He shook his head. "For what our families pay, they should be getting better advice than this."

I was surprised. It had never occurred to me that the

school might not be doing everything possible to get the kids into the best colleges; that was what people expected from a private school. Getting into the right colleges matters more than anything to private-school families. "I hope you aren't shouting that from the street corners."

"No, I have some sense of self-preservation," he said, smiling, "and by this time next year it will be better, maybe not fixed, but at least better." He closed the file. "I'm sorry. I haven't asked you to sit down. Please do."

He had already read the documents that Blair and I had sent, and he was interested and approving, but suggested that we have some activities for the high-school students. "The ones who were at the school as little kids remember loving the Spring Fair. They would come back if there was something for them to do."

It was a good idea. It really was. He seemed to have talked to more students in his two months on the job than our last headmaster had done in two decades. But provide something that would interest the high-school kids? "What will they like?" I asked. "Isn't the after-prom party a disaster because the activities aren't all that interesting?" In the spring the juniors and seniors were supposed to go straight from the supposedly alcohol-free hotel ballroom where the prom was held to the definitely alcohol-free after-prom party at the school. They didn't.

He winced. "Oh, I hadn't heard that about the after-prom." I could sense him making a mental note. That, too, was something that would be improved in the next year or two.

"Let me give the Spring Fair some thought. And now tell me, do you know what"—and he glanced down at an actual note—" 'clear elastic' is?"

That was some change in subject. "I do know." It was a sewing product that I'd been aware of for only a couple of years; I don't know when it was actually put on the market. "It's what it sounds like. It's clear, but it's got much more stretch than regular elastic. It's very useful. I usually carry some." I dug into my purse and pulled out the little zippered pouch in which I had two sizes of Band-Aids, Children's Chewable Advil for Thomas and his friends, Junior Strength Advil for Erin and hers, and maximum-strength capsule-shaped Advil tablets for Jamie and me. The pouch also had safety pins, a little sewing kit, a small pocketknife that I had to replace regularly because I always forgot that I had it until I tried to go through airport security, a book of matches, a twenty-dollar bill, three quarters, an extra battery for my cell phone, and many, many "hair things," the covered rubber bands that girls use for ponytails. I found the clear elastic, undid the twist-tie wrapped around it, and handed it to Chris.

He stretched it out, regarding it curiously. "You routinely carry this?"

"I'm a mom." I shrugged. "I used to have this cool little flat packet of duct tape, but it disappeared. So why are you interested in clear elastic?"

He had his hand over his head and was letting the elastic dangle in front of him as if it were an interesting earthworm. "If a high-school girl ties a piece of this to either side of her flip-flop and loops it behind her foot, is the flip-flop now in compliance with the dress code?"

"Oh, my God, I have no idea." I waved my hand. This seemed so unimportant. "Who cares?"

"Unfortunately a lot of people."

"Then I would say absolutely, yes, that is compliance, and we should award the girl who thought of it extra credit for inventive thinking, but you're asking the wrong person. I wish we didn't have a dress code at all."

"I have some sympathy for that position," he admitted, "but I'd also like us to have better diversity recruiting and more AP science classes, and if that means sticking with the dress code, I'll make that trade-off in a heartbeat."

"But it's so much more fun to fight about the dress code."

"My point exactly. People who like to fight can fuss endlessly about the dress code while the rest of us can outflank them on the minority recruiting and the AP science."

I smiled. Chris was obviously a "fixer," a person who likes to get things done. "You think like my husband does."

Chris thought for a moment. "I haven't met him, have I?"

"No, and you probably won't, at least not anytime soon. He's involved in a big court case, and we won't be seeing much of him until it is over."

On the surface my husband is your normal, all-American, resourceful, reliable, pigheaded guy. He gets annoyed with drivers who tie up rush-hour traffic because they don't understand how the lanes change at 3:45 P.M. He gets outraged when the poor schmo at the other end of the 1-800 customer-service line can't answer his questions. When he plays tennis, he wants to kill his opponent. There is nothing gentle about him; he is alert, ambitious, and competitive, looking and sounding like every other successful D.C. lawyer.

But there is a difference. Jamie is a Quaker. The kids and I go to St. Peter's Episcopal, and sometimes Jamie comes with us, but just as often he goes to Meetings by himself. As far as I can tell, he never says anything at the Meetings; his faith is personal and private.

But it is strong and has given him a fundamental decency that is based on respect for other people's individuality. It's part of why he is successful with jurors. He knows that every person wants to be treated with respect and dignity, and he believes that everyone is entitled to that.

His being a Quaker fascinates the wives of other driven, successful men. "Your husband is a Quaker," they will marvel. "That's so unusual." Sometimes highly successful men seem completely defined by their jobs. Their self-respect comes out of their professional success; their moral code is indistinguishable from their professional ethics. But Jamie, so like such men in manner, dress, and habit, also has a spiritual life. He never talks about it to other people, but simply the fact that some mornings he gets up and chooses to go to a Meeting by himself gives him depth and mystery.

Because of his Quaker heritage, Jamie wanted the kids to go to Sidwell Friends School, a private school on Wisconsin Avenue affiliated with the American Society of Friends. I, on the other hand, did not want the kids to go there because I think that it is one of the least Quakerish places on the planet.

Sidwell is a fabulous school. At Alden we have great music and lousy sports. Other schools spend more money on their athletic fields than they do on their science labs. Sidwell is great at everything. Theater and science, sports and language, you name it, Sidwell offers its students every opportunity.

The administration of the school does all that it can to foster Quaker values. The problem comes from the families. Although old-line Wasp traditionalists think of St. Albans as the most prestigious school in the city, up-and-coming annoying strivers like us worship at the Sidwell shrine. Sidwell is where the political—as opposed to social—elite send their kids. Its prestige attracts families who care about being first in all things, all of the time, and the atmosphere is, as a result, tense and competitive.

We started the kids at Alden, which was my choice, because its location virtually makes it a neighborhood school for us, but I had agreed that we would periodically review this decision. The first reassessment was coming up. Third and seventh grades are "entry" years at Sidwell, points at which the class size is increased and additional students are admitted. Thus we had long ago agreed to file applications for the following year when Erin was in sixth grade and Thomas in second. At the beginning of the school year, I had suggested that we talk about it before we went through the stress of applying— since I couldn't imagine we would ever take them out of Alden.

"I'm not ready to rule out transferring them yet," Jamie had said. "We don't make a final decision until April. A lot can happen between now and then. Let's just have them apply."

So stipulating that I was only agreeing to have them apply, I initiated the process.

Of course, since the whole world was also applying to Sidwell, the school was impossibly hard to get into, but being the children and grandchildren of active, committed Friends would give my kids the same advantage given to a student whose great-grandparent's name was on the gym.

Erin needed to take the SSAT, the secondary-school version of the SAT that had gotten me out of Indiana and into the Ivy League. She took it on a Saturday morning. She had a noon soccer game, so when I picked her up afterward, I had her soccer uniform with me. If she changed in the car, we would make it to the field for the start of her game. Her coach got angry when kids missed practices, much less actual games.

"How was the test?" I asked.

"It was okay, I guess," she said as she pulled off her shoes. "Some of the math seemed so easy that I wondered if I was on the wrong track. But I couldn't figure out how to make any of the other answers make sense, so I don't know."

I wasn't entirely sure that I followed that. "It doesn't matter. This isn't the be-all and end-all of your life."

While I had been waiting for her to emerge, I talked to the other mothers in the waiting room. For some of them, this test did feel like the be-all and end-all. They had hired tutors, bought vocabulary flash cards, and critiqued practice essays.

They had described what they had done in detail designed to make the other mothers feel inadequate for not having gone to these lengths.

"Oh," I had said with studied casualness, "Erin didn't need any of that. We have confidence in her own natural abilities."

Now that was a pretty bitchy thing to have said. If I wanted Erin to go to Sidwell, I would have done what those women had done and probably more, but I didn't think either of the kids should change schools.

Erin pulled her soccer shirt over her head, but kept her arms inside it so that she could worm her way out of the shirt she had worn for the exam. "You do know that I'm not going to Sidwell, don't you? Not ever."

"No one is going to force you to do anything. We're just exploring options."

"You promise you won't make me, that it's my decision?" She thrust her arms through the sleeves of her soccer shirt.

"I wouldn't go that far." I wasn't going to lie to her. "In the long run, it is Dad's and my decision for both you and Thomas, but you certainly have a voice. We will listen to you, and your preferences will probably be the biggest factor."

"Well, if it's the biggest factor, then can't we just say that it will be the only factor?"

She was trying to get into an argument with me, but I remembered the advice from my books on raising teenaged girls and avoided engaging in the battle. Of course, when the books demonstrate such techniques through italicized passages of dialogue, the authors have the kids ending up saying, "Oh, yes, now I understand, and I love you, too." Erin didn't get anywhere close to that, but when we got to the soccer field, she didn't slam the car door shrieking that she hated us, the house, the potted plants on the back deck, her little brother, and all her clothes, so I guess I had not been a complete failure.

She had a great game, scoring every goal that our team made, and her teammates flocked around her, hugging her just as if she were still one of the four drawstring cotton-fleece skirts. And maybe, to all eyes except hers, she still was.

It helped that the coach had gotten upset with how much Faith had distracted the girls during the previous week's game and had told her that she could talk to the players only during halftime. At first she had tried talking to two injured players, but the coach waved her off even from them. For a minute or so, she was standing by herself—which is, of course, a fate worse than death for a sixth-grade girl; you can't ever, *ever* let someone see you alone, how geeky is that?—but then she had the sense to go to the playground with the little sister of one of the players.

After the game Erin danced up to me and asked if she could go to Brittany's the following Friday.

I was a little surprised. I kept track of Faith's tyrannical schedule and I thought that next week was Faith's own turn to have the girls over. On those Friday nights Erin was always home alone.

"Of course," I said, "but I won't be able to drive you." I had just made arrangements with Mimi for driving our sons to a birthday party on Friday. "You'll need to walk."

"That's no problem," she said cheerily and skipped off.

It was nice to see her happy again, but three days later she asked, with an edge in her voice, if I was sure that I couldn't drive her on Friday night.

"I really can't, at least not until after eight." Thomas and Mimi's son, Gideon, had been invited to a birthday party in Rockville, one of the Maryland suburbs outside the Beltway. The party was from five-thirty to seven on a Friday evening. I couldn't imagine why anyone would think that was a good time of day to assemble a bunch of second graders, but some parents are clueless. And getting out to Rockville at the height of rush hour wasn't going to be any fun for the parents, either. The trip was long enough and the party short enough that I had said I would drive out there, drop the boys off, kill some time at G Street Fabrics, and then bring them home. "Is that going to be a problem?" I asked Erin.

"I don't know," she muttered and started to leave the room.

I followed her. "I'm doing a big favor for Rachel's mom. I'm sure she would be happy to run you over to Brittany's."

"We can't ask her to do that," Erin said instantly. "It's not fair."

It certainly wasn't fair. Mimi would be making a four-block drive in exchange for me investing at least three hours on Friday night, but I didn't suppose that that was what Erin meant.

I didn't give Erin's Friday-night plans much thought the rest of the week. Once the other second-grade parents heard that I was driving both ways to the Friday birthday party, they were determined to get their sons into my car. One of the delights of driving a "big-ass" station wagon is that sometimes you find yourself sharing the car with eight seven-year-old boys, which is the sort of thing that you probably need a day-care license for.

Even at the best of times, being the only adult with eight seven-year-old boys is no fun, and seven o'clock on Friday night with the boys on screeching sugar highs was not going to be the best of times. But long experience had told me that some of these families absolutely were not going to take "no" for an answer. They would, if necessary, go to court, getting an injunction that would force me to take their kid to this party.

I did at least draw the line at having kids share seat belts. "I'll be on an eight-lane expressway at rush hour," I said to the families of the ninth and tenth boys. At this rate we could just stage the party in my car. "I'm not double-buckling kids."

"Well, I would have called earlier," snapped one of these mothers, "but I was out of town. On *business*. It would have been nice of you to have held some spots in your car for people who *work*."

The Kennedy Center holds some tickets for senior citizens and students. American Express has a platinum card that reserves tickets and restaurant reservations for really rich people. But since when are the seats in my car such entitlements that the nation needs a system for allocating them to the most deserving?

The other thing that kept me from thinking about Erin's Friday-night plans was that Blair and I faced our first Spring Fair crisis that week. Once we had seen the list of women on the auction committee, we had known that we were going to have problems. Three people on the committee thrived on confrontation, and two prided themselves on being free spirits and independent thinkers.

Most of the funds raised at the fair come through the live and silent auctions held during the evening dinner. Only ten or so items are included in the live part of the auction; the rest are sold silently with bidders entering their bids on a sheet of paper.

All of the items for the auction are donated, and some of the donors are extremely generous. At the live auction last year we offered a private tour of the Supreme Court chambers and lunch with one of the justices, who was the grandfather of an Alden student. People also could bid on a week in a five-bedroom house in a French village; airfare for eight people was included in the package, as one family owned the house and another dad had an extremely senior position at the airline. Last year the organizers had put together a package of tickets to a home game for each of our major sporting teams with all the seats being in the owners' boxes. Most of these live auction items sell for more than ten thousand dollars.

But this year a grandmother, who had, during the fifties, a small career as an artist and still fancied herself a marketable professional, had donated five of her paintings to the auction with the understanding that the grandest one would be in the live auction. It would, needless to say, have a reserve price that corresponded to the grandmother's sense of her value as an artist. One of the "freethinkers" had agreed to this without clearing it with the rest of the committee, having done so because her own best friend was the daughter of this artist.

I couldn't imagine that someone would bid on any of the

pictures, especially the one in the live auction. The silence that would follow its introduction would depress everyone's spirits and embarrass the donor's family. The rest of the committee, now pretty upset with the freethinker who had not been assigned to solicit live auction donations, wanted her to tell the grandmother that her grand painting wouldn't be in the live auction and that at most only one of the other works would be in the silent auction.

She refused to do that, and so in the end, Blair volunteered to do the dirty work. Summoning all of her semifaux Southern graciousness and some of her University of Pennsylvania art history training, she called the artist. *Oh my, but your paintings are so striking, such vivid instances of early fifties realism—and your use of space and light—*Blair really could shovel the lingo when she put her mind to it—*that's almost Hudson Rivery, isn't it? The difficulty, of course, is that people will have been drinking, and the stark dignity of your work blurs . . .*

And somehow Blair managed to persuade the artist that her work had too much depth and intelligence to be appreciated by the blithering, drunken mob that would populate this event.

So with these grand operas chewing up my week, I didn't ask Erin about her plans until I picked her up after school on Friday. I winced as I did so because now it probably was too late to ask Mimi to run her over to Blair's, though I didn't understand why that was needed in the first place.

"I decided that I didn't want to go," Erin muttered.

That was hard to believe. "Oh, sweetie, was it just not having a ride?"

"It's okay, Mom."

Her voice didn't sound as if it was okay. I tried six different ways to ask the same question and got the same response.

So I left her at home as I set out to round up my little army of birthday celebrants and transport them to the wilds of Rockville. On the way there the boys amused themselves by taking off their seat belts to see if I would notice, which fortunately I did. On the trip home they amused themselves by yelling. Then one of the boys wet his pants, and that provided a whole new dimension of fun.

Back home I took Thomas right up to his room although I had no great hopes of him calming down. Erin was in her room reading. Now when she felt abandoned by her friends, she read rather than watching the Disney Channel, choosing books from a series of paperbacks written for middle-school girls. I had read a few, and they depicted girls solving mysteries that I thought would be better left to the police, but the girls had really cute clothes, and I suppose that that made their disregard for all laws about trespassing and privacy okay. It was a good thing their villains ended up confessing because no prosecutor could have gotten admitted the evidence that the girls had so charmingly collected. The Disney Channel might actually be more morally uplifting than these books, but I was enough of a snob about the printed word that I was just glad she was reading.

Jamie got home as I was getting Thomas settled. I could see that Erin had already made herself some macaroni and cheese, and so I switched on the Jenn-Air indoor grill to prepare some deboned chicken breasts for Jamie and me.

We were just about to sit down when the phone rang. I could see from caller ID that it was Blair's cell phone.

I wondered why she was on her cell. If the girls were at her house, surely she was home.

I could hear a lot of background noise. "Where's Erin?" she said, her voice rushed.

"She's here, upstairs, reading."

"But she was supposed to be at the movies with the other girls."

"What movie?" I asked carefully. "I don't know anything about a movie. At the beginning of the week she was going to spend the night at your house and then suddenly she wasn't."

"After rehearsal Mary Paige took the girls to Mazza." That is a mall on the D.C.-Maryland line. "They were going to eat at McDonald's and go to the movies. I was picking them up. It was all planned. I assumed that Erin would be with them."

"Well, she's not. She's here."

"Then does she want to meet us at the house? We'll be back in fifteen minutes."

"Let me talk to her. Call me when you get home."

I went upstairs. This did not add up. There was no way that Blair could have been planning to pick up all five girls from the movie theater; she had only four extra seat belts. If she had given the matter any thought, she would have realized that either someone else was also driving—which she would have heard about—or Erin wasn't being included.

But she hadn't thought. *You're my friend; you are supposed to think about my child, you should have noticed whether she had been included.*

I knocked on Erin's door. "That was Mrs. Branson," I said when she told me to come in. "I realize that there was some sort of confusion about the movie, but do you want to go over to Brittany's now? Dad or I can run you over right now or as soon as we're done eating."

"Was it Mrs. Branson on the phone or Brittany?"

I took a breath. How I wished I could have said that Brittany had called, that Brittany had grabbed her mother's cell phone. *Oh, Erin, I am really really sorry, I don't know what happened but we really really did mean you to come and it really really wasn't any fun without you and you just have to come to my house for the night. You just have to.*

But the mom had been the one to call. Erin didn't want an invitation from one of the moms; she wanted the girls to invite her.

And indeed twenty minutes later when the call came reporting that they were back home, it was again Blair calling, not Brittany.

Erin was still upstairs, so I could speak frankly to Blair. "She says that she doesn't want to come, but I think that she feels slighted about not being included."

"But she was included," Blair insisted. "In the car Brittany said that they sort of thought that Erin would be there."

We are not families that "sort of" make plans for our children; all the i's are dotted, the t's are crossed, the seat belts counted. I would never simply drop my daughter at the mall, assuming that she would get a ride home.

And Blair knew that. She continued quickly, "Brittany also said that she wasn't sure Erin wanted to come."

That was nonsense. Of course, Erin would have wanted to come. This would have been an exciting outing—the girls being dropped off at a mall by themselves, ordering and paying for their own food, then going up the escalator and purchasing their own tickets. It would have been quite an adventure for these kids. There was no way Erin wouldn't have wanted to go.

So what had happened? Had the other kids not noticed that she didn't have a ride? They were so new at making their own plans. Or had they noticed and not cared enough to mention it to one of their mothers? It didn't particularly matter because the message was the same to Erin—she had not been wanted.

Annelise called in the morning, tracking me down on my cell phone because I, loyal member of the Alden community, had taken the big-ass station wagon to the varsity girls' volleyball team's fund-raising car wash. Although we were a lower- and middle-school family, we supported the high-school kids' fund-raising.

Annelise was full of the endless apologies so typical of her. "Oh, Lydia, I feel so awful. I don't know what happened. Erin was part of the plan at first, and then I thought everything was all arranged. I really don't think it was deliberate. I don't think any of them were trying to exclude her—"

"But when she couldn't come, they didn't do anything."

The rasping bitterness in my voice surprised me. Maybe the varsity girls' volleyball team was using such harsh chemicals to clean the cars so that all their supporters would sound like hostile shrews for the rest of the day. Or maybe I was managing to sound like a hostile shrew all on my own.

"Yes," Annelise gasped, "and I feel so awful, but it can't have been on purpose, Lydia. It just can't have been."

Mimi was more blunt when she called later in the day. "I'm going to murder you if you knew that Erin needed a ride to and from the movies, and you didn't ask me." She has no patience with people who set her up to be in the wrong.

"I didn't know anything about it, or I would have asked you."

"I'm glad of that," she said. "I'm not sure why Erin fell through the cracks like that. It seemed that the plans were changing every three minutes, and I guess when Mary Paige called the rest of us to be sure that we knew she was leaving the girls at McDonald's, I thought everything was set."

"Mary Paige didn't call me."

"That's where the slipup must have occurred. She only called for the kids who would be in her car. Is Erin all bent out of shape about not being included? Rachel says that she didn't go over to Blair's afterward."

"Erin does feel slighted."

"I'm sure it will blow over," Mimi said confidently. "It's all playground politics. They've been friends for too long for something like this to get in the way."

And that's what Blair said later in the day, too. That all this would blow over, that everything would be fine in the long run, and that I shouldn't encourage Erin to dwell on this one little incident.

Erin didn't need the least bit of encouragement in order to dwell on this incident; she was managing fine all on her own.

The following week I urged her to call some different girls—if not girls from school, then perhaps some from church. But no, she couldn't do that. If her own friends didn't like her, why would anyone else like her? She wasn't ever going to have any friends again for as long as she lived, and no tornado, hurricane, or other gale-force wind would ever blow this over.

6

What was I going to do about my annual holiday pictures of the four girls?

Why pretend that the four of them were still a foursome? But if I didn't take the picture, would that be saying that I thought the friendship had ended permanently? And wasn't that a suggestion that might become a self-fulfilling prophecy?

I wanted one of my friends to say something about the photo. I wanted one of them to say that she, too, didn't like this split among the girls and that she hoped that I could rise above the fact that her daughter was being, if not an absolute shit to my daughter, at least not a loyal friend. She would beg, she would grovel, and I would be gracious and accommodating.

That was not going to happen. While Annelise would

have been perfectly happy to beg and grovel, she did not want
to make me take the photo if I didn't want to. For their part,
Mimi and Blair probably assumed that I was a rational human
being who needed to make my own decisions, doing whatever
I thought was appropriate.

Were they ever wrong. My daughter's tendency to whining
martyrdom didn't come from those Quakers on her dad's side
of the family tree.

But good friends are supposed to bring out the best in you.
If Mimi and Blair had decided that I was a mature adult, then
perhaps I could act like one. As soon as the soccer season was
over in early November, I e-mailed the other three about the
pictures just as if nothing different was happening this year.
We agreed on a date. The girls already had blue jeans with a
light-washed finish, and Mimi said that she had time to get
four matching white T-shirts.

A few days later my phone rang. "Mrs. Meadows, this is
Rachel."

"Hi, sweetie. Erin's not here." It was Sunday afternoon,
and Jamie had taken both kids out to a movie. I had some
clients coming over in a few minutes.

"That's okay. The rest of us wanted to know if we could include Faith in the picture this year. She really wants to be in it,
and it doesn't seem right to leave her out."

Leaving her out certainly seemed right to me. "I don't
know. Let me think about it. It's not anything personal. It's
that there has always been the four of you."

I wasn't just being vengeful—although surely that was part
of it—excluding Faith simply because she had excluded Erin.

The pictures of these four girls had gotten me my professional start. Even when I was still working at EPA and had only had a few classes at the Corcoran, people would see the pictures at one of our homes and would want to book a session for their own children with whoever had taken these pictures. If anyone now wanted to see a sample of my work, I showed them the most recent pictures of the girls. "This is what I do," I would say. "I use film, black and white. Very simple clothes on a white background." My pictures weren't about the red plaid dresses the subjects were wearing or the Christmas trees they were standing in front of or the bunnies they were holding. I took pictures of children. Individual, interesting children.

So I wanted to continue the series for professional reasons. But refusing to let Faith come would alienate the other girls. This time they had spoken up when someone they liked had been left out. So the solution was simple. I would take two sets of pictures, one with four girls and one with five. Faith could come, but she needed to come late.

I called Mary Paige. She sounded pleased and grateful . . . having apparently forgotten how exquisitely painful it would be for anyone in her family to set foot in my house. "We couldn't be happier that you're including her. She is so fond of the other girls."

Not of mine. She wasn't fond of my girl. "There is one thing." I explained to her how I used the foursome in my portfolio. "So could you bring Faith at eleven o'clock?"

"Of course," Mary Paige said. "That's fine, I will bring her over at eleven."

But Faith showed up with the other girls at ten.

"Why is she here?" I whispered to Annelise, who had been driving.

"I don't know. Is it a problem? Mary Paige just called and asked if she could drop Faith off at nine. She had a hair appointment."

A hair appointment on Saturday? Women who didn't have jobs shouldn't have Saturday hair appointments. That wasn't fair to the women whose schedules weren't so flexible, who could only go on Saturday. "I told her to bring Faith at eleven."

"Oh, I'm sorry." Annelise was her ever-apologetic self. "I didn't know that."

"I'm not blaming you." I just felt sorry for all the women who needed to get their hair done on Saturdays.

My capacity for self-delusion is breathtaking.

Our house had a finished attic. Much of the space wasn't very usable as the roofline slanted sharply, but the back half was a playroom and the front half was where I photographed. I had a large soft light, two strobes on stands, and a twelve-foot-wide roll of white seamless paper that served as a background.

As I predicted the minute I saw Faith, the session with the four girls didn't go well. Faith talked only to the other three girls and ignored Erin. The amount of boy-girl talk startled me. "He *likes* you," Faith said to Rachel about a boy whose name I didn't recognize. I guessed he must be a seventh grader. To Elise she said, "You know you like him; you know you do."

That boy was *definitely* a seventh grader. She teased Brittany about a sixth-grade boy who was easily five inches shorter than she was. Faith said nothing to Erin. She made it very clear that no boy was interested in Erin.

Did I want boys interested in Erin? No, not yet. Did I want Erin to be the only one of her friends whom no boy liked? Of course not.

And seventh graders! Since when had our girls started hanging out with older men?

I was finding Faith's chatter distracting, and the other girls could think about nothing else. I was about to send her downstairs to watch TV with Thomas when she started imitating the teachers. She really was very good at it, and soon even Erin had to laugh. But there was an uneasiness to the laughter. None of them were used to disrespecting their teachers; their expressions would, I knew, reveal their uncertainty.

I reloaded the camera and told Faith to join them. She skipped over and the other three girls clustered around her. I didn't push Erin too hard about making herself a part of the group. I didn't care about these pictures. I simply needed one that was good enough to give Mary Paige.

I developed the pictures that afternoon. I held my magnifier up to the contact sheet and examined the pictures of the four girls, marking which ones to enlarge.

Then I scanned through the ones with all five girls. Mary Paige would like them because Faith was in the middle and she looked pretty. I continued looking. And suddenly stopped.

The ninth picture was fabulous. Everything about the

composition, the balance, the proportion ... technically it might have been the best picture I had ever taken. Once I enlarged it, I could see a series of interlocking isosceles triangles. The bend of Rachel's elbow was a triangle that was the exact size as a triangle formed by the crossing of Faith's and Elise's arms. Elise's, Brittany's, and Faith's heads made a triangle that was mirrored exactly in one formed by the hems of Faith's, Rachel's, and Erin's jeans. I could have posed and reposed the girls for days on end and I would have never gotten this.

It was also strong emotionally. The message wasn't blatant. It wasn't like the cover of a book on childhood mental illness with one somber-looking kid standing alone in the foreground while in the background is a group of other kids laughing. This picture conveyed its message in a more subtle way. All of the lines of the picture flowed away from Erin. In every triangle in which she had part, the triangle was long and narrow, and she was at the apex. The two girls at the base of the triangle were close together, but distant from Erin. It formed a starkly beautiful portrait of exclusion.

I looked at their faces. They all looked quiet, even a little weary. That was no surprise in the four original girls; they had been tired of posing, but even Faith looked weary.

I picked up the magnifier again to look into her eyes.

The game this girl was playing was exhausting. *Pick me. Don't pick her. Here is our schedule of whom we invite when. Be sure and tell me when your games are so I can come. Will you call Erin's mom and get me in the picture?*

She was twelve. She had lost her father and her home. She

was an unhappy child, and her mother had given her a mission—to be one of the popular girls—and she was doing it the only way she knew how.

I had taken the pictures on Saturday morning, and as she always did, Blair had us over to tea Sunday afternoon to look at the proofs.

For all that we thought of ourselves as a unit, it was rare that the four of us ever sat down together in a room by ourselves unless we were counting the school's Sally Foster gift-wrap orders or processing new library books. But once a year Blair got out her set of beautiful hand-painted cups and saucers, unique because instead of being porcelain, they were glass. I think this was the only occasion from one year to the next that she used them.

The day was cool but bright, so Mimi and I walked over to Blair's with me carrying the proofs in a canvas tote bag decorated with hand-drawn stick figures who had huge heads and spiky hair. Thomas had made it for me for Mother's Day two years before. As we walked, Mimi and I talked a little bit about the new second-grade teacher; neither of our sons had him. We were sorry; we wanted the boys to have a male teacher.

The girls' relationship was the big pink elephant in the corner of the room that we were trying desperately not to talk about.

I was dreading this tea. Blair might have invited Mary

Paige. Twice these teas had occurred when Mimi's mother had been in town, and, of course, Bubbe—as we all called her—had been included. But Bubbe never spent the afternoon complaining about the price my family had paid for Mrs. Chester T. Paige's house.

As always Blair had set out her ornate silver tea service on the skirted table between the two windows of her Tiffany-blue living room. I was pleased to see four—and only four—glass cups.

Blair had decorated her house without any professional advice, and she had done a spectacular job, following the style of Dorothy Draper, who had—as I now knew—freed American interiors from dim, cluttered Victoriana. Each of the first-floor rooms was painted a vivid, cool, almost piercing color—periwinkle, melon, saffron—the kinds of colors that Blair wore herself. The colors were unified by the mirrorlike gloss of the stark white moldings and by the cabbage-rose fabric that tumbled through the rooms. Personally I prefer to live in a more restful style, but I always find myself smiling whenever I walk into her house.

I wondered what Mary Paige Caudwell, an "interior-design professional," thought of Blair's house. She must have seen it. They must have had the sort of conversation about it that Blair and I had always had.

I present my proofs to people in silver-toned binders with plastic page protectors. Each of the pictures is framed with a thick black line that duplicates the effect of a frame. Once Blair had poured the tea, Annelise and Mimi moved their chairs closer to Blair's while I sat on the other side of the skirted table, looking at the pictures upside down.

The pictures of the original four girls came first, and I knew that they were not as good as the pictures I had taken the year before. Three of the girls had braces, and none of them felt as comfortable with themselves and their bodies as they had the year before. All the boy-girl talk had made them uneasy, and the ridicule of their teachers had made them additionally uncomfortable.

But that's what preteen girls were—uneasy, awkward, and hesitant. When compared with the marvelous leapfrog picture of last year, whatever picture we chose would make a poignant statement about how hard adolescence was going to be.

In the second half of the binder were the pictures of all five girls. No one spoke as they looked at those pictures until they came to the one that I had taken ninth. They glanced at it, each probably checking how her own daughter looked. Mimi was about to turn the page when Blair, who had a better eye and more art training than the others, stopped her.

She looked up at me, her hand on the plastic-encased proof. "This is really good."

"Yes."

The others bent their heads to look more closely. Blair started talking about the lines and the balance. Then she noticed the triangles and was beginning to explicate that when Annelise interrupted her.

"That's not it. What's important in the picture is the emotion. It's—" She stopped.

She didn't know how to say this. But I did. "It's the relationship of Erin to the rest of the group."

Everyone was quiet.

So I went first. "You all keep saying that this will blow over, and I know that's what we all would like, but the other three girls really do like Faith."

"Maybe they will become a group of five," Annelise said.

"I don't know how you can think that will happen." My voice was high and thin. "Whenever Faith Caudwell organizes something, Erin is not included. When she came to my house for these pictures, she did not speak to Erin. If the difference between a group and a clique is that a clique is defined by the fact that who it *excludes* is more important than who it *includes*, then Faith is creating a clique by excluding Erin. She's showing how much power she has when she can get the others to leave Erin out. Not inviting, say, Suzanne Singer demonstrates nothing. Not inviting Erin shows real power, and this isn't just about the number of seat belts Mary Paige has."

"We know that," Blair said. "We've talked about it—"

We? We've talked about it? That hurt. When had there started being a "we" that didn't include me?

"—and we haven't been sure about what to do," Blair continued. "Insisting that they include Erin is becoming counterproductive. Inviting Erin became a symbol of having your parents too involved in your life."

"But when did they stop *wanting* to have her?" I needed to know. "What happened? What did she do?"

"It is a two-way street," Mimi said a little crisply. "Erin is telling the other girls that she doesn't want to come out with them."

"She's hurt," I cried. "She feels rejected. Saying that she doesn't want to come is her defense because she feels that they don't want her."

"But there's no reason for her to feel that way," Mimi said. "Of course they wanted her . . . at least until she got so defensive."

"So this is *her* fault?" I was furious.

"I wouldn't go that far," Mimi said.

But she had.

Blair spoke quickly. "None of us understand this, and if you are right, Lydia, that Faith is orchestrating a clique, then she has more control over our girls than any of us can like."

I couldn't sit here anymore. I couldn't listen to my friends try to talk their way out of this. I flipped shut the book of proofs and thrust it into the bag. My hands were shaking.

Startled, Mimi picked up our two cups and hurriedly carried them into the kitchen, then followed me through the front door, thrusting her hand out so that I couldn't slam it. We had come together so she was going to have us leave together.

Stay here! I wanted to shriek. *Stay here and talk about me and how this is all Erin's fault and be all smug because this isn't happening to your daughter.*

We were at the end of Blair's drive before Mimi spoke.

"This isn't like you, Lydia."

I was almost too angry to answer. "Isn't this how you felt when Rachel wasn't going to be in the ensemble?"

"That was different. That was—"

"No, it wasn't. We feel the same way. The difference is that you could keep your kid from being left out."

"And a lot of good it's done her," Mimi snapped back.

I looked at her.

"You can gloat," she said. "You were right. Mrs. Barton is making Rachel pay and pay for my interference. Rachel would have been better off if I'd just let her learn to deal with not being in the ensemble, even though it was completely unfair."

And Erin would have been better off as well. This whole fall would have played out so differently if Rachel hadn't been in the ensemble.

"Don't be like Candace Singer and assume that the cool girls don't have problems." Mimi was lecturing me. "Brittany's headaches are getting worse and worse; Blair's worried sick and she doesn't dare talk to you because she knows that you are still pissed off that Erin wasn't invited to that movie. And Rachel's not operating from a position of strength right now. Ensemble rehearsals are a nightmare for her; Mrs. Barton picks on her constantly. She comes home and is awful to her little brother. But you don't have to withdraw from the adult friendships," she went on, "just because the kids are realigning themselves."

"I'm not doing that." I was going to stand up for myself. This was not my fault. This was *so* not my fault. "I'm not withdrawing. I got in touch with everyone about these stupid pictures. You just feel guilty because your kid is avoiding my kid, and so you're not confiding in me about other stuff. Don't blame me for that. And do not, do *not*, talk about me when I'm not around."

"We aren't doing that," she protested. Now she was on the defensive.

"Yes, you are. Blair just said you were."

"Okay, so maybe we are. But, Lydia, what do you expect?"

"I'd expect you not to act like we're the ones in middle school. Don't shut me out the way the girls are shutting out Erin."

Mimi jerked at one edge of the big antique paisley shawl she was wearing, flinging it over her shoulder. The fringe caught in one of her big jingling earrings, and she winced as she tried to pull it free. I put down my canvas bag and untangled her.

We were looking at each other, standing close. "Okay," she said, "we feel guilty. We feel awful. But none of us want to hear other people, even you, criticize our daughters. Rachel, Elise, and Brittany are being lousy friends. Faith Caudwell may be piping the tune, but they are her little dancing sheep. Now it's one thing for me to call Rachel a 'dancing sheep,' but I don't want anyone else to. Even when her father criticizes her, I feel attacked and I can't see straight. So what I want is for you to tell me that either none of this is Rachel's fault or it doesn't matter and Erin doesn't mind, but you aren't going to say that."

"No," I said slowly. "I'm not."

"Then I'll say what you want to hear. What's happening among the girls stinks, and my little angel isn't doing one thing to make it better. But we've all got our egos so caught up in our daughters that it's really hard to admit that they aren't perfect."

Because Mimi had been so honest, we were able to part on good terms. I knew that neither of my kids was going to be home: Thomas was playing with some Sidwell kids who were on his soccer team, and Erin had a baby-sitting job. I was glad of that. I felt exhausted. When I opened the door, I heard the sound of a jazz recording that only Jamie liked. I followed the sound into the dining room. He was sorting papers at the table.

I wish he wouldn't do that. He has his own study upstairs, but he likes to work in the dining room and then he leaves his stuff there forever. The tabletop had been clear when I left for Blair's; now it was covered with papers. Jamie was standing at the long side of the table, picking up papers off a six-inch-high stack.

I pulled out one of the chairs and sat down to watch him. He was dressed in jeans and a long-sleeved, faded red polo shirt. He had started wearing red when he was an undergraduate at Haverford, a Quaker-affiliated college outside Philadelphia, because that was the school color, and he had just kept on buying his casual shirts in red even though with his auburn hair, he didn't look particularly great in the color.

Apparently it took him a minute to notice me. "How was your thing?"

"It was okay."

He could tell from my voice that it wasn't.

I could sense the struggle in him. He was, no doubt, doing exactly what he wanted to be doing, listening to jazz and getting these papers sorted. He was almost never alone in the house, and he did occasionally enjoy it.

So he didn't want to stop what he was doing and listen to me recount what he had in a fit of bad temper once called the "trivia of the universe," but he knew that he should.

I did not want to be anybody's "should" right now. If he didn't want to listen to me, screw him. I stood up to leave.

"Lydia, wait." He put down his papers and crossed the room to stop me at the door. "It wasn't okay, was it?"

His eyes are greenish brown with a lighter hazel circle around the pupil. Whatever he might have felt when he laid down the papers, he was paying attention to me now.

"Oh, Jamie." I could feel my throat thicken and my eyes start to sting. "I am so sick of this. You can't believe how sick I am of all this."

He put his arms around me. I pressed my cheek to his chest and I could feel him breathe. "What exactly do you mean by 'this'?" he asked.

"This whole business with Erin and her dramas and her unhappiness. I feel like it is taking over my whole life."

He stepped back. "I don't understand it," he admitted. "I've tried, but I can't."

"You understand what Erin's going through, don't you?"

"Yes. It's the intensity of your involvement that baffles me."

"But it's affecting my friendships, too."

Jamie listened to me with extreme patience for another ninety seconds or so, and then, guy that he is, wanted to go straight to the problem-solving, fix-it mode. "You know, Lydia, you can always rethink some of the choices you've made."

"Like whether to go back to work?"

"Not necessarily. Just how to have some more balance in your life."

Balance? Okay, this was really annoying. "Achieving balance was precisely what I had been trying to do when I quit work."

"Stop focusing on the working–not working thing. Your whole life is about relationships. That's what's not balanced. Even your work, your photography, when you talk about it, you always talk about individuals or relationships."

"So? That's what people want when they bring their kids to me. What pictures of our kids do you like the best? The perfect head shots? No. You like the ones that show a brother and a sister who love each other."

He admitted that was true. "So that might make it harder for you to find balance, but—"

I waved my hand, interrupted him. "A balanced life is supposed to keep my heart from breaking when my child is miserable? I can't imagine any weight big enough or heavy enough to balance out that."

I left the book of proofs on the front-hall table where we put the mail, thinking that Erin would see them when she went up to her room and could look at them in private if she wanted. Although it was clear from the position of the binder that she had looked at the pictures Sunday evening, she didn't say anything about them until Tuesday.

It was on that day that her SSAT scores arrived. The envelope was addressed to "the parents of," and so I opened it before she came home, thinking that if her scores were awful,

I just wouldn't tell her about them unless she remembered to ask. Why add to her sense of disappointment and failure?

I'd been warned not to expect dazzlingly high percentiles. Only students applying to academically challenging high schools take the SSAT, so the percentiles compare the test taker only to the best and the brightest. My eye went to the verbal percentile. Seventy-three. Ouch. We had been hoping for the high eighties, low nineties, and would have been happy with mid-eighties.

But, I reminded myself, we hadn't had her prepare. We hadn't hired tutors, hadn't made her memorize lists of vocabulary words. It was clear from the other mothers in the waiting room that many families had.

Math: ninety-nine.

I looked again. Ninety-nine. I ran my forefinger over the number, making sure that there wasn't a crease in the thin paper that had made the second digit seem a nine when it was really a zero. No, it was a nine. Her score was really ninety-nine.

Farther down the page was a section called "Test Question Breakdown." On "Number Concepts and Operations" Erin had gotten twenty-one right, none wrong, and had omitted two. On "Algebra, Geometry, and Other Math" she had again gotten none wrong, having answered twenty-three right and omitted three.

This was really amazing. She seemed to have been in complete control of the math section of this test. She knew what she knew, and she knew what she didn't know.

Mathematical ability does run in both our families. My father was a C.P.A., and Jamie's dad teaches high-school math. My mother is a crackerjack bridge player, my brother is a math professor, and his son, my nephew—God love him—dropped out of college to become a professional poker player. The numbers gene skipped Jamie and me, but clearly it had surfaced in Erin.

Ninety-ninth percentile—this was something. I couldn't wait to call Jamie.

Erin was walking a neighbor's dog after school this week so she tended to drop her backpack on the front steps, go walk the dog, and then come into the house through the front door.

As soon as I heard her come in, I hurried to the front hall to show her her scores. "Erin, this is fabulous. You did a great job. Dad and I are so proud of you."

Clearly she hadn't been giving the test any thought. She shrugged. "I told you that the math part was easy. It was probably just a fluke."

"I think they design the tests to avoid that." I started to explain the significance of her being able to distinguish between what she knew and what she didn't, but since she wasn't listening, I shut up.

She was looking down at the silver binder with the proofs in it. She jerked her head in its direction. "Are you going to use the picture with just the four of us or the one with Faith?"

I was sorry that she couldn't enjoy the success of these test scores.

"What do you think?" I tried to be neutral.

"They all look the same to me." Erin shrugged. "But the ones with the five look wrong."

"They do to me, too."

"What will you say to the rest of them if you use one of just the four of us?"

"I don't need to say anything. It's none of anyone else's business what I choose. It's my gift to them; I can do whatever I want."

I selected the best pictures of the four original girls and framed them to match the previous years' pictures, and as I had done for the past few years, I printed a smaller version for Mimi's mother, Bubbe, who was quite fond of all the girls. I also gave my friends the second best of the five, the one that revealed Erin's isolation less starkly, but I cropped it to a different size and framed it differently so that they would not be tempted to hang it with the others.

And what did I do with the best picture of all five girls, the best picture that I had ever taken?

Not a thing.

I also sent one of the pictures of the five girls to Mary Paige. She sent me a thank-you note so perfect that it was a little annoying. Then she called.

"Really, the picture is so wonderful." She sounded completely sincere. "I love it. We both do. And my mother wondered if she could get one just of Faith, with the other girls cropped out. I realize that it wouldn't work on this one, but Annelise said that there are others, and that one of them is a marvelous picture. I'd pay you for the print, of course."

I hate that. *I'd pay you, of course*. People only say that when they are trying to get away with asking you for a favor without being accountable for the favor aspect of it. And they also think that because it is a favor, but not really, they can get away with paying you a lot less than a service is worth. So from your point of view it is a complete loss. You aren't paid what you are entitled to and you don't rack up the credits for having done a favor.

"I don't really work that way."

"But surely the others have wanted a picture just of their child."

If they had, they hadn't said. I had done portraits of the girls with their siblings. I did all their prints at cost, which was a huge savings, but their mothers—even though they were my best friends in the whole world—had paid me the sitting fee.

It was that sitting fee that Mary Paige was trying to avoid.

"Could I just come look at the others and see if there are any that I'd like? I'd pay you for the print, of course."

"I don't really think that any will work in the way you want them to."

"But I'd still like to come see."

She didn't give up, did she? Did she really care this much about avoiding a sitting fee? "You'll have to trust me on this," I said.

"This is my child. I'm entitled to see the pictures of her."

"Do you mean to make this a legal issue?"

"It *is* one, isn't it?"

Frankly, I didn't know. "We didn't study it in law school. I do retain the copyright."

"I really must insist."

She was making much too big a deal out of this. I think she was just determined to have her own way to show that she could. For my part, I didn't want her to see that one picture. I didn't want her to see the extent to which her child had hurt mine. But I had numbered the proofs in the binder so I couldn't remove that ninth picture.

Actually I could. I could develop and enlarge one of the ones off the contact sheet. I could substitute it for the one I didn't want Mary Paige to see.

But what was the point? This wasn't between her and me. It was among the girls, and the damage had already been done, whether she saw that picture or not. The only way to win was not to care. I did care about what had happened between her daughter and mine, but whatever Mickey Mouse power struggle was going on between her and me, I didn't need to care about that.

I tried to be as gracious as I could. "Then, of course, you can come look at them."

Once again she had forgotten what agony setting foot in her grandparents' former home would be. She was very interested in how I had decorated the house. In the front room, she picked up the hem of one of the drapes to look at the workmanship, which seemed inappropriate, but I suppose she would have excused herself because she was an "interior-design professional." She fingered the lining, establishing that the drapes were indeed interlined with flannel. She was probably disappointed at that; now she couldn't tell me that the drapes would have been better if they had been interlined.

That wasn't fair. I had no reason on earth to think that Mary Paige would have relished lecturing me about the importance of flannel interlinings. That was my mother's specialty— offering "constructive criticism" when it was too late to be of any use. It was too easy for me, whenever I felt a little threatened by another woman, to invest her with my mother's tricks.

Instead Mary Paige was extremely complimentary about what I had done with the house. Any cutting remarks she saved for the woes of living in a rented house. "It's perfectly dreadful. You can't do anything to make it your own. I can't wait until we are more settled."

"How long is your lease?" I asked.

"It's a year, but I certainly hope to be out of there long before that. We really do need to be close to school. I want Faith to have what I had with this house. Alden can really be a neighborhood school if you live in the right house."

But this house had belonged to Mr. and Mrs. Chester T. Paige, Mary Paige's grandparents, not her parents. I wondered where they had lived.

When we went back into the kitchen, I began to doubt that she had really been in the house as much as she had claimed. By eliminating the butler's pantry, we had gotten an el extension at one end of the kitchen, but clearly she was puzzled by the space, unable to figure out where it had come from.

Mary Paige was, however, gushingly sweet about the pictures. Why not? She had won. "It was so good of you to include Faith. She was delighted. She is so fond of the other girls."

She flipped right by the good one. She was only looking at

Faith. She had no appreciation for the aesthetic composition of the whole picture and certainly no sense of any message or meaning.

I hadn't reexamined the proofs before she came, but as we leafed through the booklet, I spotted a picture that could be cropped to come up with a nice head shot of Faith. I used Post-it notes to show Mary Paige how the finished product would look. "It doesn't have the rhythm of the whole picture, but Faith looks very pretty."

"Doesn't she though? And this is much nicer than the ones my sister had done of her kids. So I think we should make it bigger than those . . . just because you're such a talented photographer, not because I am competing with my sister although I suppose it sounds like that."

It certainly did. "How big are those?"

"Oh, like this." She gestured with her hands, and I guessed that her sister had made an eight by ten. So we were talking about at least an eleven by fourteen. "I'd pay you," she kept saying.

Fine. I handed her my standard rate sheet.

"These aren't per print, are they?"

"Yes, and there is the cropping fee as well."

"You certainly do think well of your work, which, of course, you should. It is lovely."

Clearly the cost of prints was much more than Mary Paige had ever imagined.

"On second thought you were right," she went on, careful not to look at me, "cropping really doesn't work. I should have trusted you."

She looked at her watch and thanked me, but declared that she had to run. I felt sorry for her. She knew that she had bullied me into this. She had wanted me to jump through her hoop, and then it turned out that she couldn't afford the hoop.

7

We spent Thanksgiving with Jamie's parents in Pittsburgh. I like them; they are gentle, observant, intelligent people. Jamie's older brother married into a big, close-knit Polish Catholic family, and the joyous excess of their holiday celebrations has subsumed the Meadowses' quiet Quaker traditions. The rest of us—Jamie's parents, Jamie and I, and his unmarried younger brother—have chosen to accept the exuberant hospitality of the other family, but we do all feel as if we are at the edge of someone else's party.

Jamie and I went for a walk Saturday afternoon, and he warned me about his upcoming trial, scheduled to start after the first of the year.

I looked at him oddly. "We've been through trials before. This is going to be longer. Is there more than that?"

"There will be a level of publicity that we've never experienced before."

Jamie's firm specializes in corporate civil litigation. Civil court is where you go when your neighbor builds a new deck and the steps end up on your property. Of course, since his firm's clients are large corporations, the issues between the disputing parties are much larger and much less personal. Most of his cases have very little "human interest." Rarely is there one good guy and one bad guy. Both companies have probably done something wrong, and Jamie's job is to devise a legal strategy that ensures the best outcome for his client.

He compartmentalizes better than I do. If I were a litigator—something I do not have the personality for—I would do best if I loathed my client's adversary. I would want to be on a crusade at all times, carrying the banner of freedom. I would burn out in a week.

Jamie does not want to be on a crusade. He doesn't want to demonize individual people. He doesn't want to make things personal.

I used to think it odd that here he, a Quaker, dedicated to respecting other people's individuality, didn't like it when things got personal.

"That's just it," he had said. "I don't want *things* to get personal. I want people to be personal. Things need to stay things."

So while he had often been extremely busy, working long,

long hours, no case had ever left him feeling as if he had been tied to an emotional train track. He would be physically weary, but not emotionally or spiritually.

But this case was different. It was a criminal case.

Jamie's clients in this case were the senior executives of a major utilities/telecommunications/everything else now-bankrupt corporation, and the federal government had been investigating their accounting procedures. Because the clients had been far too creative in their accounting, Jamie's firm had been expecting that a civil suit would be filed in federal court.

The clients' alleged actions had caused real hardship for many of the company's employees. People in Texas wanted to punish the fiends that had robbed these nice working folks; they wanted justice, they wanted a crusade. Too many previous high-profile cases against the executives of failed Texas corporations had come after federal investigations that had seemed to last forever. This time political pressure was forcing the state to act quickly.

The district attorney's office had filed criminal indictments. They had charged Jamie's clients with crimes, go-to-jail crimes.

Jamie's firm almost never did criminal work, and in the normal course of things, it would have passed this case along to another firm. But this firm's speciality was preparation. Its lawyers always knew more than the opposing counsel. Their documents were better indexed; their arguments were supported by more citations. This case was particularly complex, but Jamie had thoroughly mastered its intricacies. Although none of the clients trusted one another anymore, they all trusted Jamie. So, even though they were each lawyering up individually, they wanted Jamie to be lead counsel.

At first he relished the challenge, but he had soon remembered why he had always avoided criminal work. In a criminal trial, a jury does want there to be a good guy and a bad guy. Furthermore, this case was getting considerable publicity, and the media personalizes everything in a way that Jamie couldn't stand. Complex accounting procedures do not interest *People* magazine. An unflattering picture of someone's expensively dressed second wife getting into an expensive car . . . now that's clear evidence of criminal wrongdoing.

On the Monday after Thanksgiving, Jamie went down to Houston for more pretrial work, and as we had agreed, I sat down and filled out the kids' Sidwell applications. Erin had to write an essay. When she handed it to me, it was folded and she was glaring. I was not to change a word.

I disciplined myself not to read it until she had left for school. It was about her cousin, my brother's son, the professional poker player. She wrote about how he could do any mathematical equation in his head and about how well he had explained probability to her. She wondered why he wasn't going to college if he was so smart.

It read like a first draft. Her ideas were interesting, but she kept circling back as she thought more about each issue. She did have a strong thesis, but it was in her conclusion because it hadn't occurred to her until then.

I know my weaknesses. If this had been a college application or if I had felt that the honor of our family was riding on the children going to Sidwell, I would have "edited" this essay, reordering the argument and fixing the sentence fragment that was glaring, zitlike, out of the third paragraph. Families who had hired tutors to prepare their twelve-year-olds for the SSATs were doing just that. Their kids' essays wouldn't have any sentence-fragment zits in them.

But I couldn't imagine ever taking Erin and Thomas out of Alden. So I refolded Erin's essay and added it unchanged to her application.

Tuesday I filed a request with the Alden registrar to have the kids' transcripts sent to Sidwell. The following day I got an e-mail from Chris Goddard asking to see me the next time I was at school, offering to come down to either the lower or the middle school. I was helping with a writer's workshop in the second grade on Thursday, so I e-mailed back, adding that I could come to his office at the high school.

Which was a mistake. His beautiful office with its high ceilings and gracious windows was freezing. He was, not surprisingly, dressed in a heavy sweater and a thick tweed blazer.

"No wonder you offered to meet me at the lower school," I said. "It's so cold in here. How do you stand it?"

"Because it's useful. Any time I want a meeting short, I hold it here. People become remarkably efficient."

My stupidly girlish vanity was pleased that he had been

willing to meet me elsewhere. "I suppose you're wanting to know why we are applying to Sidwell."

He looked momentarily puzzled. Clearly that hadn't been why he had wanted to see me. "Actually not. We believe families should explore all their options."

That sounded canned. "Did you read that on a greeting card?"

"No. I wrote it on the back of my hand." He hooked his shirt cuff aside as if to show me the lettering. His hand was narrower than Jamie's, his fingers were longer and more tapering, and needless to say, there was nothing written on it. "What they say in the lower school is that your husband is a Quaker and so this is a bit pro forma."

I grimaced. "I fully support my husband's interest in educating the children in a school affiliated with his faith."

Chris tapped the back of his hand and peered across his desk as if trying to see the crib sheet written on mine, but beyond that he said nothing.

"So why am I here?" I asked. "What do you need?"

"I suppose it goes without saying that I need something," he said, his tone not one bit sheepish. "I need someone to host a buffet to launch the new Capital Campaign next spring."

The Capital Campaign was a fund-raising drive designed to, among other things, improve Mrs. Chester T. Paige's gym. "When next spring?" The fair was going to blow a great big hole in my spring. I really didn't think I should take on anything else, especially as we couldn't predict how long Jamie's trial would last.

"The week before Spring Break. We're not asking you;

we're asking for someone like you. A big house in Northwest, a family with kids in the lower and middle school, probably without a strong alumnae connection. I don't know who picked this campaign committee, but there aren't enough lower- and middle-school families, and almost none of what people call 'new' "—he used his first fingers to make quotation marks—"families. If this isn't a schoolwide campaign, it will be a disaster."

I knew that Chris's fund-raising abilities had been a big part of why he had been hired. "Julie Rossi would be a prime candidate." Julie had three kids in the school; her youngest was in Thomas's grade. "But she is redoing her kitchen this year. And Tricia Shepherd is about to rip up all her bathrooms. So you might try my neighbors Mimi and Ben Gold. They aren't redoing anything at the moment."

He was shaking his head. "Why aren't you on this committee? Who else knows the status of everyone's plumbing?"

"There are actually quite a few others," I answered. "When you live in an old house, plumbing is an interesting subject."

"I'll remember that the next time I am stuck for conversation. I will ask about wall flanges and ball-cock assemblies."

"And we will have answers."

Then there was silence. His mission had been accomplished, and we had exchanged the necessary amount of parent-headmaster pleasantries, probably more than was really necessary. But Chris was not pushing his chair back, glancing at his phone, or sending any other messages that the meeting was over.

"Is that your son?" I gestured to the photograph on the credenza. It was the one in which the boy had an odd shadow along his nose. "Is he at Cornell?"

He nodded. "Did you go there?"

I had. "I recognized the building." I asked him if his son liked the school, and he said he thought that he did.

"You only *think*?"

"No, no, I know. Considering everything, he and I do have a reasonably decent relationship. His grandparents did a very good job with him."

"Do you see him often?"

"As often as I see anyone whom I'm not paid to see."

Chris said this with such a light, pleasant tone that I could not take it personally even though he clearly was being paid to see me.

I suddenly had a vision of him not as a lonely person, but as an isolated one, someone who had deliberately chosen to have few intimate relationships. That was probably what would make him a success as the head of this school, his ability to remain disengaged.

Whereas I—as I kept having to tell my husband—was all about relationships. All of my various pursuits—raising my kids, keeping my house going, staying married, and taking pictures of people without shadows on their noses—involved relationships. Jamie and Chris had goals; I had relationships.

So true to my relationship-nuturing self, I went home and warned Mimi that she would get a call asking her to host the kickoff dinner for the school's Capital Campaign. As I had anticipated, she liked the idea. "But you've got to have the dog at your house and let people park in your driveway," she said.

Our very pretty, very theme park–looking street was narrow. The city maps labeled Mimi's side of the street as No Parking, but there was only one sign, rather randomly placed in someone's forsythia hedge. A widower on our side of the street kept posting very official-looking No Parking signs in front of his property. This was, of course, illegal and morally indefensible, but the family on Mimi's side who had chosen to fight the battle were using such very heavy legal weaponry that the rest of us were cowering, hoping not to get caught in what was still a metaphorical crossfire.

We theme-park residents do like our lawsuits.

Then it was December. Needless to say, I took on way too many projects, but the massive baking binges and the overly elaborate decorating schemes were lots of fun. Thomas had a party with twenty seven-year-olds decorating gingerbread houses that I had made out of graham crackers and hot glue. For weeks afterward we had sugar sprinkles in the carpets and dried-up streaks of colored frosting under the first-floor faucets.

Of course, all these happy little reindeer games could not conceal that my family was not living up to the ropes of evergreen garlands that festooned the front-hall banister. Jamie was MIA. He was spending most of every week in Houston, and he did not go to a single Christmas party, including the one put on by his firm.

Erin, while not quite roadkill, continued to be knocked down by Faith Caudwell's relentless pursuit of popularity. Fortunately some of the other mothers in the ensemble had become incensed that their daughters had been left out of Faith's little rotation of Friday-night sleepovers, and so a few social events for all eleven girls in the ensemble were scheduled. This, of course, angered the mothers of the girls who weren't in the ensemble. They took their complaints to Mrs. Shot, the principal of the middle school, and she answered them by saying that she had warned Mr. Goddard that this was precisely what would happen if he enlarged the ensemble, that there was really no point in coming to her, it hadn't been her decision.

I stayed out of that battle.

Rather than being by herself on Friday night, Erin started baby-sitting a lot, which certainly made her very popular among the parents of small children. Concerned about her mood, I took her to the pediatrician, and he spoke to her privately for almost twenty minutes, which is a very long time in that practice. He asserted that she was not depressed, and then he made me feel like an overreacting private-school mom (which wasn't a great leap), but I decided that it was better to worry about your child being depressed when she wasn't than fail to worry about it when she was.

At least I decided to trust him and not insist on Erin seeing an adolescent psychiatrist. Such a person would have, no doubt, recommended that she be institutionalized as being pre-verbal because she wouldn't have said a word.

Blair's daughter started her period, the first of our girls to do so. It gave her great status. A week later, Faith announced that she had gotten hers as well. Now Erin had something else to feel defective about—she hadn't started her period. Menstruation had become a competitive sport among these girls.

Erin started carrying a little zippered pouch with a Kotex pad in her backpack, but she still hadn't needed to use it when we went to my mother's for Christmas.

After I quit working at EPA, I felt that I needed to justify myself to my mother. She had not been happy staying at home, and so I felt that I needed to explain why, despite all the societal resources invested in my education, I was go-ing to stay home, too. Then I realized that she was taking my contentedness as a reproach. She did not view her un-happiness as her own fault—nothing was ever her fault. It was society's fault. Intelligent women could not be satis-fied in a capitalistic, patriarchal culture. The fact that my sister-in-law and I were happy with our differing mixes of domestic and professional activities—Suzanne was a busy orthodontist—suggested that perhaps Mother's thesis was wrong.

And my mother was never wrong.

. . . .

Jamie went straight from Indiana to Texas. Jury selection was scheduled for January 10.

His clients had almost certainly engaged in some dreadful accounting procedures that had made a lot of people lose jobs and savings, but Jamie believed that he could put on a viable defense. The indictment wasn't well-written, and so while Jamie would have been in trouble in the face of a well-crafted federal civil suit, this criminal charge was questionable. Furthermore, the prosecutors handling the trial didn't fully understand all the dreadful accounting procedures, and Jamie did.

So he felt confident that he would be able to persuade a judge to throw out a lot of the evidence and several of the charges. He also felt that there was a good chance that he could get the jury to acquit on what was left. Whatever the clients had done, they hadn't done this.

But clever legal tactics weren't going to be enough. When the trial was over, the jurors had to go home and face their neighbors. The jurors, the press, and the public needed someone to hate, and Jamie needed to find someone for them to hate besides his clients.

Many of the clients had second wives—gorgeous, ambitious, ill-educated young women who had gone almost overnight from shopping at Target to shopping on the top floor of Neiman Marcus. Their spending patterns made for delicious reading; their clothes, their parties, and their interior-design extravagances. Jamie's firm was making a "court of public opinion" case not against the wives, but against the people who had helped the wives spend the money. Personal shoppers, stylists, and florists sensed the insecurity behind these young women's aggressiveness. These young women were pursuing social status as wholeheartedly as a middle-school girl would pursue popularity. The lifestyle advisors only had to say, "The best people do this," and the wallets opened up.

It made for fun reading. In one client's home, an interior designer had noticed the envelope of a kid's school pictures and had offered to "pick up" a little frame. Three weeks later the client got a bill for a three-hundred-dollar custom mat and frame created for this routine, standard-sized photo of a stepchild whom the second wife barely knew. A florist managed to persuade one young woman that she needed a weekly standing order so that she would have fresh flowers in all of her "principal rooms"—whether the rooms were going to be used that week or not—and the deliveries continued even when the family was out of town. Interior designers took "oh, how nice" for an approval. When one young thing said that she didn't really like the orange tiger lilies in a wallpaper, the designer ordered a custom run of the paper with magenta tiger lilies. Fashion stylists helped the wives put together ensembles, but not a wardrobe. One of these wives bought seven very expensive black knee-length skirts in sixty days, and she still didn't have anything to wear. Each skirt had detailing or an embellishment that kept it from being combined with anything but the one jacket it was purchased with.

The popular media picked up on the theme quickly, using

it to create a backlash against the cable-television makeover shows and every other kind of stylist. The coverage quickly outgrew Jamie and his case, but that was fine. An antistylist culture was in the air, and Jamie's clients would benefit.

The strategy had not been Jamie's idea, but he had authorized it.

He appeared on every talk show that would have him. He needed the public to think of him as one of the good guys. There was no live television coverage of the trial itself, but once jury selection was over, Court TV spent an hour each evening summarizing the day's proceedings. Jamie was having his fifteen minutes of fame.

Chris Goddard called and asked if there was anything the school needed to be doing for my kids.

"I don't think so."

"I was assistant principal at a private school in California. We had a lot of high-profile parents, some of whom didn't behave very well. So we had some challenges."

I made a face. "I can imagine."

"No, you can't imagine, and you should be grateful for that." Then he sobered. "Have your kids said anything?"

"Thomas says that kids have seen snippets of Jamie on TV, but, of course, they are clueless about the case itself."

"Aren't we all?" I sensed that he was smiling. "What about Erin? Has she said anything?"

"No." I took a breath. "But she wouldn't. What's going on?" Obviously something was.

"Most of the attention she is getting is positive."

I didn't like the sound of "most." "Is someone saying that the other kids shouldn't talk to her because her dad is representing bad people?"

"More or less."

"It's Faith Caudwell, isn't it?"

He couldn't answer that directly, but, of course, it was. "The sixth-grade teachers are spending some time on the case where John Adams represented British soldiers, emphasizing how everyone is entitled to legal representation."

I sighed with grateful relief. This really was a wonderful school. The teachers were changing the curriculum in order to provoke some meaningful discussion of an issue that might be used to torment my child. This is what you are paying for when you get the tuition bill . . . and it is worth it.

8

Blair was giving a party. Looking at our houses, you would think that we entertained all the time. The big kitchens, the open spaces, and the multilevel decks are ideal for crowds. In my cellar are bays of shelving where I keep two thirty-cup coffee urns, boxes of wineglasses, a folding banquet table, twelve stackable catering chairs, and twenty-four bamboo trays for guests to use at buffets. Mimi has twelve more chairs identical to mine, Blair has two more folding banquet tables and fifty white china dinner plates, Annelise has a portable coatrack, three beautiful copper tubs for chilling adult beverages, and countless bright plastic ones for kiddie drinks.

And so what kinds of parties do we give? The end-of-the-season soccer–family potluck and the going-away party for the one kid in the fifth grade whom no one really liked. The only times we have adults-only parties are when we host the Parent Service Association Volunteer Appreciation Tea or when we open our homes for fund-raisers, as Mimi will for the school's Capital Campaign in a few months.

We keep meaning to entertain a lot, we think of ourselves as people who entertain a lot—that's why we buy all this stuff—but in truth, we have what the etiquette columnist Miss Manners calls "faux social lives." We rarely just have friends over although we look as if we do. More life in the theme park.

Blair's party was for adults, but its basic impulse was professional, not personal. Her husband, Bruce, is a lobbyist. His firm was merging with another firm, and I didn't understand the details, but Branson—their last name—was going to be part of the firm's title.

Bruce Branson is vibrant, smart, and persuasive, and he does not sweat the small stuff. He never worries about the whereabouts of his car keys, his attaché case, his umbrella, or his passport. He is the sort of person who always leaves the last page of his original document in the copying machine. He has instead allied himself with two detailed-oriented women, his wife and his assistant. Blair rescues him at home; his assistant at work.

Blair never seems to mind dropping whatever she is doing and taking him an extra set of car keys. She never buys expensive umbrellas because Bruce will lose them. I would mind having a husband who was so unable to take care of himself, but I suppose being the rescuer makes her feel powerful.

She was giving a party to celebrate Bruce's success. His parents were coming in from out of town.

"It's going to be Presidents' Day weekend," she said right after finding out from me which caterer Mimi was using for the Capital Campaign party so that she could use someone different. "And you have to promise that Jamie will come."

"What?" Promise that Jamie would come? Why? "You know I have no idea whether or not he will be in town."

"But he was home last week for Martin Luther King Day. Surely the trial will take a long weekend for Presidents' Day, too."

I was suddenly feeling cautious. "That doesn't mean he will be home." The lawyers at Jamie's firm prided themselves on always being more prepared than the other guys. If an unexpected issue arose during a trial, they instantly invested the hours and hours required to master the subject. They hammered their opponents with the breadth of their knowledge. "Don't ask us a question," was their motto, "unless you want an answer that will take you eight hours to read."

"But if he's home, he will come, won't he?" Blair asked.

"Blair, I have no idea. He didn't go to any Christmas parties, and that was before the trial had even started. So if it's a sit-down dinner with place cards and such, if you need to know, then I'd better say no."

"I don't need an answer right away," she said, "but you know how it is. Everyone knows that we know you. And Bruce's parents have been following the case on Court TV, and they really do want to meet him. You know how it is."

Somewhere during that speech, well before the second "you know how it is," she had stopped looking at me. My husband, my very tired, very absent husband, was now a sought-after commodity.

Oh, no, now *he* was popular.

I certainly hoped that his popularity wasn't going to be as painful as Erin's.

I was at Blair's to drop off some Spring Fair contracts, but I needed to get home to cook. One of the mothers in Thomas's class was on jury duty for what might be a two-week murder trial. The other second-grade moms had set up a three-day-a-week meal rotation. A family from church was also needing dinners brought in because that mother had broken one ankle and sprained the other.

So I thought I would be clever, and I grabbed the same date for both families. Since people in crisis usually like comfort food, I bought about seven hundred pounds of pot roast and just as I was flouring the meat, the person in charge of the jury-duty meals called to confirm that I was providing the dinner that evening and to ask me what I was making. I told her.

"Oh." Her voice was timid and anxious. "You didn't know that the Eriksons don't eat beef?"

I paused. "Obviously I did not."

"Didn't someone tell you?"

I paused again. "No, no one did."

"Oh, I guess we must have assumed that all their friends knew."

Maybe they did, but Patricia Erikson and I weren't, in truth, friends. I didn't have anything against her; I'd certainly talk to her a mile a minute if we were stuck together in the grocery-store line, but that had never happened. I was making this meal more out of institutional and sisterly solidarity than out of a particular closeness to Pat.

"I'm sorry," the voice on the phone apologized again, "but this is something that they feel quite strongly about."

"And I suppose that they don't want lasagna or a casserole."

You might think that people who were getting free home-cooked meals would be more grateful than fussy, but you would be wrong. Maybe in normal parts of the nation you could take people a casserole, but here in theme-park, aging-yuppie, food-snob land, the organizer of these meals always specified "no lasagna, no casseroles," although you could never be sure if it was the family who was so picky or the high-control, messiah-complex organizer.

In some ways I could understand. No-boil noodles, sauce from a jar, and pre-shredded packaged mozzarella the family in distress could have made for themselves. But Mimi made a lasagna with spinach, four kinds of cheese, and a béchamel sauce that everyone adored. And Annelise, who described her cooking as nouvelle Wisconsin, had a three-sausage, sweet-pepper hot dish that was fabulous, but definitely a casserole.

I stared at these masses of bloody animal tissue oozing on my big cutting board. Droplets of blood had hardened in the flour, forming purplish pellets. I sent a quick e-mail to the organizer for the church-family's dinners. "They do eat beef, don't they?"

No, came back the answer almost instantly. They were vegetarian. Didn't I know that?

Obviously I didn't.

I am from the Midwest. We eat beef. I have no decent vegetarian recipes except Mimi's spinach lasagna. So I called my mother. She is a very good cook. Smart women are allowed to be good cooks. *Mastering the Art of French Cooking* is worthy of one's intelligence. But she is reluctant to share recipes.

"Mother, I'm in a bind, and I'm your only daughter. If you are going to give a recipe away to anyone, it's me."

She is not without a sense of humor. "I don't want to come to your house and have my own recipe served to me."

"Mother, I need a vegetarian recipe. I'm not going to serve it to you."

She thought for a moment. "You can get fresh basil and fresh thyme, can't you?"

We theme-park residents can always buy fresh herbs. I copied down a recipe for a zucchini thing. "I used half-and-half instead of the heavy cream," she said, "and cut the butter by a third."

But when I went back to the grocery store for the zucchini, basil, and thyme, I bought a quart of heavy cream and two pounds of butter. I was so seriously pissed off at these two families for their eating habits that I decided to kill them in the only way I knew how—with dairy fat.

While I was cooking, my laptop kept chirping at me from the kitchen desk, indicating that I was receiving e-mail. While my beautifully minced shallots were browning themselves, I opened my in-box. The request for silent auction donations had just gone out, and unbeknownst to me, donations had to be—or so announced this set of high-control volunteers—accompanied by a .phb file. It was mandatory. The number of subsequent e-mails that I had received with the subject line "silent auction" suggested that this was a problem.

Before I could read any of them, the phone rang. The caller shrieked that she had no idea what a .phb file was.

"It's from a digital camera."

"I don't have a digital camera," she snapped. "Well, I mean, we do have one, but I don't know how to use it."

"Maybe your kids could take the picture." Kids always knew how to work digital cameras.

"My kid? He's a junior. Do you know what junior year is like? Do you have any idea how hard those kids have to work? And he is doing winter track. So when he is supposed to take a silent auction photo?"

I had no idea. "Let me look into this."

But before I could I got another call. "Every year my husband's mother makes a perfect copy of a Disney princess dress for American Girl dolls."

"I know. They sell for the earth."

"And do you think that she has a digital camera?"

No, I didn't suppose that she did.

I called the chairman of the silent auction catalog subcommittee.

She was belligerent. Obviously mine was not the first such call she had received. "We spent hours and hours last year scanning pictures for the catalog. If people just submit a file, it will save us so much time."

"But what if people can't submit a file? What if they don't have digital cameras?"

The thought hadn't occurred to her. She was a lower-school parent, and half of the kids in the first and second grades had had Web sites created for them within eighteen hours of their births. Grandma and Grandpa would log on to the Internet (assuming that Grandma and Grandpa could log on to the Internet) to see the pictures of the newborn. This mother couldn't imagine a family without a digital camera any more than one without a DVD player, a fax machine, or toothbrushes.

I would loathe being a scholarship family at this school.

I raised the possibility of not having pictures in the catalog. Last year had been the first year we had had pictures. In fact, until three years ago, there hadn't even been a catalog. People just roamed through the tables looking for something that they wanted to bid on.

"We can't do that. We can't have pictures of some items and not of others."

I didn't see why not.

Eventually I got them to admit that the .phb files weren't mandatory, but they were unwilling to send out a note saying that. If people called and asked, they would say that it was all right, but people had to call them.

Or people could just not donate. That was what was going to happen.

• • •

Then Chris Goddard blew his first snow-day call.

The Washington metropolitan area does not handle snow well. We don't get heavy snowstorms often enough for people to learn how to drive well in the snow. Some drivers happily barrel along at sixty-eight miles an hour and then are startled to discover that the road is turning and their car isn't, or vice versa. Others start driving five miles an hour at the first snowflake, which drives the people going sixty-eight miles an hour nuts, and people going sixty-eight miles an hour on ice really ought to remain as calm as possible.

The big suburban school districts close a lot. The outer edges of their jurisdictions are virtually rural with narrow, winding roads that quickly become impassable. So if the kids along those bus routes aren't going to be able to travel safely, the suburban schools take a snow day.

The District of Columbia—the city—tries never to close. Most of its students walk to school or take public transportation along well-traveled roads. Furthermore, too many of those kids are dependent on the school-provided breakfasts and lunches for their daily nutrition. For middle-class kids, a snow day means a fun day of sledding and watching videos, but a lot of kids in the city public schools aren't middle class, and a snow day for them means a cold apartment and an empty refrigerator.

The private schools in Northwest each make their own assessment, and when I got up Thursday morning, two days after my cooking adventure, I logged on to the Web site and saw that Alden was opening two hours late, which seemed like a good call. That's what Sidwell, Maret, and the Cathedral schools were all doing.

But at 7:35 A.M. which is much, much too late for this kind of decision to be made, the phone trees and the e-mail lists got activated. The Alden School would be closed for the day. The parking lot hadn't been plowed. There was nowhere for the teachers to park and nowhere for the parents to drop off the kids.

Two of the reasons that it was much, much too late for this decision were sitting in my kitchen—Jake Rabern and Charlie Carruthers, two second-grade boys. Their mothers both worked full-time, and they had an agreement to trade snow days. But for delayed openings they often dropped the boys here, which was fine. I didn't mind having them for two hours. I didn't really want to have them for the whole day.

It was Jill Rabern's turn to have stayed home, but she was a reading specialist in the Arlington County schools, a system that was opening on time. By the time I had finished my share of the phone tree, I knew that Jill would already be in her classroom. Unlike the classrooms at Alden, Jill's didn't have a phone or Internet access. Any message I left for her she wouldn't pick up until lunch, and then she wouldn't be able to leave until a substitute could be found.

So I called Sue Carruthers, who worked at a trade association, but she said that it was Jill's turn to take the kids and so she was not coming home. I should call Jill. I pointed out that it was impossible to call Jill. No, it wasn't, Sue replied. All I had to do was reach the principal of the school and persuade him that this was an emergency. He would take the message to Jill, and he would cover her classroom himself if she truly needed to leave.

I did not want to make that call. I didn't think I should have to make that call. But Sue said that she was in a meeting. She couldn't call Jill. I would have to. After all—and she came very close to actually saying this—I wasn't in a meeting; I wasn't at work.

I try very hard to fight the idea that working mothers and nonworking ones are adversaries, but at the moment I did feel adversarial. Sue was trying to take advantage of me, and she was going to get away with it because I wasn't going to call Jill's principal. There was no point. I would have to lie my head off before I would be able to convince a principal that this was a true emergency.

A half hour later Sue called back. Her son might be at my house, but his noon dose of Ritalin was at school.

"Do you have anything you can give him?" she asked. "He does best on short-acting Ritalin, but if you only have long-acting, that's probably okay. Even Focalin would be all right."

As trendy and with-it a family as I like to think we are, neither of my kids is ADHD, and so we don't have those medications in the house. Furthermore, most of the various drugs used to treat that disorder are carefully controlled substances. Doctors can't call in refills. You have to show up at the drugstore, a written prescription in hand.

Sue's suggestions for getting her son's pill were absurd. I could go to school—with its unplowed parking lot—and see if someone was there and see if that someone had a key to the nurse's office and then see if he or she would be willing to violate school policy and federal law and give me Charlie's Ritalin.

"Or I could meet you at your house," I said.

"Oh, I'm in a meeting," she said. "And it *is* Jill's day, not mine. She has a dose for him in case this happens."

I asked if there was any way I could get into her house. No, the neighbors who kept her key spent the winter in Florida.

I had to wonder if they were therefore the best people to have charge of one's key.

"Oh, well, I'm sure he'll be fine," she said. "I'm sure of it."

That she had left this incredibly important meeting to call me suggested she knew perfectly well he was not going to be fine.

I called Annelise, but her younger daughter took Adderall, which was apparently not interchangeable with Ritalin. The family who lives behind Mimi had Stratera, which was again something else. My third call also turned up Adderall, but the mother thought she might have an half-used bottle of Concerta around somewhere and offered to go look for it. But I was growing uneasy about the liability issues involved in playing doctor, so I gave up and did what people must have done with ADHD kids before the days of Ritalin—sent him outside to play with orders not to come in until he was too tired to move. That was fine with my son, but the other kid, Jake, was a whiny number; he was cold, he complained, he was tired. He kept coming in the house to use the bathroom, to get a drink, to track in mud, and I finally let him stay inside, lying on the sofa in the sunroom under a blanket, watching a video.

All of this sent Erin across the street to Mimi's house where she met up with the other girls. I didn't see her again until dark.

The snow had extended along much of the Mid-Atlantic, and I had spoken to Jamie's parents early in the day. Yes, Pittsburgh was catching the edge of the storm system, but it shouldn't be bad at all.

The following morning, however, my father-in-law called. Pittsburgh's slush had frozen overnight, and Jamie's mother had been in an accident. Another car had slid into hers, forcing it into the car ahead. Her airbag had inflated, and she had been wearing her seat belt, but she had broken her sternum. She was going to be fine, but her recovery was going to be long and, for a while, rather painful.

The kids and I drove up Friday after school. I was prepared to be the perfect daughter-in-law, but the other daughter-in-law and her million Polish relatives had gotten there first. The house was spotless, and the freezer was full of neatly labeled little packages. So there wasn't much to do. My mother-in-law slept; my father-in-law did guy-type stuff out in his workshop with Thomas and taught Erin how to use a slide rule. "No one ever uses them anymore," he said, "but the learning is good for you."

As soon as he heard about his mother, Jamie said he would fly up to Pittsburgh on Saturday, but his dad and I agreed that there wasn't much point. I tried not to hear the relief in Jamie's voice.

Sometimes I wondered how much I was missing Jamie. I did miss the Jamie whom I knew and loved, but the fellow who had been coming to our house for the occasional weekend wasn't him. That individual was a cantankerous bachelor.

Jamie had been finding it hard to come from the pristine order of a hotel room to the normal chaos of a family home. So whenever he was going to be coming home, I spent Friday afternoon frantically tidying up so that our house was within hailing distance of a pristine hotel room, and nothing makes me bitchier than when I am doing something to meet someone else's standards.

In Houston he had been falling asleep listening to sports talk shows. So when he came to bed at home, he unthinkingly turned on the clock radio to listen to complete idiots yammer about major-league hockey. He found it restful, a way to stop thinking about the trial; I didn't find it restful, and I wasn't thinking about the trial in the first place. He'd walk in the room where someone was watching television, pick up the remote, and change the channel. When the kids or I shrieked at him, he blinked, startled at himself, and apologized, but then sat there, obviously unable to relax because he couldn't channel surf.

What he truly wanted was for all four of us to be sitting quietly in the same room while he channel surfed. If we really did live in a theme park, I could get three automated dummies to sit with him and then the kids and I could go about our business.

• • •

Jamie did come home the following weekend, and I brought up Blair's party with him since Blair had not stopped bringing it up with me. "Bruce's parents really do want to meet him," she had said over and over.

"If you are home next weekend," I said to him, "will you come?"

"I am not going to want to," he said, not very apologetically. "Either people are going to insist on talking about the trial, which I do not want to talk about, or the whole conversation will be about the carpool line."

The second half of that was true. It's easy for group conversation to find the lowest common denominator, the easiest thing to talk about, and in our case, at least for the women, that's the kids—the school and the carpool line and the teachers. And although the men do love their own children and even feel considerable concern for their kids' little friends, they aren't interested in talking about who is getting which lane on the swim team. At the end of some evenings I'm embarrassed at how trivial and boring the conversation has been.

When we moms are talking about the Spring Fair or the cotton-fleece drawstring skirts, we're talking shop. In some ways it isn't any different from when the men talk about how their firms are billing. We are talking about our jobs, too. The difference is that we don't acknowledge it as shoptalk; we think that any discussion of children's issues must be universally interesting . . . and it's not.

I suppose that that's how we differ from the fifties' moms, the June Cleavers. They didn't come to parties expecting to talk about what they cared about. They were there to be pretty and to listen to the men. We, on the other hand, would never dream of silencing ourselves in favor of the men.

Jamie did make it home for the Presidents' Day weekend. He got in very late on Friday night, and when I asked him Saturday morning if he was planning on going to Blair's party, he said no. He hadn't come home to go to a party.

"We don't have to stay long. Won't you please come?"

He had the sports section of the paper spread out on the kitchen table. Ever since the trial started, he had been following college-basketball statistics obsessively. He turned a page. "Nope." He was keeping his voice even and pleasant.

All day long I kept hoping that he would change his mind. Wasn't it enough that I wanted him to go? Couldn't he do this for me?

At six-thirty he was sitting on the floor of the sunroom, his back against the sofa, shuffling cards at the big square coffee table. Erin was in the kitchen, putting a bag of popcorn in the microwave, and Thomas was sprawled halfway across the coffee table, resting on his elbows, watching his father shuffle the cards. "Will you tell Erin that she can't keep track of the eights?"

"I will not," Jamie replied evenly. Clearly they were settling in for an evening of Crazy Eights, a game at which Erin had long since revealed herself to be a vicious card counter. "Why don't you keep track of them yourself?"

Jamie was clearly not going anywhere. I sat down.

He shuffled the cards again, then looked at me. He knew exactly what I was thinking. "Why do you care so much?"

I paused. I didn't understand Bruce's career or this merger. I had no special relationship with his parents. There was nothing about this evening that I was looking forward to.

But it was a test. Blair had made it into a test, and one thing I've always been good at is tests. "Are you not going just because you think my priorities are out of whack?"

"That's probably part of it, but I also don't want to go."

I guess there wasn't anything else to say. I stood up.

"It doesn't sound as if you want to go either," he said. "Why don't you stay home, too? We'll deal you in the game. It will just be the four of us. Erin will beat the pants off of us, but you can view it as an opportunity to teach the kids how to be gracious losers."

It was tempting. God knows the last thing on earth I wanted to do right now was go upstairs and doll myself up in the world's most boring outfit—a long black velvet skirt with a black velvet shell and a black velvet blazer. It would be fun to stay home, having popcorn and playing cards with the three people I loved the most. This wasn't a theme-park moment. This was real; this was family.

But I couldn't blow off Blair's party. I couldn't not show up. It was bad enough that Jamie wasn't going. I might as well paint a sign and put it on the front walk: "The Meadows family does not value Blair Branson's party."

Once again here we all were, back in middle school. So I stood up and went upstairs for my rendezvous with black velvet. I do not look good in black.

The snow of two weeks ago had long since melted, and the pavement was dry as I walked from my car to Blair's in my thin-soled party shoes.

Blair and Bruce were at the door. Bruce greeted me heartily, but Blair looked over my shoulder. "Jamie didn't come?"

"I'm *so* sorry." And over her shoulder I could see that the furniture had been taken out of her Tiffany-blue living room and was replaced by rounded ivory-draped tables with centerpieces, silverware, wineglasses, and place cards.

I had told her. Countless times I had said, "If this is sitdown, if there are place cards, then don't count on him," and every single time she had said, "I don't need an answer yet." I was angry; I felt as if she had set me up.

I turned my wrap over to the catering staff and went to find Bruce's parents. They recognized me immediately.

"We're at your table!" Mrs. Branson exclaimed. "We can't wait to meet your husband. We've told everyone at home."

"Then I'm so sorry," I said. "He isn't going to be able to join us tonight."

Isn't going to be able to join us. That isn't me. I don't talk like that. I'm straightforward; I'm impulsive. I explain and explain and explain. Apparently I am going to have to become a different person if I continue being related to popular people.

Bruce's parents were looking at me expectantly, waiting for me to say more. Mr. Branson finally spoke. "You tell him that we think he is doing a great job."

"It's hard to know who to root for," Mrs. Branson said. "I mean, we went in thinking that these were such bad guys, but I don't know . . . that prosecutor gal, I don't like her."

That was exactly why Jamie hadn't wanted to come to-night. He hated that in this trial personalities were mattering so much. The likability of "that prosecutor gal" was irrelevant to the cause of justice, but it was not irrelevant to the verdict. Jamie was consciously exploiting people's dislike of her abrasive, shrill persona. And he was not proud of it.

He was not the only no-show. I saw Blair discreetly ease into the dining room to rearrange a few place cards and direct one of the waiters to remove some place settings. Annelise went to help her. I didn't think I would be welcome. Annelise was wearing a fitted sheath of a glowing bottle-green Dupioni silk. She looked very good in it, which meant, of course, that I, too, would have looked very good in it or at least better than I did in black.

I felt frumpy.

Why hadn't I gotten my hair cut? Or had my nails done or something?

I looked around. Should I make an effort to introduce myself to Bruce's colleagues or should I join one of the familiar carpool-line conversations?

The bar was set up in the dining room so I went in there. Blair had had the room painted apricot, and her window treatments were wonderful—gloriously simple waterfalls of shimmering apricot silk. The room was crowded, but as I moved in, someone stepped aside, and I saw—to my surprise—silhouetted against the glowing apricot, dressed in a perfectly cut black dinner jacket, Chris Goddard.

I hadn't known that Blair was inviting him. Now that I thought about it, I realized that I knew very little about this party; normally Blair and I would have discussed the menu, the centerpieces, the guest list, everything. This time we had only talked about Jamie.

I started toward Chris, then stopped when I realized that he was talking to someone else I hadn't known Blair was inviting—Mary Paige Caudwell.

Why had Blair invited her? Mary Paige might have wanted to get her daughter included in our daughters' crowd, but she had—thank God—shown no interest in being friends with us. Our daughters might be cool, but we weren't.

I had no interest in being friends with her, either, so I started to make my way to the bar, which was on the far side of the room. Mimi's husband, Ben, was there, and when he turned, he spotted me.

He lifted the glass of wine that he was probably getting for Mimi, and since there were too many people for him to call across the room, he pointed to the glass, inquiring if I wanted one. I nodded a yes, and as I waited for him, I glanced back at Chris and Mary Paige.

When I had first seen them, they had both been standing in front of the silk drapes. I was sure of it; that was the kind of detail I noticed. Now Chris was silhouetted against the wall. Although the wall and the curtain were the same color, the wall had less sheen. It held on to the light instead of reflecting it back as the silk did.

But the distance between Chris and Mary Paige was the same—another detail a photographer is not going to be wrong about. I guessed that Mary Paige had moved forward, and Chris had stepped back. Still waiting for Ben and my wine, I continued to watch them. Yes, Mary Paige eased herself forward, and as if they were a little physics experiment, Chris moved himself back.

This must be an ongoing problem for him—the single mothers who, even if they didn't want an actual relationship with him, were eager for some occasional masculine validation of their womanly charms.

The warm apricot reflections in the dining room were flattering to everyone, but Mary Paige did look particularly well in her high-necked, sleeveless sheath. She could wear black, and even from across the room, I could see that her earrings were perfectly shaped, so perfectly that I was annoyed. Sometimes I can be way too much like my mother—unable to be at peace until I have found at least one fault with every person in the known universe.

I thanked Ben for my wine, and before I could decide if I should talk to him about world peace or next year's Cub Scout popcorn sales, we were joined by one of Bruce's business associates. Surprisingly he wanted to talk to me, not Ben. He reminded me that he had a son on Thomas's soccer team, and that his son went to Sidwell Friends School.

"People are eager to get your boy at Sidwell," he said. "You will enroll him, won't you?"

Sidwell parents can't imagine anyone ever choosing to send their kids elsewhere. "He hasn't been admitted yet."

The man looked a little alarmed. "That's not going to be a problem, is it? I could make a few calls if you'd like."

"No, no," I said. If their father being a Quaker wasn't enough to get Thomas and Erin into Sidwell, no calls from other parents would. But people like to believe that they have clout, that their "making a few calls" could advance the Second Coming.

He then asked about Jamie, and I went into my "nondenial denial" routine that lasted until Blair started gesturing people to come in to dinner.

I wouldn't have been surprised if, during the place-card rearranging, she had demoted me from Bruce's parents' table, but my place card was still there along with seven other place settings. Clearly rather than leave this table short, she had moved someone into Jamie's place.

Before I could look at the place cards, the answer to my question strolled up in his beautifully cut dinner jacket.

"I've been promoted," Chris said, "and I get to sit at your table. I take it that your husband got held up somewhere and couldn't make it."

If that was Blair's story, I wasn't going to add the fact that the "somewhere" was the family television set.

On the other side of the room, Mary Paige, her lips narrowed and her face a little hard, was taking a seat at one of the tables now having only seven people. Blair was an alert hostess. She must have noticed the same little physics experiment that I had witnessed. Her "promotion" of Chris had been a rescue, and Mary Paige wasn't happy about it. She was now the extra woman at what must seem to her like a losers' table.

Chris was going to be sitting in Jamie's place between Mrs. Branson and a woman whose name I recognized because she wrote for the *Washington Post*. But neither of them had come to the table yet, so Chris and I remained standing.

He spoke lightly. "Now it is your turn to tell me how you suffered during the snow day."

"Charlie Carruthers was at my house, and Charlie's Ritalin was at school."

Chris winced. "You have my sympathies."

I waved a hand. "It was nothing." In fact, I decided that the snow day had been a good thing for our family. Erin had spent the whole day with Rachel, Brittany, and Elise and had come home tired and happy. Apparently Faith had kept calling, pleading with Rachel to get her mother to bring all the girls over to Faith's house in Virginia, but Mimi had refused. Mary Paige too often needed to drop Faith off early or pick her up late, or simply had made no plans for the girl's transportation. Mimi was starting to say no to arrangements designed primarily for the convenience of Mary Paige, who, in truth, had a far more flexible schedule than Mimi did.

"The Building and Grounds guy," Chris said now, "kept assuring me that the contract-snowplow people would show up any minute, and the contract-snowplow people kept assuring me that their plows would be there. I was going to call the football team to come shovel the parking lot, but it seemed easier to cancel school."

"Since we don't have a football team."

"Oh, no, you are wrong there. Haven't you heard? As Spring Fair chair, you should have. Remember how we wanted the high-school kids to get more involved in the Spring Fair? Last week they came up with the idea of the girls' varsity soccer team playing the girls' j.v. team in a Powder Puff football game."

What a good idea. That would bring out the older kids. "Do the girls have any idea how to play football?"

"No," he said cheerfully, 'but they don't know what powder puffs are either."

Bruce's parents came to the table, and I introduced them to Chris. There were two other couples at the table. The husband of one couple was from Bruce's firm; his wife was a lawyer for a child-services nonprofit. The other couple worked at the *Washington Post*; she was a reporter for the "Metro" section, and he was one of the senior marketing people for the Web site. We were all grown-ups, quite able to make dinner-table conversation with people we weren't likely ever to see again.

But I was surprised at how easy and interesting the conversations were. Whenever the discussion started to drift into the "easy to talk about" topics such as traffic or housing prices, Chris would refocus us by asking one person questions, using his conversational skills rather as a talk-show host would, making a conversation between two individuals interesting to everyone. He asked me what I had learned about people from taking portraits, which turned out to be a topic that the rest of the table could get involved with.

I stayed much longer at the party than I had planned.

When I did finally leave, after saying a rather stilted thank-you to Blair, Chris came up to me. "Are you all right walking to your car?"

I paused. He was offering to walk me to my car. I had gone to parties alone all December, and no one had thought to go with me to my car. How nice of him. No, *nice* wasn't the word. The word was *gallant*. This was a gentleman offering to escort a lady.

Black might not be my best color, but the jacket was exactly the right length, and the neckline couldn't have been better. The skirt was beautifully cut and neatly lined. I felt light and feminine.

"If you do," he continued, "I will go find Mr. Branson."

Bruce's father? I didn't want Bruce's father to walk me to my car. Bruce's father wasn't going to make me feel light and feminine.

And Chris Goddard shouldn't. I had almost put myself on the Mary Paige side of the little physics experiment.

"I'm completely fine," I assured him. "Absolutely."

I hurried down Blair's front walk, mortified with myself, feeling that somewhere in my heart I had crossed a line, wanting something from Chris that I had no right to expect and which, if he stepped forward to provide it, would lead to unhappiness for all.

But sometimes I get so tired of just being a mom.

Jamie and the kids were all in bed when I got home, but the family room had been picked up.

As a family we are not great picker-uppers. Our house isn't hopeless; we don't have the seven cities of Troy layered on top of the coffee table, the Legos permanently mixed up with video adapters and little plastic combat figures. We never have more than a day or two's worth of newspapers, coffee cups, and sneakers, but we often do have that.

Tonight, however, the popcorn bowl was in the sink, the

cards had been put away, and the sofa cushions had been straightened. The kitchen counter had been wiped.

It was Jamie's way of apologizing.

I was grateful. Of course, I was. But what had happened to the days when he had made me feel light and feminine? Was I so completely a mom that the most romantic gesture left was putting the popcorn bowl in the sink?

9

Sunday morning Jamie came to church with the children and me. As he had remained a Quaker, he only occasionally came to St. Peter's with us, but I suppose he was trying to make a point—that the four of us going to worship together was more Mom, America, and apple pie than two adults getting all liquored-up together Saturday night at a party they didn't want to be at.

Except my self-esteem was, at the moment, far too heavily dependent on the Mom-America-apple-pie thing. I could have used a little of the liquored-up hot babe.

Jamie slept most of the afternoon; we had a quick supper at home and then took the kids to a movie in Bethesda. The same movie was showing at closer theaters, but we thought it would be fun to go to Bethesda.

This close-in Maryland suburb has actually made a success of the "urban village" concept. It has restaurants, art galleries, delis, bakeries, and clothing boutiques, all open late. In the warmer months the sidewalks are so crowded in the evenings that the pedestrians spill out into the street. Bethesda also has places that a real village—urban or otherwise—actually needs: grocery stores, shoe repairmen, and even a hardware store, something that we don't have down in theme-park land since hardware stores can't afford theme-park rents.

Washington weather is erratic, and although it was February, the evening was pleasant. When we came up from the movie theater and walked toward Woodmont Avenue, we could see that there were plenty of people out and about on this Sunday of a three-day weekend. Groups of teens were hanging out in front of the Barnes & Noble bookstore. Its broad, well-lit diagonal entry at the corner of Woodmont and Bethesda Avenues made it a popular gathering place. I supposed that next year we would have to face that parenting challenge—how much time you let your kids hang out in public places.

No, I was wrong. That challenge was already here. As we drew nearer to Woodmont, I could see that among those teens were Rachel Gold, Brittany Branson, Elise Rosen, and Faith Caudwell.

"Look," I exclaimed, very surprised, "it's the other girls."

The girls didn't see us. The sidewalk leading up from the

theater ran perpendicular to Woodmont, and this side of the street was less well-lit. But the flood of light spilling from the Barnes & Noble windows put the girls onstage. They were at the edge of a group of clearly older teens, most of whom were boys, but only Faith was talking to those kids. She was very animated; the other girls were standing back, looking more hesitant. It was the inverse of the first-day-of-school scene. Now our girls were hovering uncertainly, feeling awkward and self-conscious.

"This can't be right," I said immediately. "Let me—"

"Mom, *no*," Erin almost shrieked. "You can't go over there. You can't. I'll die."

"I'm sorry." I could sympathize. She didn't want everyone to know that she was with her *parents* when every other one of God's creatures was hanging out in front of the Bethesda Barnes & Noble with cool-looking older kids. "But I need to know that they are all right."

"They're fine. Can't you see that? They're fine."

No, they weren't. Even Brittany, the prettiest of the three and the one who had gotten her period first, had her head down and her arms wrapped close around her body. The body language of all three girls screamed of discomfort and uncertainty.

"What's going on?" Jamie asked. He and Thomas had been walking more slowly and had just now come up to the street.

"Erin's friends are over there, and—"

"For God's sakes, Lydia," he exploded, "can't we have one family evening that isn't all caught up in other people's issues?

Can't the four of us go to a movie, walk down the street to get some ice cream without having to rescue the entire world?"

"But—"

"Don't give me that 'it takes a village to raise a child' crap. It also takes a family, and you need to start putting our family first."

Thomas was wide-eyed. I don't think he had ever heard Jamie so directly angry with me. Erin was too caught up in her own mortification to care.

"Me?" I hissed at him. "You're telling *me* to put our family first?" He had slept in our house eleven nights since the beginning of the new year.

"That's right. I'm saying that you need to put the family first because right now I can't."

And just why couldn't he? He had made a choice. This was a criminal case. His firm didn't do criminal cases. Yes, the senior partners had urged him to take the case, but no one would have held it against him if he had said no.

The three girls were inching closer together. They were clustered at Faith's back as if she were an overly hot campfire in the middle of dark night. You wanted to get away from the heat of the fire, but the darkness, while cooler, was too scary.

"They aren't supposed to be here," I said. "I can't imagine that Mimi, Blair, and Annelise have any idea that they are just hanging out here."

"I don't question that, but Lydia, what is going to happen to them? This is downtown Bethesda at nine o'clock. It isn't exactly a slum at midnight. They're as safe here as they are on the school playground."

He had a point. Within the next year or two we were going

to let them do this. But it was the overall behavior that worried me and, I knew, worried my friends. Kids who are spending their evenings on the streets of Bethesda at age twelve are going to find that activity too tame by fourteen.

But, of course, this single evening wasn't going to launch an inevitable slide into drug addiction. "Let me just speak to them, let them know that we are here in case they want to leave with us. I'll be back in a second."

I checked for traffic and started to cross the street. I didn't stop to think about what would happen; I suppose I secretly imagined being welcomed as a rescuer. *Oh, Mrs. Meadows. You're here. Could we use your cell phone or get a ride home?*

It was always nice when you could help other people's kids. I loved it when the kids knew that they could count on me.

Elise saw me first, and she clutched at the others. They shot nervous glances across the street, and then so quickly that I couldn't tell who moved first, they whisked into the bookstore.

They were running from me. I wasn't their rescuer. I was the bad guy, the eternal, ever-spying, East Berlin mom. Humiliated, knowing that Jamie and Erin had seen this, I went into the bookstore.

The store has three levels and most of the racks were five feet high. The girls could easily hide from me if that's what they were trying to do, and clearly that was what they were trying to do.

I took out my cell phone. I knew that Blair and Bruce were taking his parents to the Kennedy Center, and I had seen Mimi's car pull out just as we did. So I called Annelise.

"But they can't be in Bethesda," she said, "they are at Faith's tonight, and they were going to go to a movie in Virginia."

I didn't want to hold a meeting about this, not with my family across the street glowering at me. "Annelise, I know what these girls look like. They were in front of Barnes and Noble, talking to a group of older guys."

"Then tell them not to move. I'll be there in fifteen minutes."

"I'm not with them. As soon as they saw me, they dashed into the bookstore."

"Lydia! You let them wander off?"

Why did I have to defend myself? "There was no 'let' about it. They think that I am pursuing them and they are hiding from me."

"Could you go look for them?"

"No, Annelise, I can't. They are safe inside the store, and I am not going to humiliate myself even more. You can call the store's security and have them paged."

"But that will embarrass them," Annelise said. "They will hate that."

"Annelise! Don't you think that they deserve to be embarrassed?"

"I suppose." Then Annelise came to her senses. "Oh, my God, they deserve to be strung up by their thumbs." She ended the call quickly, and I went back across the street.

"Is everyone ready for ice cream?" I tried to sound lively. I wanted the rest of the family to believe that we were having fun. Wasn't that part of my job? To make sure that everyone was having fun?

If so, I was failing. Erin and Jamie were silent as we walked toward the ice-cream parlor. Jamie didn't order any ice cream, and Erin didn't finish hers.

My compromises were terrible. Just as my going to Blair's party without Jamie had appeased no one, this plan just to speak to the girls had alienated absolutely everyone except my sweet Thomas. He told me twice that his ice cream was yummy, and back at home, he was more cuddly than ever.

"I love you, Mommy," he said when I went in to get him organized for bed.

My heart melted and my stomach turned—if your body cavity can have that much going on at the same time. My son thought that no one else loved me so he needed to love me extra hard.

Monday was Presidents' Day. Jamie went up to see his parents and would fly straight to Houston from Pittsburgh. The kids were, of course, off school, and in the middle of the morning Mimi's son, Gideon, came over to play with Thomas. Mimi followed him and filled me in on what had happened.

Annelise had the girls paged, and so they were sitting in the manager's office when she arrived, every bit as mortified by this public roundup as Annelise predicted they would be. "At first," Mimi said, "they told us that they had been planning on going to a movie near Faith's house in Virginia. But they arrived late, and the movie was sold out. Mary Paige had already left, and so they decided to get on the subway and go to Bethesda to see the movie there. At least that was the first version of the story."

"They took the Metro?" Late last summer we had let the four girls take the subway by themselves from Tenley to Friendship Heights, a five-minute trip with no intervening stops. They had walked across the street, bought themselves ice cream, and come back home. We had figured that as city kids they needed to know how to get around, and they had been thrilled with themselves. But that carefully controlled daytime experiment was very different from a long, after-dark trip that involved changing trains at Metro Center.

"Yes, they took the Metro," Mimi said with such a steel-eyed look that I knew her daughter was in a whole peck of trouble. "But it gets worse."

As soon as Annelise had made it clear to Elise that she was calling the movie theater to verify that the movie had sold out, poor Elise had caved and spilled the whole story. The girls had never planned on going to the movie in the first place. After Mary Paige had dropped them off, they had gone directly to the Metro station.

Even though the plan was unquestionably Faith's, the other three girls had gone along with it, and their mothers grounded them for two weeks. Not only couldn't they see their friends, but they couldn't use the phone or the Internet, either. And my friends didn't fool around. *You have a question about homework?* they would say to their loophole-seeking daughters. *Fine, you tell me what it is, and I will make the call.*

This punishment was the talk of the sixth grade, and at first Faith gloated that she had escaped any consequence. But whatever the sixth-grade kids thought of the punishment, the sixth-grade moms were pleased at how sternly Blair, Mimi, and

Annelise were dealing with the escapade. *You see what will happen,* they said to their own kids, *if you go somewhere without telling us.*

This was the advantage of being in the village that it took to raise a child. Now it was clear to a greater part of the sixth grade what the standards were, and all the village dwellers were hoping that because three women had enforced the consequences of misbehavior, the rest of them wouldn't have to endure two long weeks of living with an outraged, sullen twelve-year-old.

But because she hadn't been willing to face her daughter's displeasure, Mary Paige Caudwell had not conformed to the standards as the community now understood them to be. She had pitched her tent outside the village wall.

At the beginning of the second week of the girls' punishment I went to the lower school. The silent auction catalog subcommittee—the lower-school moms who had been insisting on the .phb files—had decided to take a tiny fraction off their huge printing bill by having volunteers collate and staple the catalog. It made no sense; leaving the color graphics off one page of the catalog would have more than paid for the collating and stapling, but the egos of this subcommittee were deeply invested in these color graphics, As a result, five grown, well-educated women were going to be spending their morning collating and stapling. I showed up just to be sure that there were enough volunteers, and when I saw that there were—the lower school always had enough volunteers—I went over to the middle school to see what had been left in the Spring Fair mail drop.

A coffee urn had been set up in the hall outside the

middle-school office. A group of sixth-grade mothers was idling around it. There were both boys' mothers and girls' mothers; my best guess about the nature of the group was that all their children took Spanish and so the coffee urn had been set up for some event related to the Spanish classes.

Mary Paige Caudwell was among them, and she came straight up to me. "I suppose you've heard about what Rachel, Brittany, and Elise are enduring?" Her voice sounded a little forced. "Isn't it the silliest thing to punish them like that? Hanging out is what teenagers do. It's so unrealistic to expect anything else."

Did she expect *me* to publicly criticize Mimi, Blair, and Annelise? Clearly she was hoping that I would.

Not having a village map, Mary Paige hadn't intended to pitch her tent outside its walls, but now that she realized she had, she wanted back inside. But she was not going to move her tent; she wanted me to move the village wall. She wanted me to say that she was right.

"I think that the issue was the long, unauthorized subway trip," I said.

"So they forgot to call." She shrugged, dismissing the elaborate planning that had gone into the escapade. "They're kids. Kids forget."

She had no idea whom she was dealing with. I had decades of dealing with a mother who was never wrong, and I knew what to do. It's impossible to get such people to admit to being wrong, so what you did was just not care. If you stood up to them, trying to show that they had been wrong, they fought harder. What killed them was the notion that you didn't care.

"I wasn't involved in this," I said. "It's none of my business."

"Oh, yes, but come on, surely you think their families are being more than a little overprotective?"

"It doesn't concern me." Then I looked straight at her. "As you well know, my daughter wasn't there."

She blinked, surprised. She hadn't been thinking about the fact that had any of the other families initiated this plan, my daughter would have been included.

How dare she be surprised? How dare she forget what her daughter had done to mine?

Prepared only to defend herself against being a poor disciplinarian, she was caught off-guard now. She faltered. "Ah . . . I only have five seat belts."

Blair only had five seat belts; Annelise only had five seat belts. They worked it out. When there were more than four kids, they both drove. So if this was some sort of belated excuse for what she and her daughter had done to mine, I was not going to listen. "Again I wasn't involved." And I turned away, a flat-out snub, and instantly began speaking to another one of the mothers—every one of whom had been listening to my conversation with Mary Paige—inquiring with great interest about the Spanish-language curriculum even though Erin was taking French.

Mary Paige had apparently left this encounter smarting with a sense of defeat. She had gone home—of course, I had all this fifthhand—and tongue-lashed Faith. Then at school the next day Faith, who had inherited the "I'm never wrong" gene, tried to convince the other three girls that they had had a really great time in Bethesda that night, even though I had seen at first glance that they hadn't.

That evening our phone rang. I answered it, and well-mannered Alden alumnae offspring that she is, Faith Caudwell identified herself and asked to speak to Erin. As far as I knew, she had never called Erin before.

Erin was doing her homework at the kitchen table. I covered the mouthpiece of the receiver. "It's Faith," I said. "For you."

"For *me*?" Erin sounded horrified. Four months ago she would have bubbled with delight to get a call from Faith. "I don't want to talk to her."

"Shall I say that you are asleep?"

"No. It's eight-thirty. I'll sound like a big dork. No one goes to sleep this early."

"I could say that you are doing something with Thomas."

"But he *is* asleep."

"She's not going to know that."

"Okay. That's good. Then say that."

So in my best prim secretary voice, I informed Faith that Erin was engaged with her brother, but that I would pass along the message.

"Will she be able to call back afterward?" Faith asked.

"No. We don't let her use the phone after nine." That was true.

"I guess I'll see her at school," Faith was suddenly not sounding so confident.

"I suspect so," I said sweetly.

. . .

The prosecution case in Jamie's trial had gone on way too long. Every single commentator said that. Jamie had just started presenting his case, and he said that the jury was too weary to listen. Someone in the press corps had had a particularly nasty cold, and it had spread to the other journalists, the lawyers, and now the jury. Newspaper accounts recorded that everyone in the courtroom was slumping, looking bewildered and miserable.

And now, after being a media darling, Jamie was getting negative publicity.

Trial observers were seeing what he had sensed all along—as guilty of so many things as the defendants probably were, there was a very good chance that they were going to dodge a criminal conviction. So where Jamie had once been described as "affable," he was now "slick." He had gone from being "intelligent" to being "crafty." "Longtime Quaker roots" had become a "background of traditional privilege."

He said that it was all in a day's work. "We fed the media machine every day; we used it as long as we could. We knew there would be a backlash."

But he did mind. He wouldn't admit it, but he did.

Talking to him on the phone was getting more and more difficult. I never knew when to expect his calls—he didn't have much control over his schedule—and then he was so distant from our lives here that I didn't know what to say. *The kids are fine. I'm fine. The weather's fine. The house's fine. And oh, wow, I bought some new hangers for the front-hall closet, and man, oh, man, is it ever great to finally have enough hangers in there.*

Sunday afternoon, two weeks after Presidents' Day weekend, he called. I actually did have news for a change. Rachel, Elise, and Brittany had finished serving their punishment, and right away they had called Erin—not Faith—wanting her to go to a movie. I mentioned that to Jamie, but he did not appreciate the significance of it. So I took the cordless phone over to the sofa and sat down, pulling a pillow across my lap, determined to be a good listener. "So how are things?"

"They just suck." He had never been so negative before. "There's no describing what an ordeal this is. It's like we are all trapped in this horrible thing. We just can't seem to move any faster. I see the jury. They are completely confused, but they don't care anymore."

"You know that in the long run, once they start to deliberate, most juries really do want to do the right thing."

"But it will be too late by then. They'll have to go with the last thing they remember understanding, which happened back in January."

"Or maybe they will just decide that they trust you more than anyone else."

"Which is the wrong reason for coming to a verdict. I'm never doing another criminal trial again."

I knew he felt that way now, but I had to wonder if six months after this trial was over, he would find himself missing the visibility and the intensity. He would remember the legal strategizing; he would forget the emphasis on personality. If that happened, then he would do this again. And again. "I wish there was something I could do."

"You could be here."

I paused. "What?"

"I wish you were here."

I was startled. He wanted me there. This wasn't us. This wasn't what we did. We loved each other, we were loyal, and we were both completely committed to our marriage, but this "I need you," this "I can't do it without you"—that wasn't us.

"Are you asking me to come to Houston?"

"I don't know . . . I'm too tired to know what I'm asking."

"But you want me to come?"

"Stop trying to pin me down on this." He was suddenly defensive. "I just said that I wished you were here. What's the big deal about that? Of course I wish we were all together."

Now he was turning this into the meaningless "wish you were here" of a postcard. But he had meant it. For whatever reason, he wanted me there. I got up and walked toward the calendar. "I could probably get down for a couple of days; the kids could stay with—" I looked at the calendar. "Oh, crap."

"Don't worry about it," he said. "It's no big deal. I don't even know why I mentioned it."

"I'll try to work it out, Jamie, I will try."

"Like I said, it doesn't matter."

But it did matter.

The problem was that starting Wednesday of this coming week, the lower- and middle-school kids were taking a series of standardized tests, the ERBs. I have no idea what the initials stand for, but the school takes them very seriously. Not only are the results used to evaluate the individual child, but also the teachers and the curriculum. At any other time I could have asked Mimi, Annelise, or Blair to take the kids, but during the standardized tests, every kid needed to be home in his or her own bed, getting a good night's sleep.

There were two nice widows in the neighborhood who came into people's homes for overnight baby-sitting. Although I had never used either of them, I knew plenty of people who had. A quick e-mail produced their phone numbers, but it turned out that both of them had been booked for months. Two families, in which the mom and the dad each traveled a lot in their jobs, had put these women on retainer for the duration of the ERBs just in case both parents were called away.

Whom could I call? Jamie's mother was still recovering from her broken sternum. My brother was in California, and both he and his wife worked full-time. In a life-or-death emergency, of course, my sister-in-law would throw herself on a plane to help me, but this was not life-or-death. Jamie's younger brother was, he always claimed, terrified of children, and I knew that he had deliberately trained himself to be incapable of putting a meal on the table to ensure that no one would ever expect him to do so. Jamie's older brother and his wife had young children of their own at home and were busy helping Jamie's parents.

Reluctantly I picked up the phone and called the person whom I wished I could have called first—my mother. "Is there any chance you could come out and stay with the kids this coming week?"

"I always told you and your brother that I wasn't going to be at your beck and call for baby-sitting."

I lived on the East Coast; Frank lived on the West. We were hardly in the habit of asking her to sit with the kids while we ran out to a movie.

"Mother, don't you think you should have first asked me why I needed you?"

She didn't say anything for a moment. I closed my eyes, knowing that I had made a mistake. That had been the worst thing I could have said. Of course, she should have asked—she knew that—but there was absolutely no way that she was ever going to admit that she was wrong.

Her voice was tight. "I would assume that if it had been a life-threatening situation, you would have said that immediately."

I was not up for a long conversation about whether she had been right. Such a conversation would probably end up with her agreeing to come, but it just didn't seem worth it. And did I really want her with her critical eye and prima-donna airs running my house and taking care of my kids? "Fine, Mother, fine."

"Now don't take that tone with me, missy."

"I won't." I was hanging up; there wouldn't be any tone. "Good-bye."

I took the phone back into the kitchen, swamped with weary failure. Was I letting my difficulties with my mother get in the way of being with Jamie?

Before I could replace the phone in its cradle, it rang again. It was Blair. "Oh, Lydia, I'm so glad you're off the phone. Can you come over and help? This is such a mess."

Her voice was frustrated, not panicked. "What is it?"

"I've got those stupid Styrofoam peanuts all over my yard, the street, my neighbor's yard, and it's getting worse by the minute."

I really wasn't sure what she was talking about, but I said I would come. Since Erin wasn't home, I had to bundle Thomas into the car and take him with me. When I turned down Blair's street, I could see that Mimi's van was already parked at the curb.

What had happened was a mishap, the results of which were so time-consuming that it didn't feel like a mishap but a crisis.

Blair's husband had put out at the curb for Monday's trash collection two shipping cartons full of white foam packing pellets and had then gone off to a Wizards game, neglecting to tape the boxes shut. Blair's neighbor had called her angrily to report that wind had knocked the cartons over and the peanuts were being blown everywhere. She had to come clean them up right now, or he would take steps.

Blair didn't believe him about the taking steps, but she acknowledged that the pellets were her moral responsibility—or at least her husband's—and the sooner they were cleaned up, the easier the job would be.

Blair's yard was beautiful even at the ragged end of winter. The holly and the boxwood were glossy and green all year-round. The oak-leaf hydrangea, even when stripped of its leaves and lush flowers, had a silvery-flecked bark, and the weeping cherry trees were elegant even without their clouds of pink blossoms.

But gleaming in the fading winter sunlight, scurrying along in the wind, were thousands and thousands of those awful foam pellets. Blair and Annelise were trying to corral them with leaf blowers. Mimi was scooping them up into a trash bag that her son, Gideon, was holding, and Blair and Annelise's younger girls were sweeping the street.

I started raking the pellets out from under the neighbor's bushes. I found packing peanuts annoying in the best of situations; this was the worst. The air was dry. Charged with static electricity, the pellets clung to my gloves and the sleeves of my coat.

It wasn't possible to talk over the sound of the leaf blowers so I worked silently, and the absurdity of the task suited my mood. Even after the others finished with the leaf blowers and had come nearer to me to fill the trash bags, I said nothing.

Eventually we were close enough to being done that Blair sent the kids inside. I was tying up one of the bags when Annelise put her hand on my arm. "Lydia, you don't seem yourself. Is something wrong? I really do think things are better with the girls. None of them wanted to call Faith this afternoon. They're all ready to have things be the way they have always been."

I supposed I was glad of that, but right now Jamie's misery was what mattered. I told my friends about him asking me to go to Houston, but with the ERBs I didn't see how I could go. "And don't even think of offering to take my kids, Annelise. You know it isn't fair to yours."

She sighed. "I suppose you asked your mother."

They knew about my relationship with my mother. "I did, and I am not supposed to take that tone with her. I can't remember if I was addressed as 'young lady' or 'missy,' but the conversation was short."

"That's such a shame," Annelise said.

"I sometimes think," Mimi said, "that's why you are the best of us. Your mother was the worst and so you need to spend all your time being better than her. My mom is great, and—"

"Wait a second," Blair interrupted. "Mimi, is there any chance that your mother could come and stay with Lydia's kids?"

"Bubbe?" I exclaimed. "Come here?" Mimi's mother lived in New York. Why should she drive five hours to come take care of my kids?

But Mimi was already snapping her fingers to get Blair's cell phone from her. She moved off to call.

Bubbe was no picture-book grandmother. She was forthright, and she didn't have a sentimental bone in her body. She believed in right and wrong, but she never expected that anyone would find it easy to do what was right. A former pediatric nurse, she treated children as individuals. She believed that one five-year-old was as different from the next five-year-old as one adult from another. My kids adored her, and so did I.

Would I mind turning my kitchen and my children over to her? Of course not.

Blair tapped at my jaw, closing it. "It is a perfect solution. Your kids certainly know her a lot better than they know those other women you would have hired."

"But this is way too much to ask of her," I protested.

"But you're really asking Mimi," Annelise said. "You're the one who said that we're here to back up our kids' throws. We want the girls to think that they can catch a ball themselves, but if they can't, we want to be standing behind them. Mimi wants to help you, but she can't. So her mother is going to do it for her. Isn't that the kind of relationship you want with Erin when she grows up?"

"Yes." Outside the Barnes & Noble store two weeks ago, I had thought about how exhilarating it was to feel that you've helped other people's kids, how much self-congratulatory joy you felt for living that kind of life. And why would that stop just because you didn't have schoolchildren in your home anymore?

Mimi was coming back toward us, sliding the antenna into the phone. "She'll pack tonight and then leave first thing in the morning. She'll be here long before the kids get home from school."

It all fell into place quickly. Mimi made my travel arrangements, and Blair and Annelise came over to help me get organized. Erin and Thomas were surprised at the notion that their friends' grandmother was coming to stay with them, but after a moment they both declared that it was okay.

Although she didn't say, I was pretty sure what the issue was for Erin. *What if I get my period for the first time and Mom is out of town?* After a moment's secret thought, she probably concluded that, if nothing else, Bubbe would have at least seen the video about menstruation and so would know enough to be able to help out.

I didn't have to guess why Thomas was agreeable about Bubbe's coming. He told me. It was fine that she was going to be staying with the two of them, he said. Her scrambled eggs were better than mine.

10

I dropped the kids off at school the next morning and went in to tell their teachers what was happening. At the offices I added Bubbe's name to the list of people who could pick them up in an emergency. As I was heading back to my car, I saw Chris Goddard.

"You are looking very professional today," he said.

I was in one of my formerly-a-lawyer pantsuits, and I had blown my hair dry instead of letting it do its usual "finding itself" thing. "I'm going to Houston to spend some time with my husband. Mimi Gold's mother is staying with the children."

"You'll be at the trial?" he said. "That's exciting."

"I don't know that I will actually go to the trial. I'd be taking someone else's seat if I did." I didn't like the idea of being the wife who sweeps in and grabs a perk from a hard-working young associate.

"So you're going to give your husband support?"

"Yes."

"I'm sure it will make a big difference to him."

"Let's hope," I answered pleasantly.

I hadn't meant anything by that. It was just something to say. But I suddenly realized while I might be hoping to "support" my husband, I didn't have a plan. I had no idea what I was going to do, what he needed me to do. If Jamie needed legal help, I would have dusted off as many of my brain cells as I could find and pitched right in. If he needed someone to make nice dinners for him, I would have been there with pot roast, zucchini, and quarts of heavy cream. And if he needed someone to set up car pools, that was my specialty.

But he had a staff of lawyers and paralegals. The hotel was feeding him dinner, a caterer sent lunch to the courthouse, and a car service picked him up at the hotel in the morning and fetched him from the courthouse in the afternoon.

Jamie didn't need a mom, and unfortunately, at the moment, that's what I was best at.

Chris and I had started to walk, and I could feel my shoulders and torso start to turn toward him. I wanted to confide in him, wanted to tell him that I had no idea why I was going to Houston or what I was going to do once I was there.

But I couldn't do that. There was a line between us that he didn't want to cross any more than I did.

And what possible advice would he have for me? What experience had he had with the ups and downs of a marriage? He had been the road manager of a rock band, and the mother of his son had probably been a groupie.

I left my car at home and took a cab to the airport. It wasn't easy to get to Houston. There was only one nonstop flight a day, and it took off from Dulles and landed at Bush Intercontinental. Both these airports were long drives from the center of town. By changing in Charlotte, I could fly out of Reagan National and into Hobby. That's what Jamie usually did.

Would my friends know how to "support" their husbands? I think so. Bruce would have called Blair because he had lost, forgotten, and/or broken everything in his life, and Blair would go find, remember, and/or fix all of it. If the ever-critical Joel called Annelise for support, he would have a list of all the things that she should have known to do yesterday even though he himself had not known that they had needed to be done. Mimi would have expected Ben to be straightforward. If he had started to backpedal in the way that Jamie had, she woud have taken him at his word that he had changed his mind.

And I didn't think that their marriages were any better than mine, and judged by objective standards about equal partnerships, Annelise's and Blair's were probably worse.

So why did I feel so uncertain?

Until I met Jamie, I had never felt sexy or feminine. My mother had had a two-columned chart in her head. One column was labeled "smart" and the other "not smart." Sexy, feminine, domestic, and athletic were all in the "not smart" column. I had always had a boyish figure—small chested with almost no indentation at my waist. But it wouldn't have mattered if I had been built like a Barbie doll. Because I was smart, I couldn't be sexy or feminine.

But Jamie thought I was all three.

During law school I lived, as did many students, on a residential street in a semidetached house that had been cut up into student apartments. The houses on the block were brick and they sat close to the street. Across the street from me was a lady in her early eighties, still living in her own home. Mrs. Murray had a narrow driveway to park her car in, but the sidewalk between the driveway and her front steps had cracked, having been pushed up and out by a rising tree root. I noticed that she was careful when crossing the fissure, her gloved hand resting first on the tree trunk and then on her stair railing. I sometimes helped her with her groceries. Once I noticed that her porch light was out and so helpful midwesterner that I was—*helpful* didn't appear in either column on my mother's chart so I could be helpful—I rang her doorbell and changed the light for her. She gave me two unopened gift packages of scented lotion, dusting powder, and cologne. I protested; she was being too generous, but she showed me her closet. She had at least five more such boxes. They were all that anyone gave her anymore.

Their scent was sweet and flowery, what people assumed that old ladies will like, but I used them and felt clean and fragrant. I looked like a boyishly built, first-year law student, I lived and acted like one, but I didn't smell like one.

Jamie noticed.

We had already discovered how compatible we were, neither one of us given to procrastination or high drama. He could see that I was a behind-the-scenes kind of leader, the person who kept everyone else on track. And even though he would become by far the better lawyer, I was a better first-year law student, so he treated me as someone valuable. We organized a study group together, carefully admitting people who would complement us.

A week after I had started using Mrs. Murray's scent, I was in the library with him and unthinkingly reached across him for a book.

He dropped his pen. "I can't deal with this."

There was a lot on this table that neither one of us could deal with—that no human being should have to deal with—but he was not talking about the curriculum. "What do you mean?"

He was not looking at me. His eyes were focused on his college-graduation pen, its cobalt enamel almost black in the dim light. "The way you smell."

I hesitated. Did he like the way I smelled, or did I remind him of his grandmother?

He kept looking at his pen. "In all this mess, in all these gray papers, suddenly you smell so . . . I don't know . . . like a girl." Then he looked at me, and it was the first time that I noticed the light hazel circle around the pupils of his greenish brown eyes.

So that's how our relationship started, in a state of sleep-deprived scent intoxication. He told me later that he had felt so detached from his physical self that it took seeing how much smaller my hand was than his to remind him that he had a Y chromosome.

The one Barbie-doll thing I had going for me—in that time long ago, in that galaxy far, far away—was a very flat stomach. If I wore a loose shirt tucked into snug jeans, I looked like I had a shape. Of course in the middle of a New Haven winter, you wanted bulk, but I didn't let that stop me. I removed my heavy sweater at every opportunity.

Then I started baking. Cooking was the one domestic art that my mother allowed into the "smart" column. Julia Child was smart. A thinking woman could admire Julia Child. Cooking was creative, not degrading. While I would not have dared a hollandaise sauce in my student kitchen, I was perfectly willing to make cookies. I brought still-warm chocolate chip cookies, snickerdoodles, and peanut butter cookies to study group. I was so engrossed in pleasing Jamie that I didn't worry, as my mother might have, about whether this made me look less serious to anyone else.

I had never before met another person's needs so well. He wanted to feel masculine, I wanted to feel feminine—the world's most fundamental win-win situation. When my bottles of lotions and scents from Mrs. Murray were empty, I bought more for myself. Part of why I loved Jamie was that it was the first time I had ever loved myself.

And so what happened to all the sexual deliciousness? Life, marriage, the kids. Thomas had slight signs of cough asthma, and the doctor suggested that we use as many unscented products as possible around him. We didn't have to be compulsive about it. He could use scented toilet paper in someone else's home—this happened at a moment in Thomas's life when the thought that he could be relied on to use any kind of toilet paper was welcome indeed—but there was no reason for Mom (as the doctor called me) to be wearing a lot of products.

But Thomas wasn't with me, was he?

Okay, so I didn't know what I was doing, but when had that ever stopped me? Sometimes I faced the world with lists, schedules, and spreadsheets. Sometimes I didn't even wait for someone else to hum a few bars, I just started singing along. I had ruled out being lawyer, caterer, and chauffeur. But what about being a groupie? That was a role I had never tried before.

I rented a car at the airport and, following a map carefully, drove into the heart of Houston, passing by miles of motels and park 'n' ride lots. Jamie's hotel was owned by a high-end national chain. The lobby of the hotel was sleek and European with strong horizontals and lots of smoky Plexiglas. I left my suitcase with the bellman and wandered down the little arcade of stores, finding a Crabtree-and-Evelyn type of shop. Although the saleslady clearly found me so far beneath her that it was going to be painful for her to conduct a transaction with me—a real Crabtree-and-Evelyn store would have fired her in a minute—I stared her down and managed to buy scented oils, lotions, and candles. By the time I heard Jamie unlocking the door to his suite, the rooms and I were smelling like an orchid who had mated with a vanilla bean.

He paused at the door. "Lydia?"

"You got the message that I was coming?" I asked lightly.

"I did, I knew it, but . . ."

I understood. He had known it as a fact, he had left word at the front desk so that I could pick up a key, but beyond that he had given my coming no thought. I crossed the room and hugged him. At first his clasp was routine, but then I could tell that he noticed my perfume. We kissed, open-mouthed.

And then I—soccer mom, curriculum committee member, former assistant Girl Scout leader, orchid-scented Spring Fair cochair—dropped to my knees and gave my startled husband a blow job.

"Lydia!" He laced his hands through my hair when he realized what was happening. This was not like us. Oral sex was a part of our vocabulary, but it was always nice married-in-bed sex. Never like this, fully dressed, him standing. But when I didn't stop, the hands in my hair grew firm, holding me there.

And it certainly didn't take long.

I sat back, laughing, while he—poor guy—was leaning against the wall, his pinstriped suit pants slipping down around his knees, looking exhausted, ridiculous, and very, very dear.

"That was unbelievable." He shook his head. "I don't know what to say."

"Don't say anything. You go take a bath, and I will order us dinner."

"A bath? I don't take baths."

"You do now."

I had the tub already partially filled—"be prepared" is the Girl Scout motto—so it only took a minute or so to add more hot water. I had lined up scented candles along the edge of the tub, and the water glistened with a perfumed oil. The orchids had abandoned the humble vanilla bean and were carrying on a mad fling with something richer and spicier. The bathroom smelled exotically tropical. I closed the door, hoping he wouldn't fall asleep and drown.

The suite had two rooms, and it was spacious and comfortable, decorated in hunter green and sand with maroon accents. Everything was designed to give a welcoming first impression. The soft furnishings were deeply upholstered. The sofa and chairs in the living room were tufted; the bedskirt was lined; the headboard was padded. The living room had a chair rail and both rooms had a wallpaper border running around the ceiling. But after the first impression, there was nothing interesting to look at. Everything matched too well, and there was nothing intricate or unexpected in any of the prints or textures. The wallpaper borders gleamed with the pebbly sheen of a commercial-grade product. Although it would have been a great place to stay for a night or two, I knew that Jamie now viewed the suite as a sensory-deprivation tank. So I had brought some pictures I had recently taken of the kids and set them around the rooms.

As soon as he came out of the bath, he noticed the pictures. "Oh, you've brought the kids!" he exclaimed.

That was a potentially revealing comment. I had not brought our children. I had brought pictures of them, and a person would like to think that their father could tell the difference, but Jamie crossed over to the pictures so eagerly, and picking each frame up, looked at the images so attentively that I kept my mouth shut.

He shook his head. "They look so great. Don't you miss them?"

Actually, I didn't. I'm sure I would start missing them to-morrow, but I had just seen them about ten hours ago.

"How did you manage with them? Are they across the street?"

"No, they were able to stay home. Mimi's mother came down to take care of them."

He paused, trying to figure this out. "Mimi's mother is stay-ing with our kids? Why?"

"It's a long story, but they're fine, or they will be until Bubbe brings a live carp home." I had called and spoken to Erin and Thomas when they got home from school. Gideon, Mimi's son and Bubbe's actual grandson, had obviously felt a little jealous and so had terrorized Thomas during the day with stories about Bubbe making gefilte fish out of a live carp that would swim in our bathtub until the time of its decapitation, an event that Gideon, right-minded second-grade boy that he was, had described in awesome and fantastical detail.

"He has never seen such a thing in his life," Bubbe said af-ter I told her the story. "It was *my* bubbe who made her own gefilte fish. My mother bought hers, and I certainly do, too."

Jamie smiled. "I do like it when the kids get chatty on the phone, but I'm having trouble knowing what to say to Erin. I do okay with Thomas. He will go on forever about whatever games they are playing during recess. Erin, on the other hand . . ."

I knew. "'School is fine.'" I drawled out the word *fine* with the flat, contemptuous sullenness of a preteen. "'Homework is fine, the weather is fine, the post-Soviet Russian economy is fine.'"

"That's about it. Doesn't she want to talk about anything?"

"Probably not. You could try asking her what she wore to school, but if you do that, you've got to act interested and ask a follow-up."

"A follow-up question about her clothes?" He sounded suspicious. Either he didn't think much of that idea or he doubted his ability to execute it or both. "I don't want to talk to her about her clothes. I want to talk to her about her."

"Her clothes and her friends are what she understands about herself, and she isn't going to talk to us about her friends. So clothes are your only hope."

"Then I'm in a peck of trouble."

Jamie had said that he was sick of looking at the hotel menu. Earlier in the afternoon I had spoken to the chef, and the kitchen was preparing a simple veal dish especially for us. I had asked for a tablecloth and candles to be sent up with our order, and I carefully moved the stacks of papers that had probably been sitting on the table for weeks.

He commented on the table and noticed the veal, but I could tell that, within moments of sitting down, he was swamped by a wave of weariness. He hardly spoke. So I chattered away, talking about the book I had read on the plane. I could tell that he was listening. Perhaps it was only in the way that you half-listened to a program on NPR, but that was enough to keep other things out of his mind. Because he wasn't responding, I felt as if I was giving a book report. But that was okay. I was better at book reports than I was at blow jobs.

. . .

Jamie told me to stay in bed in the morning and call for room service, but I was determined to be Ms. Energy, Mrs. Perfect-at-your-side wife. His legal team had an office in the hotel, and breakfast was laid out in the conference room so that everyone could touch base with one another first thing in the morning. I rode down the elevator with Jamie, thinking nothing of the fact that he was in a well-fitting business suit and I was in suitcase-creased khakis. At our breakfast table at home we never looked as if we were going to the same party—because we weren't.

There were nearly ten people in the conference room, and all of them looked surprised to see me. With few exceptions they had no idea who I was, and even those who knew me had not known that I was coming. As soon as Jamie introduced me, everyone was very polite, very, very polite. After all, I was the boss's wife.

I didn't like that. I was suddenly conscious of how I was dressed. Almost half the people were women. They were dressed for success in dark suits and shoes with inch-and-a-half heels. Their hair was neat, their makeup fresh, and their blouses were made of woven fabrics, not comfortable knits.

I'm an attorney, too. I suddenly wanted them to know that. But I wasn't here as an attorney. I was staying in this expensive hotel, eating this expense-account food, simply because I was a wife.

Did Jamie think of me that way, just as a wife? I glanced at him, and the answer to that was clear—Jamie was not thinking of me at all. He was already engrossed in a planning session with one of the individual clients' attorneys, a local man who belonged to the Texas bar.

Jamie hadn't been only loving and grateful when he had suggested that I sleep in and order room service. Even if he hadn't admitted it to himself, he knew that I would be in the way at breakfast.

So I ate as quickly as dignity allowed and then laid my hand on Jamie's shoulder in a cheerful but proper farewell. Steve Ellsworth, the local attorney, half-rose and said, "Are you going to be here through the weekend? My wife and I would love to have you and Jamie out to the house for dinner on Saturday night."

The plan was that I should stay through Sunday. So I nodded. "Do you want to check with her about a time?"

By which I meant "don't you want to check with her at all?" Steve Ellsworth had learned of my presence fifteen minutes ago, and he had not done anything to communicate with his wife. She was not being consulted about the invitation.

"No need to do that. Six-thirty or seven will be fine. You can't be any more precise than that, not with our traffic," he said genially.

So I thanked him and went back to the suite to figure out what on earth a perfect at-your-side wife was supposed to do with her day when there was no one to stand next to. What did women do when they accompanied their husbands on business-related travel?

I suppose a trophy wife would spend the day polishing the chrome so that she would glitter in the evening. So I read until the hotel's beauty salon opened, and then I went and got my hair cut, highlighted, and colored. The color was warmer than I usually had, and the cut was edgier. I liked it. The manicurist had been available during the various processing stages so I also got a manicure and, as long as I was at it, a pedicure. I read so many issues of *People* magazine that I was really sick of looking at people who were far prettier than any human had a right to be.

It was now noon. Jamie said he usually had dinner around seven or eight.

I'm not used to being alone. At home, even when I'm the only person in the house, I don't feel alone. The phone is always ringing and the laptop is chirping.

I suppose the other thing that trophy wives do is shop. The padded leatherette notebook of "Guest Information" had indicated that the fifth-largest mall in the United States was only eight miles away. How could you pass up the fifth-largest mall in the nation? I called for my car.

The valet parking guys urged me to take the hotel courtesy shuttle, but resolutely independent, I drove myself. And that was the right thing to do. The horrendous Houston traffic and the immense and crowded Galleria parking lot had the happy effect of killing almost an hour. Now I only had five or six hours to shop.

I took off my clothes fifty million times and bought almost nothing. I was trying to expand my wardrobe horizons, to buy things that I wouldn't usually buy, and so I would try such things on and realize why I didn't usually buy them. At the end of the afternoon, I was tired, my feet hurt, I was frustrated . . . and I was lonely. As I sat in traffic on the way back to the hotel, I called Annelise and whined.

She listened patiently for five minutes and then told me gently I had done this to myself. "Lydia, you know what looks good on you. You always say that the problem with your wardrobe is that you don't stick with what you know is right."

She had a point. I do know what looks good on me—V necks, diagonal lines, warm colors, prints with small figures and low contrast—and the reason that I don't look spectacular every minute of the day is that I let other things override those rules. Sometimes I will buy a color that I love in a garment that isn't great for me. Or I will pass up a pair of trousers that might be utterly perfect if I would just try them on in a bigger size, but I can't bear the thought. And if something is on sale then all the rules fly out the door. The more times a garment has been marked down, the more I am willing to forgive. I'll buy anything if the price is really great, and then I will never wear it.

It was much harder to be the perfect groupie at dinner that night. Jamie seemed more distracted, and whatever initial relief my appearance had created had worn off. I mentioned having gone shopping, but despite yesterday's lecture on follow-up questions vis-à-vis wardrobe issues, he couldn't ask a follow-up question because he didn't ask an opening one. He also didn't notice my new haircut. I was quiet for a while, and

he didn't seem to notice that, either. So I talked about what I
had read, and he did seem to be listening to that.

Had I dropped my whole life, hauled Mimi's mom across
however many states to stay with our kids, so that I could give
book reports? I could have sent Jamie some books on tape; it
would have been a lot cheaper and just as effective.

The following morning I skipped the group breakfast. "I'm
sure you have people to talk to."

He seemed relieved. "We do have a routine. People often
get ideas late at night." He paused. "You are going to be okay,
aren't you?"

"Me? Oh, goodness, Jamie, of course, I'll be fine. This is a
luxury for me, all this time to myself."

"Oh, yes." Now he really seemed relieved. "I suppose it is."

He wasn't supposed to have believed me. He was supposed
to have nodded and said that he appreciated what I was trying
to do, appreciated that I didn't want to add to his burdens by
whining about myself, but, of course, he knew perfectly well
that I didn't like roaming around Houston with nothing to do.
I waited until I knew that Mimi would be in from walking her
dog. Then I called her and whined.

She listened to me for ten minutes and then told me that
if I didn't want to shop for myself, I should shop for her. "Just
make sure that it is short and that two of you will fit into it."

This time I did let the hotel courtesy shuttle take me to
the Galleria, and I got to work with grim efficiency. In each
store I looked for the saleslady who most closely resembled me
in age and build and treated her neither like a hang-those-up-
for-me-won't-you-darling underling nor like a bitch-goddess

put on earth to scare the bejesus out of me. I introduced myself and treated her like my partner. I told her what I thought I looked good in and then followed her around as she showed me what the store had.

I purchased things with crisp decision. I set very high standards and if the garment met those standards, I purchased it. I felt completely detached from myself and my life. I was a little robot with a mission. I don't think it was the CIA that had planted a chip in my brain—although I suppose it might have been. More likely it was the mall's management or the Federal Reserve or who else cares about people spending money.

I completely lost track of what I spent. Without a car to store my purchases in, I had everything shipped back to D.C. As I rode the shuttle back to the hotel, I pulled my receipts out of my purse to add them up, but the numbers didn't seem real. I started to feel an odd churning in my stomach. Yes, we have enough money, but I knew that I had spent more than I needed to.

Shopping makes some women feel good; spending money on themselves makes them feel pampered, nurtured, taken care of. Not me. I was feeling icky. I didn't want to become the sort of person for whom spending money solves things.

I called Blair. "Shut up," she told me briskly, "and stop thinking about it. All those stores have branches around here. Come home, look at everything here, let me look at it, and then we can return whatever was ridiculously overpriced."

That made me feel better. The van got completely stalled in traffic. So I called home. I chatted briefly with Erin—who had worn her Gap low-rise, slender-fit, boot-cut black jeans to school with the Haverford College hoodie Jamie had bought for her the last time he had visited his alma mater.

"I thought you weren't supposed to wear anything with writing," I, the queen of follow-up wardrobe questions, asked.

"Mr. Goddard said that the high-school kids could start wearing things with college insignias on them."

Good for him. I started to ask Erin if he had explicitly told the middle-school kids that they could as well, or if she and her friends were pushing the dress-code envelope, but I decided to give that question to Jamie.

Bubbe reported that Mimi's husband had taken Gideon and Thomas to Cub Scouts.

Why wasn't I home? I wished I were with them.

Dinner was even more difficult that night because I could no longer believe that I was doing Jamie any good.

I couldn't think of what to talk about. Relationships, personalities, and individuality are what interest me, and right now Jamie was sickened by how his legal case had become about those things, instead of about law or justice.

The silence continued. I thought about the dinner at Blair's, how Chris had gotten me to talk about photography in ways that would have been interesting even to Jamie.

Jamie looked up from his plate with a sick, watery smile. "I'm not very good company," he said.

"Don't worry about that," I chirped. "You don't have to put on a dog-and-pony show for me."

I suppose that at Blair's Chris had been thinking of himself as at least the pony part of a dog-and-pony show. He had been trying to be interesting and engaging. Jamie just didn't have the energy to do that now.

Thursday I went to the art museums, and I was lonely. I wanted to talk to someone about what I was seeing. One of the paintings was so sublime that I felt as if my eyeballs were being fried. I had an intensely physical reaction to the work, and I ached to talk to someone about it.

When I got back to the suite, there was a message from Jamie that the legal team was having a dinner meeting in the office suite, and I should join them there.

I wanted to go home. I missed the kids, Thomas even more than Erin. I missed how cuddly he still was, how sweet and serious. I missed the clumsy relish with which he and his friends were growing into stupid male humor. They were gleeful at even the most hackneyed potty joke because, however tedious the joke seemed to me, they were hearing it for the first time.

So why not go home? I could tell Jamie that Bubbe was having to leave unexpectedly or that something had come up with someone. He wouldn't ask for details.

But I wasn't going to lie to him. If I was going to leave, I was going to be honest. *Jamie, I'm not doing you any good. I should go home.*

But he would protest. *Oh, no, Lydia, having you here is important, you do make a difference.* He would say what he thought I wanted to hear. He tells the jury what they want to hear, he tells reporters what they want to hear. Why should I be any different?

Saturday morning there was no breakfast in the conference room, and so I called for room service. "Shall we do something together this afternoon?" he asked. "I can take off a couple of hours."

Was this the big thank-you for my having come? A couple of hours on Saturday afternoon?

I was angry. All week long I had stifled every impulse, every need of my own, so as not to be a bother to him . . . and he had let me do it. "You do remember that the Ellsworths are having us to dinner?"

"Oh." He had forgotten. "But I can still take some time off this afternoon."

"I need to get something halfway educational for the kids." So far I had only bought them instant-gratification junk. "I was thinking about going to the gift shop at the Houston Children's Museum, not to any of the exhibits, just the gift shop."

"Just the gift shop? Isn't that a strange way to go to a museum?"

"Give Erin that option next time we take her to a museum and see how strange she thinks it is. She would love it."

"Oh, I suppose." So he came with me to the museum, but stood at my shoulder like the ghost of Christmas past.

In the evening we took my rented car out to the Ellsworths' house. The directions we had were simple enough, but it quickly became clear that the distances were considerable. I couldn't imagine commuting that far every day, and I started to say something to that effect when Jamie spoke.

"You know, we need to be careful this evening."

"About what?" I asked.

"Steve represents only one of the clients."

Each of the defendants had his own set of lawyers, and as lead counsel, Jamie was trying to keep the entire cast singing the same tune, something that was becoming more challenging by the minute.

"In fact," Jamie continued, "our going to the Ellsworths' at all is making some of the other lawyers nervous. It looks as if we are playing favorites."

This was a little too much like the sixth-grade parents' coffee at the beginning of the school year. "You must hate this," I said. Jamie would want to be judged on the quality of his work, not on which parties he went to.

"You have no idea," he answered.

Marcy and Steve Ellsworth had a very large, very new house. They were a blended family. Marcy and Steve had two toddlers of their own, and apparently this was the weekend that all the various teens—the stepchildren, the half-siblings, and even a stepchild's half-sibling—were at their house. If I had been Marcy, I would not have been happy about having to haul out my china and crystal for a pair of strangers on this particular weekend. The older kids, while very polite, interrupted us all evening, needing to rearrange the cars in the driveway, check in about curfew times, and borrow money. One girl wanted to look through Marcy's sweaters because she had left all her own sweaters at her mother's house. I sensed that had we not been there, Marcy would not have allowed the girl, a stepdaughter, to pillage her closet . . . and I think that the girl knew it.

Steve was making drinks much stronger than Jamie and I liked, and the wine goblets at dinner were equally Texas-sized.

We all struggled to talk about topics of general interest—where each family vacationed, what sports our sons played—until finally Marcy rose to clear the table.

I hopped up to help her. "Oh, no," she insisted. "You're a guest. I can't have you working. And I have my own way of doing things."

The last sentence told me that she wasn't simply being polite. She really didn't want help. She wanted to be alone in her kitchen. I couldn't blame her. This evening couldn't have been any fun for her.

So I stayed in my chair.

Steve brought out a tray of after-dinner drinks. Jamie and I both refused more alcohol. Steve poured himself some cognac, then started talking about the case. Silver-haired and red-faced, he was inching toward dangerous territory, wanting to talk about the other defendants and their lawyers.

There had already been some analysis in the media about the growing division among the defendants, and so far Steve wasn't saying anything interesting or new, but Jamie was growing wary. His answers were getting shorter and shorter, and I was reminded of the way Mary Paige Caudwell had, at Blair's party, kept moving closer and closer to Chris Goddard while Chris kept moving back.

I decided to help out. Three days ago one defendant and his lawyers had started to wear Bengal-striped ties. On such ties a dark stripe alternates with a light stripe of the same width. Although conservative, such ties make a strong statement, and the supposition was that this defendant and his lawyers were trying to separate themselves from the others. I had read about this in the newspaper and heard about it on TV. I figured that it was something safe to mention, and then I could redirect the conversation. I would ask Steve if many men in Houston wore college ties or ties from their clubs. And were the connections implied by those ties more or less important in Houston than in the rest of the state?

"It is interesting—" I said, and just as Steve was turning to look at me, I felt a sharp blow on my shin.

Jamie had kicked me. Jamie was telling me to shut up.

I looked at him, startled, disbelieving. Didn't he trust me? Didn't he know that I wasn't going to run my mouth off about the case?

He looked back at me, his eyes hard, his lips tight. He was ordering me to keep quiet.

I was furious. How dare he not trust me? How *dare* he? I was not a clueless, brainless child bride. And when it came to the little dance that was going on at this table right now, I was better at it than he was.

Part of me wanted to barrel ahead with my tie conversation just to show Jamie that I did know what I was doing. I felt like a defiant child. All I wanted to do was show him that I had been right and he had been wrong.

The trouble was that I was now too angry to listen to myself carefully. Jamie's silent accusation made it likely that I would say something inappropriate. So I had to remain silent.

As soon as we got in the car, I turned to him, determined to defend myself.

"Don't start," he snapped. "I don't want to talk about it."

"Jamie, I do not take orders from you."

"I said I didn't want to talk about it. Lydia, please, don't make me fight with you, too."

So I turned away from him and stared out the window. I remained silent for most of the drive home. Then he asked me what time tomorrow my flight was.

If that was an apology, he was going to have to do a lot better.

Sunday morning he walked me through the lobby, and we said good-bye in front of my rented car. There was no point in him coming to the airport with me since I had to return the car.

"I'll try to get home next weekend," he said.

Don't, I wanted to scream. *Don't. Just stay here until this trial is over. I don't want to have anything to do with you. Stay here.*

"That would be great," I said.

"I may not be able to get away."

"I understand."

"This week's been okay for you, hasn't it?" he asked, his voice edged with concern. "A nice break from your routine?"

I like my routine. I like coming down the back stairs every morning to make coffee in my charcoal and yellow kitchen. I love sitting at the kitchen table hearing the sounds of Erin getting herself up and then the fifteen minutes later tiptoeing into Thomas's dark room and scooping my arms around his little blanketed body to wake him up. I love opening my car door and chatting with the neighbors if they are on their front porch. I love going into the kids' school, knowing that I always see someone I know.

I didn't need a break from my routine, but he wanted me to lie. So I did. "Oh, I've been fine."

I caught an earlier flight than I had planned, and I made a close connection in Charlotte so the cab dropped me off at the house hours before I was expected. I came in through the front door and saw that some of the boxes from my shopping expeditions had already arrived. I heard noise in the kitchen and eagerly went through the house to find the kids, but only Bubbe was there.

She apologized immediately. "Erin's at the movies with the girls, and Thomas is at"—she glanced at a Post-it note by the phone—"Zak Hoffman's. Mimi said that he was allowed to go there."

Zak was one of the Sidwell kids on Thomas's soccer team. Thomas was certainly allowed to go to Zak's house. I just wished that he were here.

I launched into a repetition of my profuse thanks.

"Stop it," Bubbe ordered. "I know you're grateful, and you know I had a good time. So let's not be boring about it."

I smiled. "I did bring you a scarf. It may be in one of those boxes by the front door."

"You did do a lot of shopping."

"Yup."

Bubbe looked at me. "Is that good or bad?"

I sat down at the table. Why wasn't she my mother? Why hadn't I deserved a mother like this? "Bubbe, I had no idea why I was there. I don't know that I did my husband any good."

"Did he do *you* any good?"

"No." I was puzzled by her question. "I didn't expect him to. I would have felt good if I had been able to help him, but except for the first night, I didn't make much of a difference. So I'm just mad at him."

"Does he know that?"

"No. I wasn't going to pitch a major prima-donna fit because I had to eat breakfast alone."

"That must have taken a lot of self-control."

I looked at Bubbe curiously. My mother prides herself on speaking her mind, but as my sister-in-law points out, Mother only speaks her mind when she has something negative to say. If she has something complimentary or positive, she manages to repress herself beautifully.

Bubbe probably holds her tongue a fair amount, but when she does speak, she does tell you what she is thinking, both good and ill.

"Bubbe, where are you going with this?"

My mother would have instantly denied meaning anything at all. That was another one of her specialities, making it clear that she disapproved of something without specifying what it was. You ended up designing your own multiple-choice question with all of the answers being something you were doing wrong.

Whereas Bubbe paused for a moment as if to be sure that I really wanted to hear what she had to say. "Sometimes I don't think you girls give your husbands much of a chance."

"A chance to do what?"

"To be your friend. I know things were different for me. I was working in the days when no one else was, so I didn't have the kind of girlfriends that Mimi has."

"But you didn't need friends the way we do," I argued. "Your mother was living in your building, and your mother-in-law was nearby, too. You didn't need to rely on friends to watch the kids while you went to the dentist. You had family. We don't."

"My mother and mother-in-law were a lot of help," she admitted, "but they weren't my girlfriends."

"Who did you tell your troubles to?"

"My husband."

"What about when the troubles were about him, who did you talk to then?"

"Him."

Oh. "But, Bubbe, it wouldn't have been fair this week when Jamie was so tired and miserable. And not only unfair, but also pointless. He's so drained right now that he doesn't have anything to give back."

"I'm sure you're right about this particular week. But what about the rest of the time? Is he your friend the rest of the time?"

Is Jamie my friend? "I don't think he would know how."

"That's no surprise. Men don't know how to be friends with

211

their wives; you've got to teach them. I had to take my Samuel by his ears and tell him that he just needed to listen to me. Otherwise every time I would complain about the people I worked with, he would tell me to find a new job. I didn't want a new job; I just wanted to fuss. So he learned. Sometimes I think it is too easy when you've got a lot of girlfriends. Then you talk to them and you don't have to train your husband to listen to you."

Wasn't Bubbe's advice dated, good only if you hadn't left your hometown? Certainly the messages we were getting from popular culture argued the opposite. Whether you wanted bar pals or quilting buddies, a woman was supposed to have lots of female friends. If a woman had friends, it proved that she wasn't a competitive bitch; it proved that she was not dependent on men for approval.

But did having women friends keep you from having to show your husband what you needed from a friend?

Unlike every housekeeper, nanny, or cleaning lady we had ever had, Bubbe knew how to sort mail. There was a pile of first-class letters and bills and a pile of larger first-class envelopes. The magazines were stacked neatly by the reading chair, and everything else was in a bag next to the recycling bin for me to check if I wanted.

In the pile of big official-looking envelopes were two from the Sidwell Friends School addressed to the kids. The size of the envelopes said everything. A small envelope meant you were rejected or on the wait list. My kids had gotten big envelopes. They had been admitted: Thomas to the third grade, Erin to the seventh.

I thought of how many families all over the D.C. area had been aching to get those big envelopes from Sidwell, how these acceptances would have made them ecstatic. I didn't bother to open the envelopes. The kids weren't changing schools, and Jamie had no right to insist that they should, not when he was never home.

When I went up to say good night to Erin, I sat down on her bed. "You know you got into Sidwell?"

"I figured that. Bubbe said we could open them, but a big envelope did mean that you were in."

I nodded.

"You aren't going to make me go, are you?"

"No, honey. We'll sit down and talk about it as a family. As I said before, even though the decision is ultimately mine and Dad's"—or just mine—"you will have a say. We will listen to you."

"Then I think I don't want to go."

I was a little surprised that she only *thought* that she didn't want to go. I would have expected her to be more emphatic.

I patted her quilt-covered leg. "You guys were really good sports about staying with Bubbe. Dad and I appreciate it."

"No problem."

She wasn't looking at me. Something was on her mind. I wondered if it was Sidwell or something else. Or maybe she was just tired. I decided to wait until tomorrow to badger her.

Which for once in my life actually paid off.

I was still awake at ten-thirty. I was in bed, happily reading

Threads, a sewing magazine that was always full of extremely elaborate instructions about things such as using a partial stay when installing a quarter-round godet. My door was partially ajar, and I heard Erin's footsteps in the hall. I looked up as she came into my room.

"Mom?"

I moved over, hoping that she would sit down on the bed. She did. "Is your hair different?"

"Yes." I didn't suppose that this was why she had come in. "I had it cut, and the color's warmer."

"I thought you had changed it."

We sat silently for a moment.

"And that's a new nightgown."

"Yes."

We were silent again.

"Mom?"

"Yes, Erin?"

"You know what Dad is always saying about following your Inner Light and about the primacy of the individual conscience?"

I nodded. The "primacy of the individual conscience" was probably a Reform Judaism thing that she had picked up from Elise or Rachel, but it was close enough to our family's values that I didn't think that we needed to have a theological discussion.

"Yes."

"And that sometimes people tell you to do something and even make you promise, but if you know that it is wrong, maybe you shouldn't do it?"

The lawyer, the mother, in me could think of tons of exceptions to that, especially if I were the "people" telling her to do something, but I didn't want to get us going down the bunny trail. "Yes."

"I heard something."

"Oh?"

"I don't want to get anyone in trouble, Mom."

"Of course not."

"And you have to promise me that you won't get all crazy."

"Erin, what is it?"

"It's Faith and Mr. Goddard."

"Faith and Chris Goddard? What about them?"

"He's fallen in love with her."

What? I struggled with the covers, but Erin was sitting on them, trapping me. Chris and Faith? Faith was a child. I forced myself to sound calm. "Do you believe that?"

"No, not that he loves her, but he does call her into his office and kiss her."

I did not believe that for one second. Not Chris. His face flashed before me—his neat features, his close-cropped hair, his perfectly chosen wire-rimmed glasses, and his quick sly smile. No, not Chris. "How did you hear this?"

"Elise told me. Faith made the three of them promise not to tell, but Elise told me last night. She said that they were starting to think that they should ask someone what to do."

"They were right. Erin, sweetheart, this has to be looked into. She is accusing him of sexual abuse—"

"Oh, Mom, it's not *that*." She still had a young girl's horror at the notion that people actually had sex.

"Any kind of contact like that between an adult and a minor is very problematic. Her accusations could ruin his career."

It turned out that none of the other girls had said anything to their mothers, which sort of surprised me. I wouldn't have thought that Erin and I had a better relationship than did the others, but, of course, Faith didn't exert as much influence over Erin.

Or maybe Erin and I did have a better relationship. I should give myself some credit.

She and I talked a little bit, and she finally agreed that I could say something to Chris. "Since if it is not true, he might want to know that she is saying it."

"And if it is true?"

Oh, God, if it was true that the headmaster of a school was fondling a twelve-year-old . . . at best he would leave town disgraced and unemployable. He could also be facing jail. "In this country we assume that people are innocent until they are proven guilty."

"But if we assume that he is innocent, then that means that we assume that Faith is lying." Erin wasn't being a smart mouth; she was genuinely trying to figure this out. "And so we're assuming that she is guilty."

Having intelligent children isn't all that it is cracked up to be. Of course, I was assuming that Faith was lying. "You sometimes have to be able to hold two contradictory assumptions, knowing that one will be true and one won't, but you won't know which."

"Oh." I couldn't tell if she understood. She stood up. "I think I do like your hair."

"Thank you, dear."

After she left, I called Chris's number at school and left a message. "Please call me as soon as you can. There's some fireworks that you need to know about." If Faith really had only mentioned this to Elise, Brittany, and Rachel, and if they had only told Erin, then this might quickly be contained.

Once again—oh, silly me.

II

Even though I knew that Chris got to school well before seven each morning, I wasn't too surprised that the phone didn't ring until after nine Monday morning. I hadn't said that the message was urgent; he probably thought that I had wanted to talk about the fair.

But it was Erin. "Mom—"

Her voice was shaky. "Mrs. Marlent said that I could use her phone."

This was so like a young teen. The mechanics of delivering the message were as important as the message. Figuring how to act independently was so new to middle-schoolers, and they had to think through each step—*which phone will I use*—that those logistics often took precedence over what they were actually doing. "I told the other girls that I told you—I instant-messaged them last night—and now Mrs. Shot has called them all into the middle-school office, and I don't know what is going on, and I think it is all my fault."

"Erin, it is not your fault. I will be right there. You either go back to class or stay with Mrs. Marlent"—she was the school nurse—"and lie down. I'll go straight to the middle-school office and see what's going on."

I was still in my pretty new bathrobe so I pulled on the clothes that I had flown home in yesterday.

At school I parked in the fire lane and hurried up the steps to the middle-school office. Elise, Brittany, and Rachel were sitting in the outer office, their faces blurry and frightened. They jumped up, very relieved to see me. Someone they trusted was here; this time—unlike that night outside the bookstore—I was the rescuer. I hugged them. "It's going to work out, girls. It's going to be fine."

They were so glad to hear someone say that. "But what do we do?" Rachel asked. "Mrs. Shot is saying we may have broken the honor code."

They broke the honor code?

"Tell the truth," I said. "That's what you should do. But don't say anything until you've talked to your parents. You've called them, haven't you?"

The girls nodded.

"Then wait until they get here. Tell them everything and then do exactly as they say."

The middle-school secretary was sitting at her desk, checking the attendance reports, offering absolutely no comfort to the girls. I hated her for that. "Who's in there?" I asked, nodding toward Mrs. Shot's office.

"It's a private meeting," she said.

Through the window over her shoulder I saw Mimi backing her car into the last place in the fire lane. "Mrs. Gold is here," I told the girls. "She'll stay with you."

I went to the door of the office.

"It's a private meeting." The secretary rose in her seat. "You can't go in there."

"Yes, I can," I said.

There were four people in the room. Martha Shot was at her desk. She was sitting upright, her face controlled. She had put herself in charge. Chris was standing in front of the window. With the light coming from behind him, I couldn't read his expression. Faith and Mary Paige were on the small sofa. Faith was sobbing noisily. Mary Paige, I noticed, did not have her arm around her. She was sitting forward, next to her daughter, but distant from her.

Chris should not be here. The school must have a procedure to follow when a student accused anyone—teacher, staff, other student—of inappropriate behavior, and surely the procedure did not begin by having the child immediately confront the person he or she was accusing. How unfair that would be to the genuinely frightened child.

"Mrs. Meadows, you're interrupting something private," Martha Shot said.

"Yes, I am. Because this should not be happening, and it needs to stop right now." The trophy wife was again a lawyer. "If an accusation has been made, then no one should say another word. Not one word. Chris, go back to your office and get a lawyer this minute. And Mary Paige, take Faith home and do the same."

"Get a lawyer?" Mary Paige looked up at me, surprised and defiant. "Why do I need a lawyer? My child has been abused. I don't need a lawyer."

"Yes, you do. If she has been abused, then you need someone to speak on her behalf."

"I'm her mother. I will speak on her behalf."

"And if she hasn't been, then you may get sued off the face of the earth."

"Lydia, I would nev—" Chris was about to say that he would never do that.

I wouldn't let him talk. "Everything about this meeting is wrong." I looked at him, putting every ounce of our relationship in the look. *Trust me. I know what I am doing. Get out of here now.*

He levered himself away from the window and walked out. I followed.

The girls were gone, and the secretary sat there, still typing. She did not look up.

I caught up with Chris. He was vibrantly angry, his body like a tight guitar string.

How well did I know him? Ten minutes here, fifteen minutes there. Other than that one evening at Blair's I had never seen him off of the school campus.

I knew him well enough. "I know you didn't do this, but this is ugly."

"You don't have to tell me that."

"Why were you down at that meeting? You shouldn't have been there."

"I know that . . . at least I did once I knew what it was all about. Mrs. Shot called me and said I had to come down to her office immediately. She sounded so urgent that I came right away. Then I kept hoping that the girl would stop crying and tell the truth. Or at least tell me what she told Martha. I don't even know what she said I'd done."

Erin's version of the story with its middle-school girl emphasis on love and kisses was such hearsay that I didn't repeat it.

"Martha wants me to leave the school grounds immediately," Chris continued. "She's taking an Alexander Haig 'I'm in charge here' attitude, and she's acting as if she believes Faith."

"The thing is, Chris, we are all obligated . . . not necessarily to believe her, but at least to listen to her—"

"Listen to her! What the hell is there to listen to? She's just crying."

Once again I remembered all my books on raising teenaged girls. They talked about how girls cry when they know they are in a corner. Whenever anyone tries to get an "alpha girl" to account for her behavior, she starts to cry, and everyone, even the kids she has been mean to, ends up comforting her.

"I had spent extra time with her," he acknowledged. "I knew that her unhappiness was causing problems for other kids."

Namely my daughter. "Do you have a lawyer? I can call

someone at Jamie's firm, but if this goes beyond today, you should find a firm that doesn't have any connections to the school community."

He ran a hand over his face. "I can't believe that this is happening. Lydia, I have been so careful. I've had no private life at all this year. I didn't want anything to get in the way of what I wanted to accomplish here . . . and then to be accused like this . . ."

He was a man of character, offended, wounded, and outraged by this challenge to his integrity. I followed him into his window-lined office and closed the door. I told him to call Jayne Reynolds, the chair of the board of trustees, and I used my cell phone to call Jamie's firm. I didn't know the main number, so I called Jamie's own line, and his secretary immediately connected me to the managing partner. He said that one of the partners would call Chris back in ten minutes.

Chris was still trying to reach Mrs. Reynolds. I put my phone back in my purse. "While you're waiting, get out your calendar and start listing every single contact you've ever had with the girl. Dates, times, door open or shut, everything that you've got."

"I can do that." It was clear that he was relieved to have something to do.

"And don't leave school unless the lawyer tells you to. Martha Shot is not in charge. The board of trustees is."

I went back to the middle school. Mimi was in the hall, waiting for me. She had found Erin in the nurse's office and had sent all the girls back to class.

"Martha Shot wanted me to take them home. 'It will be so disruptive to have them in class,'" Mimi mimicked Mrs. Shot at her simpering worst. "But forget that. If the school is going to suspend them, then it needs to follow procedures."

"Why on earth would they be suspended? What did they do wrong?"

"That's hard to figure, but both the secretary and the principal told them that they had done something wrong. I wonder if Martha and her cohorts see this as an opportunity to get back at Chris for the changes he's made. I'll bet all the alumnae line up with Martha. Do you think Chris's worried about that?"

Mimi always saw conspiracies in everything, but she might have a point now. "I think it's safe to say that he is worried about everything," I answered.

"He's right to be. I hope this doesn't get into the *Post*."

"Don't we all?"

I asked her where Blair and Annelise were. "Didn't the girls call them?"

"Oh, they're both at home, ready to kill. One of the embassies is having some kind of morning event, and there are three limos blocking their street, not a driver in sight. I was about to go pick them up."

We decided that there was no reason to have them come to school now. We would meet them at Annelise's. So Mimi and I got our cars and entered the neighborhood from a different direction, parking on a street parallel to Annelise's. We cut through the side yard of a family who had kids in the high school and entered Annelise's through her back door.

We had called to say that we were coming so Blair was already there and Annelise had coffee ready. Blair was dressed for the day, but Annelise was in leggings and a sweatshirt as if she had been on her way to exercise.

"I'm assuming that we all believe Chris," Blair said. The others were nodding.

"But what exactly is she accusing him of?" Annelise asked.

"No one knows," I said. "Apparently she told Martha Shot and won't repeat it to anyone else. Erin used the word *kissing*, but she got that secondhand from Elise."

"Our girls will be able to tell us what she said to them," Blair said, obviously a little disconcerted that Brittany hadn't said anything to her while Erin had come almost immediately to me. "But that won't tell us what she said to Mrs. Shot."

"What will happen if she just goes on crying?" Mimi asked. "What if she won't say anything to anyone? How does that play out legally?" She was the only one of us who wasn't a lawyer.

"I don't think any of us know much about this kind of law, but no one will charge him with something just because she told Mrs. Shot that it happened," Blair answered. "So legally it will be in limbo."

"Which means," I added, "he can't defend himself."

"That sucks for him, doesn't it?" Mimi said.

I nodded. "Career-endingly so."

"So what do we do?"

Naturally everyone's first concern was her own child. We needed to find out exactly why Mrs. Shot thought that Elise, Rachel, and Brittany had broken the honor code. Then we would think about how to help Chris.

"Excuse me for sounding completely self-centered here," Mimi said, "but I've got a caterer delivering eighty chairs and ten tables this afternoon and thirteen million pounds of food tomorrow. What am I going to do about this dinner?"

I had forgotten about that. Mimi's dinner for the start of the school's Capital Campaign was supposed to be tomorrow evening.

"I suppose you need to talk to Jayne Reynolds."

"I hate that woman," Mimi said. Jayne was almost a caricature of a girls' school alumna.

"You'll hate her more before this is all over," Blair predicted.

We talked about the dinner for another fifteen minutes, saying absolutely nothing of any use. Mimi decided to go home and see what the caterer's contract said about penalties for cancelation. We had gotten up to leave when the phone rang. Annelise waved good-bye to us as she went to answer it. Blair went toward the front door. Mimi and I were headed out the back door when a Kleenex box whacked Mimi in the back.

Annelise had wanted to get our attention without speaking, and the Kleenex box was the closest thing at hand. She had been able to grab Blair's arm. "It's Mary Paige," she mouthed when we had turned around.

Quietly we all sat back down and listened while Annelise said things like "that seems a little premature on our end" and "that probably does seem like a good idea."

And then she said, "I think that the only way you can blame Lydia is if Faith was trying to recant."

Blame me? Blame *me*? What had I done?

"No," Annelise was saying, "if Faith is telling the truth, then, of course, no one expects her to back down, but she is going to need to speak. I know it will be hard, but she will have to."

Annelise brought the conversation to a close, which was not like her.

"What is she blaming me for?" I asked as soon as Annelise had hung up.

"That everything has become adversarial, that lawyers are going to be involved . . . but she does like your hair, by the way."

My hair? In the middle of all that drama in Mrs. Shot's of-fice, Mary Paige had noticed my *hair*? None of my friends had noticed the new cut. They were looking at it now, but I waved my hand, making it clear we could talk about my hair at a later date.

"Mary Paige's not making any sense," I said. "How could it not be adversarial, unless Faith is going to say it didn't happen?"

"Of course, Mary Paige's not making any sense," Blair said. "She found out about it this morning just like the rest of us, and Faith won't say a word to her, either."

"I bet," Annelise said, "that Faith rushed in and blurted this out to Martha Shot, and now Mrs. Shot's taking it to the bank. Faith probably has no idea what to do."

"She could tell the truth," I said.

But none of us thought that that would happen anytime soon.

Mimi and I picked up our purses to leave. Annelise spoke. "Lydia, I owe you a huge apology."

"For what? I'm not going to let Mary Paige blame me, but I don't see that anyone owes me an apology."

"No, it's not for this, but for everything that's been happening with the girls all year." Annelise tugged at the neckline of her oversized sweatshirt. "Look at today. Mary Paige called me, not Blair or Mimi—"

"You're the only one home," I pointed out.

She waved her hand. "No, you'll see when they get home and check their messages. She called me first. She thinks of me as the weakest link among us, the one she can most easily manipulate."

It was a little hard to know what to say in the face of such an obvious truth.

"I think about times like the photos and her dropping off Faith at my house early. She was counting on the fact that I wouldn't fuss about spoiling your plan."

"But you didn't know what my plan was."

"Not that day, no, but at other times it was as if she and Faith were looking for the low part of the fence, and it was me. I don't think I've been a good friend."

"If we come across to the world as being fenced in," Blair said realistically, "then people are going to look for the break. That's what people do."

"And I," Mimi said, "clearly never took this seriously enough. A couple times this year Bubbe said that Faith was a troubled, power-hungry kid, but I didn't see it as anything more than playground politics."

"But ever since that night they went to the movies in Bethesda," Annelise said, "Elise has been avoiding Faith. You have to wonder if Faith knew that the girls were slipping away from her and so she told them this 'secret' to put herself in the center again."

"I wish Rachel had had more sense," Mimi sighed.

"I'm sure she will next time someone tries to manipulate her like this," I said.

"It's good of you to say that because Erin certainly suffered the most from Faith's need to be popular."

"No," I said, "Chris is going to suffer a whole lot more."

Jayne Reynolds, the chair of the board of trustees, was in Chris's office long before Monday's school day was over. The board had decided that they could not ignore Faith's accusations, that no one should ever automatically assume that a child is lying. The board put Chris on paid leave and asked him to leave the grounds immediately.

No one from the board interviewed Faith. None of the members were trained at questioning adolescents, and the lawyers among them knew that the last thing the police would want was well-meaning adults asking young victims a lot of leading questions. So the board was acting on Mrs. Shot's report of Faith describing "kissing and fondling," but none of *"that,"* which people assumed was Faith's lingo for genital contact.

But had Martha Shot's questions been leading? That's what I wanted to know. Faith might not be the only person to blame here. But Jayne Reynolds was an alumna, Martha Shot was an alumna, and apparently that counted for a lot more than I thought it should.

The repercussions of Chris's suspension were immediate. The kids in the high school were furious. The senior-class prank was planned for Friday and apparently Chris's presence was required. Without Chris, the prank—and no one outside the class seemed to know what it was—would make no sense.

At the end of the school day Mrs. Shot called the Rosens, the Golds, and the Bransons, asking them not to send the girls to school on Tuesday. Mrs. Shot was, Mimi reported, trying to avoid calling it a "suspension," and kept giving her what Mimi called this "girls' school mumbo-jumbo" about no, not technically, but wouldn't it be easier for all involved? After all, hadn't they broken the honor code by failing to report what Faith had told them?

No such command had been issued to Faith. No one said anything to her about not coming to school. Someone was wanting to protect her; her grandmother's name was on the gym.

Of course, while she might be protected by her background and her mother's maiden name, our girls were protected by us and our fierce obsession with them, by our money, and by the rottweilerish legal talent we could access. In the face of the threat of immediate legal action, Mrs. Shot had to acknowledge that oh, no, of course, the dear girls hadn't been suspended, and if they wanted to come to school, of course, they could.

But first the three girls needed to speak to the police. Accompanied by their parents and a senior member of Mimi's husband's firm, the girls gave statements. They had witnessed nothing. All of them were clear about that. It was simply that Faith had told them things.

The girls had been told that they would probably be asked what Faith had told them. Brittany Branson was able to be extremely specific about what she had been told and exactly when she had been told it, consulting a list that she had written on a piece of saffron-colored graph paper. She got very evasive when asked why she could be so definite. In fact, she started crying in a way that made everyone very concerned. Why was she so distressed? Was she lying for someone? Had she been abused herself?

Finally she admitted that she kept a diary. Her headache specialist had told her to keep a log of what happened before and during her migraines, and she had started keeping a full-fledged "who liked whom in the sixth grade" diary. When she had been told that she would need to be specific, just as children raised by wolves do whatever it is that wolves do, she, with a lawyer for a mother, had consulted her private records and drawn up a summary from them.

But she had never told anyone that she kept a diary; she didn't want anyone to know, not ever ever. "I'm going to go home and burn it so that Mom can't read it."

So then she had had to endure a lecture about the destruction of evidence. As a result she was now not only mortified because she had had to reveal a secret, but she was also traumatized at the thought that her diary was going to be subpoenaed. The resulting migraine was the worst that she had ever had.

Following their session with the police, the girls went to

school, Brittany staying long enough to be marked present once and to throw up twice.

I held down the fort at Mimi's house, helping to get ready for the Capital Campaign dinner that evening. As big as the caterer's cancelation penalty was, Mimi and her husband Ben still thought that the dinner should be postponed, but Jayne Reynolds and the lower-school, middle-school, and high-school principals wanted the dinner to go on. "The school is not just about one person," Mrs. Reynolds said.

No, to them the school was about the alumnae population. How they would love it if they could prove that they didn't need Chris.

The turnout for the dinner was great. Everyone—except Chris—came and they stayed and stayed, but for all the wrong reasons. They wanted to gossip. They certainly didn't want to be solicited about donating funds to a school currently in chaos.

Originally Chris, and only Chris, was going to speak to the dinner guests. He could be trusted to keep things short. But in his absence, everyone spoke. Jayne Reynolds spoke, and the principals of the three schools each spoke. All of them said exactly the same thing. And they went on and on and on. Chris would have spoken for exactly nine minutes. By the time the principal of the lower school stood up, people had been speaking for forty-seven minutes, and the lower-school principal was known to be the most long-winded of the bunch.

I was standing next to a high-school mother who was on the board because she was a professional fund-raiser. She was ashen. "This was why we hired Chris," she whispered to me. "This same old girls'-school pitch isn't working anymore."

She was so angry that she was shaking. "This has done years of damage to major-gift fund-raising. Years. That girl can have no idea what she has done, not just to Chris, but to the school."

Fourteen minutes later the lower-school principal was still speaking. Another board member eased up to my companion and whispered something to her. I looked at her expectantly.

"Fasten your seat belts," she said. "It's going to be in the *Post* tomorrow."

I woke up the next morning before the paper arrived and so I went online to read the article . . . and it was just awful.

Of course, everything in the article was true. The board had indeed immediately suspended Chris. That was a fact. The school's public position was noncommittal, wanting to work through the process, hoping that it would be as brief as possible. That too was a fact.

The board couldn't come out and say that they were behind Chris 100 percent even if they were. They just couldn't. For so long people had not listened to children. Children had to have a voice.

But this one was lying.

Wednesday night I spoke to Jamie on the phone, giving him a quick, unemotional account of what was happening. I didn't make too big a deal of it. He was in the middle of presenting his case, and he couldn't let himself care.

"That sounds bad," he said, but his voice was flat.

"Yes."

One-word answers aren't my style, and he knows it. "Oh, God, Lydia, I'm sorry. Of course it must be much worse than I can imagine, but I feel so distant from you and the kids. I'm still trapped in this nightmare, and I can't see anything else."

"I know that it is much harder on you than it is on us," I said.

He paused. I rarely talked about how his professional commitments affected the rest of the family. I probably worried too much about turning into my mother, whose mission on earth was to make sure that other people understood what they were doing wrong. As a result, I hadn't said things that should have been said.

And it wasn't that Jamie was doing something *wrong*. But his choices had consequences. If he wasn't going to be here, we would develop into a family that didn't need him to be here.

"You know I'm never taking another case like this, don't you?" he said.

"Jamie, I completely respect that you believe that right now."

"What are you saying? That you *don't* believe me?"

"I don't believe you or disbelieve you." I was in my careful-lawyer mode. "You aren't in a position to deal with anything except the present."

I had thought a lot about what Bubbe had said Sunday. Did I want Jamie to be my friend? Of course, I did. But you can't teach someone how to be a friend if he is never around.

The police had tried to talk to Faith on Tuesday and then again on Wednesday. She wouldn't say anything. She wouldn't say what had happened, she wouldn't say what she had told Mrs. Shot had happened. She wouldn't say what questions Mrs. Shot had asked her. She sat with her head down, staring at her hands. By Thursday the newspaper reported that unless the girl was willing to speak to authorities, there was little that the law enforcement community could do.

Chris was now being represented by a firm with no connection to the school. The youngest, least threatening-looking female associate from that firm showed up at Blair's house, dressed in jeans and a T-shirt, looking for all the world like a baby-sitter, not an attorney. She read Brittany's diary in her presence, verified all the dates, and compared it to everything Chris had been able to produce. She then sealed the diary in a manila envelope, had Brittany sign her name across the flap, and took custody of it, protecting it from unreasonable search and seizure by Brittany's mom.

Nothing in the diary had any legal weight, of course, but Brittany's record of what she had been told apparently underscored that this was Faith's fantasy. The timing of the alleged encounters never meshed with Chris's actual and easily verified schedule, and the specifics of the allegations described behavior more consistent with a teenaged hero in a Young Adult romance novel than with that of a grown man.

The tide was turning. The members of the board of trustees now realized that they had suspended Chris based on their chairwoman's version of Martha Shot's version of something a child would not repeat.

Several of the history teachers junked their curriculum and started teaching about the Salem witch trials, focusing on the dangers of false accusations. The school community was charged with a poisonous energy. I was getting fifty or sixty e-mails a day about the matter. At our final meetings of the various Spring Fair committees, people would talk and talk and talk, and go home dispirited and weary. A feverish excitement was exhausting everyone, draining life and spirit out of the school.

I couldn't seem to get anything done. I would get the breakfast dishes in the dishwasher, but before I would wipe the counters, I would go put a load of laundry in the machine and never get back to the counters. When the mail came, I read the church bulletin, but didn't enter anything on my calendar. I had to leave the bulletin on the kitchen counter so I wouldn't forget about it, and then it disappeared. I emptied out our bin of unmatched socks, lined the socks up on the ottoman in the sunroom, but then never finished pairing them, so they lay there on the ottoman for days. I went through the magazine pile, checking the tables of contents to see if there was something I wanted to read. I carefully set the ones with interesting articles aside and left them on the kitchen table for two days. Then I got sick of looking at them so I dumped them in the recycling bin along with the others. I couldn't seem to finish anything.

I had never been like this before. I had never let housework take over my days. I had always been quick and disciplined about the domestic chores. But I was addicted to this school crisis. Every hour or so I had to stop what I was doing and check my e-mail.

I couldn't stand myself.

Friday my cell phone rang. It was Mary Paige. I didn't know she had that number.

She needed to talk to me. She had just dropped Faith off at school. Could we go somewhere for coffee?

"You'd better come to my house."

As soon as she came, she started in on the usual polite girls'-school chitchat. I didn't want to hear it. "What's on your mind, Mary Paige?" I didn't suppose that I sounded very cordial.

"Mr. Christopher Goddard wants to sue us."

Her tone was a little high and mighty for someone whose child had brought this all on herself. "Has he actually filed?"

"I don't know. I don't think so. His lawyer just called, making the most awful threats."

Chris needed to get things unstuck. I didn't know exactly

what would happen if he sued Faith, I didn't know how her juvenile standing would impact the process, but I doubted that he would need to actually file. The threat would probably be enough.

"You have to understand," I said to Mary Paige, absolutely certain that she had no interest in understanding, "that Chris must want a chance to defend himself. No one knows for certain what Faith actually said to Mrs. Shot."

"But don't you understand that she had no idea how serious this would be? That, in her mind, saying this about him was no different than saying it about one of the sixth-grade boys."

"Then she can end everything right now by saying that she wasn't telling the truth."

"But if she says it didn't happen, they will expel her."

I should hope. "That's hardly surprising. A lot of damage has been done."

"And the handbook says that there is no refund of tuition."

I was careful not to react. Was this dragging on because of money? "If you want to make a deal—that Faith will recant in exchange for a tuition refund—you should be able to get that." The board would have to be out of its mind not to accept.

"Well, it's not just the money . . . there are other legal issues here. I don't want her to leave Alden. I graduated from there. Look at what my grandparents did for the school."

I remembered what Pam Ruby had told me at the beginning of the year—that Faith being at Alden was a key part of Mary Paige's divorce strategy, why she had to leave Texas, why she couldn't work.

Surely the "I can't work, I have to drive car pools" was not a realistic legal strategy—however realistic it might feel to an individual woman on a particular day—but having her daughter go to this school might have been part of why Mary Paige was allowed to take the girl out of Texas. I didn't know enough about divorce law.

"The problem is," Mary Paige continued, "Virginia public schools have these rigid standardized tests that are pegged to their curriculum, and the sixth graders are starting them after Spring Break. She can't take a test on Virginia history."

People use the word *can't* way too much. Faith could certainly *take* a test on Virginia history, she probably couldn't pass it. "See if Alden will let her finish out the year off-site." Several years ago two seniors were caught smashing a window of a fellow student's car. They were not allowed to return to campus, to attend graduation ceremonies and such, but they were allowed to submit their final papers so that they could earn their diplomas.

"You're not being any help, Lydia."

"But, Mary Paige, why would I be any help?" I'm such a major buttinski, I so like being in the thick of things, that only now did I realize how odd it was of her to come to me. "I'm not on the board; I'm not particularly close to anyone who is."

"But everyone likes you, Lydia. Everyone listens to you."

She said that as if she were accusing me of something. So now *I* was the popular one? "Mary Paige, I know you want this to go away, and I do think that you can get a lot of what you need—the tuition refund or letting her get credit for this year somehow—but I don't see how she can be reintegrated into the school community."

I couldn't hate this woman. This was the second time her world had fallen apart. She had thought that she could divorce her husband without it affecting her life, but that hadn't worked. And now her daughter was getting them exiled from this next community.

But did she really think that there would be no consequences for her? That having her grandmother's name on the gym was enough to give her the seemingly charmed life that the rest of us were working so hard to achieve?

"It's Chris who shouldn't be allowed back," she said, "not Faith."

"Chris? Weren't we just talking about Faith recanting? Why should he have to leave if he hasn't done anything?"

"When an educator threatens to sue a child in the school, when he wants to extort money from a family—"

"Chris doesn't want your money. Trust me. Chris didn't want your money."

"The threat is so completely out of line, that simply shows that he is unfit to be a member of this community."

I shut my eyes. I had been wrong. I could hate this woman. It would be no problem at all.

12

On Friday of this awful week, Spring Break began. The flood of crisis-related e-mails slowed on Thursday night as people began packing for their trips to Colorado, Spain, or Jamaica and then ceased as they left town.

The kids and I had planned to go to Houston for Spring Break, but with Jamie so focused on the trial, I knew that a visit would end up being awful for all of us. I thought about taking the kids somewhere else, but wherever we went, I would be running "Camp Mom"—me getting up each morning responsible for my two campers having a day packed with fun-filled, educationally enriching, culturally broadening, lifetime-of-memories experiences. It seemed easier to do that from home, where I could share the responsibility with the television set.

The three of us painted Erin's bedroom and went to the zoo. We hiked the Billy Goat trail out at Great Falls and made caramel corn. We sorted through all the books in Thomas's room and made more caramel corn. I was occasionally unnerved by how normal it felt not to have Jamie with us, and that thought drove me to making yet more caramel corn. When we were caramel-corned out, we took a subway trip, ending up at the Pentagon City Mall over in Virginia. There was a movie theater there, and Erin was willing to watch a little-kid movie with Thomas while I looked for new clothes for him, an activity for which he has no interest.

I was coming out of Macy's when I heard someone call my name—not "Mom," but "Lydia."

It was Chris Goddard.

How odd to see him at a suburban shopping mall. We city residents disdain the malls. They are, we pride ourselves on saying, the locus of empty, mindless experiences . . . although, in truth, I have found myself capable of empty, mindless experiences in such a variety of places that it really doesn't seem fair to blame malls.

"What a nice surprise," Chris said as he came up to me. "I don't think I've ever seen anyone from school here before. Thank you for your note. I did appreciate it."

"It was nothing," I said, not quite truthfully. Tracking down his home address had been a bit of a challenge. I looked at him carefully. There might be some unfamiliar gray shadows under his eyes and a new gauntness below his cheekbones, but the light in the mall was thin and watery so everyone looked a little gray.

The mall had a central atrium that rose up over a food court and a community stage. We were on the facility's second level, and we had stepped toward the railing to get out of the way of the foot traffic even though the mall was fairly quiet on this weekday afternoon. The public schools didn't have their Spring Break for another week or so. Public-school holidays usually result in the malls being very crowded. Those families don't automatically go to Colorado, Spain, or Jamaica every time their kids are off school for five minutes. Chris gestured down to the food court. "Do you have time for coffee?"

As we rode down the escalator, I answered his questions about why we weren't out of town and explained that the kids were in the movie theater. He was carrying a bag from Johnston & Murphy, a men's shoe store.

We got coffee and sat down at a table. I was wearing one of the new outfits I had gotten in Houston. It was just slacks and a shirt, but the silhouette was trim and stylish, the colors fresh. I'd flipped back the cuffs of the shirt and I was wearing two thin silver bangles around my wrist. I was trying to feel light and feminine all on my own.

"So how are you?" I asked. "What's happening?"

"It hasn't reached the e-mail lists yet?"

I shook my head, not knowing what "it" was.

"These are my back-to-school shoes. I will be in my office tomorrow."

"Oh, Chris." My bracelets slipped down my arm with a silvery jingle. "I am so glad. What happened? I knew that you had threatened to sue Faith. Did that get things unstuck?"

He nodded. "We knew we had to threaten someone, and Faith and her mother seemed an easier target than the board."

"I hope that you don't feel guilty about that."

"No, especially since the goal was not to have to sue anyone. But the threat got the mother to get a lawyer, and he very quickly took the position that the girl had said one thing in a private conversation with a school administrator and then never repeated it. While that might meet the legal definition of slander, it didn't make for much of a case. At that point the board had to acknowledge, at least among themselves, that Mrs. Shot may have had her own agenda."

"Does she want your job?"

"Not really. She would take it if offered, but she likes her job. What she wants is for the school to stop changing."

That wasn't going to happen. "She went about it just like a middle-school girl would have, talking about what someone had said in private but never quite saying what was actually said."

Chris liked my point. "That turns out to be a very powerful technique. Anyway, the individual members of the board are horrified that they never stopped to question Mrs. Shot. As an official body, they aren't going to say that publicly, but they are extending my contract by two years as a show of support."

"And what's happening to Faith?"

"Nothing."

I couldn't believe it. Faith wasn't being expelled or suspended? "But obviously they know that she made it all up. Is anyone questioning that?"

"They say that they believe me, but we are a school with a culture of forgiveness and redemption." His eyebrows arched over the thin pewter-toned frames of his glasses, and it was clear that he wasn't feeling very forgiving, and I can't say that I did, either.

"Does the board think that Mrs. Shot is as much to blame as Faith?" That would be one reason for not punishing Faith. "Or is it that Faith's great-grandmother's name is on the gym?"

He didn't answer. He picked up his coffee, but his eyes never wavered from mine.

This episode hadn't simply been caused by the psychology of an unhappy girl. There had been sociological forces: the old against the new, the aristocracy against the meritocracy. Unfortunately for them, the Old Guard had picked the wrong battle. They had lost, but they had managed the retreat well enough that no one was going to be held accountable. Both Faith and Mrs. Shot were going to stay at the school.

"Aren't you angry?" I asked.

"You have no idea," he said. "None. I'd leave this place in a heartbeat if staying weren't the best way to salvage something of my reputation and career."

"This is *so* unfair. You didn't do anything wrong."

Chris looked down at his coffee. "That is not correct. I do have some measure of responsibility. In the name of getting to know the school, I got involved in things that weren't my job to get involved with. People don't like that. I'm also probably too proud of my ability to deal with people one-on-one—"

I interrupted. "You're great with individuals, and the high-school kids love you. We hear that all the time."

"But that isn't the most important part of my job. I spent extra time with Faith because I thought that would help her, but if that's what I want to do, I should be a counselor, not an administrator. I need to focus on my job and step back from being the guy who can swoop in and fix anything and everything."

"But isn't fixing everything your job?"

"Not at the micro-level, and certainly not all at once. I'm still angry enough that I need to work on autopilot for a while."

"That doesn't sound so good." Not only for the school, but for him as well. What I had liked about him was the dry wit and the impish warmth behind his elegant, shrewd presence. It sounded as if we were going to be left with a lot of the shrewd-ness, some of the elegance, but the rest was going under-ground. "What can you do on autopilot?"

"Let's call it 'emotional disengagement.' I can disengage enough from the personal to get back to the fund-raising. The Capital Campaign has gotten off to the worst possible start."

"You heard about the dinner at Mimi's?"

He held up a hand. He had obviously heard too much about it. "We need to get the campaign back on track. If we can't, then someone else needs to be in my shoes. Right or wrong, if I can't be effective, I should leave, but leaving now will make it seem as if I were guilty."

Then there was one answer. He had to be effective. The Capital Campaign had to be a success. If I needed to get myself on the Capital Campaign committee, that's what I would do. Chris Goddard was not leaving this school.

School started on the Tuesday after Spring Break week. The board of trustees, with the help of hired public relations professionals, was in full "let's put this behind us and move forward" mode.

Jayne Reynolds sent a letter to every family in the school, citing the board's full support of Chris. In the next paragraph she defended the board's actions, emphasizing the need to listen to all children and to give voice to the least powerful members of a community.

Of course she was right. Somewhere there were headmasters, teachers, or coaches acting inappropriately to students. But what would happen now when one of those students spoke up? "Oh, don't you remember that case in D.C.?" people could say. "The girl was lying." The implication would be that this child was lying as well.

Faith hadn't damaged just our community, she might have damaged others, giving people a reason not to listen to children.

I longed for a simple answer.

There were two big things on the calendar for the short week after Spring Break. The Spring Fair was on Saturday, and the

Thursday evening prior to that was the middle-school Curriculum Night, at which student projects were put on display.

We have a problem at Alden with parents helping the kids too much with their schoolwork. When the second graders are doing PowerPoint presentations and the fifth graders write in Johnsonian sentences filled with series of perfectly parallel, impeccably punctuated dependent adverbial clauses, you have to wonder if maybe the parents aren't doing a shade too much. I now think that the primary reason that Erin was admitted to Sidwell was not that her father was a Quaker, but that her essay had a sentence fragment. However bad we at Alden are, Sidwell parents are bound to be as bad—if not worse—and the admissions office was undoubtedly thrilled to find a parent so stunningly well-adjusted as to let her child's essay stand or fall on its own merits, and as a result that kid was moved to the top of the list.

So the projects displayed at the Curriculum Night are done entirely at school. It's the only way to keep some parents from getting involved in their children's educations, which is, of course, sometimes a euphemism for doing your kid's work and showing the world, not that your kid is smarter than everyone else's, but that you, with your joint M.B.A./Ph.D., are really good at sixth-grade assignments.

Curriculum Night was an adults-only coffee-and-dessert event, and even though the eighth-grade families were providing the dessert, I arrived early. Unfortunately six bales of hay, designed to give a rugged Western atmosphere to the Spring Fair pony rides, had also arrived early and I had to spend twenty minutes talking to the driver, trying to figure out if this was a duplicate order and, if not, where we should store the hay in the meantime. So by the time I got to the middle school, the central corridor was crowded.

Martha Shot was reigning supreme in the lobby, greeting parents with queenlike confidence. I knew what she had been saying about her role in the Faith affair. Oh, yes, the incident was unfortunate, but she had taken the side of a student, and at Alden we always put our students first. What on earth did she have to apologize for?

I wondered how Chris could stand to be in the same room with her.

The sixth-grade projects were a joint assignment from the English and history teachers. The students had each re-searched a different time in history and had then written a first-person narrative about a day in the life of a twelve-year-old living in that time.

Parents were already crowded around, reading the pieces, and I could hear them exclaiming how wonderfully imagina-tive the narratives were, how full of detail and life. Many of the dads had come straight from work, but had left their suit jackets and ties in their cars. The light colors of their open-collared business shirts, white, pale blue, and butter yellow, made the space feel more airy and springlike than if the men had been in their dark, formal jackets.

The essays hung on the wall of the sixth-grade corridor in an alphabetical loop. The first half of the alphabet ran down the left side of the corridor and the second half came back on the other. So Erin and the mid-alphabet kids would be at the far end of the hall. Rather than push my way down there right away, I stopped and read a few others. The first essay on the right side of the hall was Chloe Zimmerman's. It was set in twelfth-century Britain. Although the girl in the essay had the authority-challenging sensibility of a twenty-first-century kid, the essay was full of striking auditory detail. The straw on the floor of the Great Hall rustled as the women crossed the room in their heavy-hemmed long gowns. The water in the girl's washbasin had a thin coating of ice on it each morning, and the ice cracked with a quick, high-pitched, silvery sound. Chloe was a very musical child, and it was interesting to someone as visual as me to see how her imagination had engaged with sounds as much as sights.

I crossed over the hall to read Brittany's essay. It wasn't as sensorily rich as Chloe's, but Brittany had obviously been struck by the amount of responsibility that twelve-year-olds had among the Incas. Although she didn't quite put it into words, she was starting to understand that adolescence was a modern concept. I glanced at a few other essays, noting how some kids had managed to find topics that reflected their own interests. One boy wrote about the domestication of dogs in the New Stone Age. Everyone else in the community tolerated the dogs because they ate the trash, but the boy in the narrative loved one of the dogs and had discovered that letting the dog curl up next to him at night had real advantages now that the nights were getting colder. Rachel's essay was set in fourteenth-century France; her character, a peasant, was seemingly cold and hungry most of the time.

There were fewer people at the end of the corridor so I

moved quickly to Erin's and started to read. *I am twelve years old and I live in Spain in 1492. I am a Jew.*

The essays had been written by hand, which seemed odd because all these kids could keyboard and the school had plenty of computers. Erin's handwriting was beautiful. The slant of her letters could have been used for a geometry lesson on parallel lines, and the spacing between each word was so exact that it looked as if she had used a ruler.

But the essay itself was horrible. *Back in 1492, our houses were . . .* My dear sweet beautiful child had simply not been able to do this assignment. Her research was extensive, but she was supposed to have imagined a character, she was supposed to have created a fictional world, immersing herself in the character's point of view. *Our primary diet consists of . . .*

Why were these put on display? Why did we need to humiliate kids like this?

I knew the answer to that. At any school everyone always knows who the good athletes are, and at Alden everyone also knows who the talented musicians and actors are, so it is only proper that the kids who could write should have their work on display, too.

And who exactly was being humilated at this moment, the child or the parent? I struggled to read on.

"Mrs. Meadows?"

I turned. It was Erin's English teacher.

"Erin worked so hard on this project," she said quickly.

"Erin always works hard."

"But I'm not sure that she relished this as much as some of

the other kids. This particular assignment did not allow her to show her strengths."

I smiled weakly.

Erin's essay wasn't the worst. There were kids who obviously didn't care, and theirs were worse than hers. But among the kids who did care, who had tried, hers was the worst.

She wasn't stupid. She would have known that hers was not like the others. After all my poor child had been through this year—the phone not ringing, her friends inviting her only because their mothers had made them—she had had to endure this. She had copied out her final draft so perfectly, knowing all the while that what she had written was bad, knowing that she was not measuring up.

Slowly I walked back up to the central lobby where the dessert was laid out. The fluorescent lights dropped a flat, directionless blanket of industrial light, giving everyone's skin a greenish cast. The lobby was tiled and its front wall was glass. Noise bounced off these bright hard surfaces, and the conversations, the laughter, the "excuse me's," and the "Oh, yes, we must get together's" reverberated in a single lawn-mowerish whine. People were balancing white foam coffee cups and thin paper dessert plates. Those who had chosen pies, cakes, or tortes were trying to eat with white plastic forks, and their elbows jostled the crowd.

The first person to stop me was Candace Singer. She had been the person who had waited outside the sixth-grade parents' coffee last September to complain to Blair about Brittany not gushing over Candace's daughter's new dress. I wondered what little treat she had in store for me, what imagined offenses she would repay with patronizing remarks about Erin's essay.

I decided not to find out. "Excuse me," I said before she had said a word.

I wanted to be with my own friends. Usually they aren't easy to find in crowds as none of us is tall. So I had learned to look between people's shoulders and waists, searching for the flash of Mimi's flamboyance or the distinctive cool, clear colors of Blair's wardrobe. But tonight the husbands had come— everyone's husband except mine, of course—and Joel, Annelise's husband, is so tall that he is easy to spot.

The others were with him. Blair held out her arm as I approached, as if creating a passage for me through the crowd. She touched my shoulder, pulling me in. That was rare; she was not one for touching.

Don't be nice. Don't be sympathetic. If you do, I will cry.

Mimi's husband, Ben, spoke first. "Hi, Lydia! We were wondering what had happened to you. Weren't all the essays—"

He broke off, his expression suddenly startled. Mimi must have pinched him, stopping him from raving about the essays.

Why shouldn't he rave about the essays? Most of them were remarkable.

No one said anything.

Finally Bruce spoke. "Did any of you have this cherry pie with the little things on top? It's really good."

Oh, come on. This is a sixth-grade essay. Why are we all standing around embarrassed and talking about pie as if Erin had been arrested for selling drugs to the fourth graders?

Because that was how I felt, humiliated and embarrassed for my child.

This is not an important failure, I said to myself, *and if it is any failure at all, it is Erin's, not mine.*

Which only made things worse. I would rather fail myself than have it happen to her.

"Erin's handwriting is beautiful," Annelise said. She could always be expected to find something nice to say.

"Yes, it is," I agreed. "But imaginative writing isn't quite Erin's thing, is it?" I couldn't remember a thing about Brittany's or Elise's essays so I looked toward Mimi. "Rachel was trying to understand how those medieval peasants could endure such daily misery. I was impressed."

"Thanks," Mimi answered. "But didn't it seem a little heavy-handed on the religious issues? I hope that no one views it as anti-Christian."

"I don't think you need to worry about that," I said.

I kept my head up, and I participated in every twist and turn of the conversation. Other people joined us, and I said that, yes, I'd heard that Adam's parents were inviting the whole grade to his bar mitzvah, and yes, that was good of them. And, oh, my yes, it was such a relief that the weather was going to be good for the fair, and Jamie really was hoping that closing arguments would start next week. No, I didn't know what would be in the judge's instructions, and yes, having people coming to the fair park in a church lot and take a shuttle to the school might work, but yes, they might all park on the neighborhood streets anyway. I then told a funny story about the hay bales and finally excused myself, saying that I needed to go check on them.

It was just an excuse. I wanted to get away from the noise and the elbows and the politeness. I couldn't imagine that anything could be wrong with the hay, but there was. The playground gate wouldn't close. That would drive the lower-school teachers nuts tomorrow. So I pushed and prodded at hay bales. It was stupid, idiotic work, and I started to get angry with the delivery person. Why hadn't he looked at the position of the gate? And why should I have to fix the mistake when I hadn't made it? I wanted to cry.

I finally got the gate to close. I was crossing back to my car when I heard a man calling my name. It was Chris. "Someone said that you might be out stacking hay. Do you have a minute?"

He was coming out of the lower school, which seemed surprising as there wasn't anything going on there this evening. I started to explain about the hay, apologizing, hoping that I had suggested the right place for it to be stored. He shook his head; he didn't care about the hay. He gestured back toward the middle school, and I followed him. Fussing with the hay had taken me long enough that most of the people were gone, leaving a few eighth-grade mothers cleaning up the food. Chris nodded to them, took his keys out of his pocket, and opened the middle-school office.

"Chris, could this keep? Is this something we could talk about tomorrow or Monday?" I just wanted to get home to Erin.

He shook his head. "I need to talk to you about your kids, and I wanted to look at Erin's file. I was just at the lower school, looking at Thomas's."

Thomas's file? Why had he been looking at Thomas's file? What did Thomas have to do with Erin's essay?

I sat down and watched him open a file drawer. It was packed with manila folders; each folder had a white adhesive label on its tab. He ran a finger along the tabs, stopping when he found Erin's.

"You read her essay?" I asked.

He nodded as he rifled through the file, looking for something.

Maybe he would have some perspective on all of this. Maybe he would know exactly the right thing to make me feel better. I know it's horrible and sexist to say this, but sometimes men can do that for you, make you step back from the details and not feel so godawful about what Jamie would call "one data point."

No, it isn't *men* who do this for me. It's always been one particular man, Jamie, my husband. Why wasn't he here?

Chris had obviously found what he was looking for. He nodded again as if the file said what he had expected it to. Then he looked straight at me. "Lydia, I've been accused of crossing all kinds of lines this semester, and now I am going to cross one. You should be hearing this from your kids' teachers or the counselors, not from me, but I don't think anyone else would say it. This is not the right school for either one of your children."

Not the right . . . I stared at him. The file-cabinet drawer was still open, and he was standing on the far side of it, looking at me. He had laid Erin's file down on top of the folders still in the drawer. "What are you talking about? That was just one assignment, Chris, just one essay. She's not going to be a novelist, but so what? It's one data point."

"Of course, she's not going to be a novelist, but she may well be a mathematician, and the high-school math curriculum is not right for her. I wish we could offer linear algebra or multivariable calculus, but I don't think enough kids would take it. And while we supposedly have BC calculus, we had one kid get a three on the AP exam. The rest got two's, so we are clearly doing something wrong."

I could not follow what he was saying. I did know that the highest score on the Advanced Placement exams was a five, and that colleges usually only gave credits for scores of four or five, but I knew nothing about the math courses at the high school. When I had been on the curriculum committee last year, we'd been working on the social studies offerings. Math had barely been mentioned.

"When it comes to math," Chris said, "we're still a fifties girls' school. Look at this." He picked up a sheet of thin blue paper out of Erin's file. "It's her second-grade report card. 'Math comes easily to Erin because her handwriting is so neat.'" He flipped the file closed and thrust it back in its place. "Can you believe that anyone would ever write anything like that?"

Erin's second-grade teacher had been an older lady, gentle and nurturing. I had loved how safe her classroom had felt.

"Math comes easily to Erin because she's gifted. Look at her scores on the standardized tests." He picked the file back up. "This year's ERBs aren't in, but you saw that SSAT score, and you heard about the math Olympiads, didn't you? That she got the highest score in the whole grade?"

"Just by two points."

"Lydia, two points on the math Olympiads is huge. With all that's been going on, I haven't had time to check to see if we've ever had a sixth grader with her score, but I bet that we haven't. And this isn't just about her. It's about Thomas, too. We don't have any standardized scores for him yet, and it does not appear as if his handwriting is particularly neat, but clearly we don't need to explain why he is good at math—and he is very good—since he is a boy."

I winced. "Surely people don't think that way."

"It's changing, but no boy will ever come to this school because he wants to do multivariable calculus or play any kind of sport. I've watched your son on the playground. We are never going to have the kind of athletic program that he will want. If he goes to the high school here, he will hate his coaches for not caring enough, his teammates for not being good enough, and you for everything in general. He needs to be at a school with a strong tradition of scholar-athletes. And let's not be sexist—Erin is no slouch when it comes to athletics either."

"But she's so small." That was completely beside the point. I knew it. But it was all I could think to say.

"But she's strong, she's coordinated, she's light, and she's tough as nails. She should try crew."

Crew? I wasn't sure what he was talking about. At Alden

crew always meant being on one of the technical crews for a stage production.

"You know," he prompted, "the sport, rowing."

Oh, yes. "We don't have a crew team, do we?"

"No, and we won't. We don't have enough kids interested and that's not how we want to spend our money. Lydia, as long as I am at this school, every decision I make will take the school farther away from what your kids need. The P.E. department wants a new weight room. Forget it. The dance teachers want to hire a professional choreographer to create a new cutting-edge dance on our kids. That's what I'm in favor of. We've got two kids at the high school who've been working on an opera all year. They think they can finish it this summer. If they pull it off, I'm finding money to stage it if I have to pay for it myself. Can you see your son writing an opera?"

No, of course not.

"They got into Sidwell, didn't they?"

"Only because Jamie is Quaker."

Chris waved his hand, dismissing that. "Sidwell would never take them if they couldn't do the work, and Erin might have gotten in on her math scores without any kind of preferential treatment."

I knew what he was saying. Sidwell did have a strong tradition of scholar-athletes; Sidwell would have every possible advanced math class. "But Alden is a wonderful school," I protested. I believed that with all my heart.

"Alden is a *great* school . . . for some kids. But not yours." Chris sat down on the chair across from me. He reached out as if to touch my hand, but stopped. "Lydia, don't you know that I would give anything to have this be different? You're the last person I would want to leave the school community. Unfortunately your kids are the last ones who ought to stay."

13

The kids leave Alden? Our family not be a part of the school anymore?

I couldn't find my car keys. I was in the parking lot, I needed to get home. Where were my keys? They were supposed to be in the side pocket of my purse. They weren't there.

The last two eighth-grade mothers came down the sidewalk. One was carrying a red milk crate full of paper products; the other's arms were cradled under a stack of serving platters. Their cars were on the other side of the parking lot from mine.

I still couldn't find my keys. I pulled out my wallet and my cell phone, the first-aid pouch and my checkbook. No keys.

Leave Alden?

Erin had started pre-K when she was four. She had seemed

like such a big girl to us. Her sneakers had closed with Velcro and had had happy puppy faces on them. She had loved those shoes. Now I see the pre-K students and they seem so much younger and smaller than I remember her being.

You don't worry about whether a four-year-old is musical or artistic. And she was our first child; we had thought that she was magic, good at everything.

I turned my purse upside-down. The pens and pencils scattered across the hood of the station wagon like Pick-up sticks. I saw the receipt I had signed for the delivery of the hay, an appointment card from Erin's orthodontist, another from Thomas's allergist, but no keys. I fumbled through the empty purse, feeling at each compartment, and there were my keys, in the side pocket just where they belonged.

I thought Alden was where we belonged. It was so close to our house, and we knew so many people. We had worked so hard, given so much, cared so much. It wasn't perfect—this year had shown that—but that was why I cared so much, because I had felt I had a part in making the place better.

How could I quit now? I had already talked to people about joining the Capital Campaign committee and next year I was going to be the first non-alumnae woman to run for the board. Every time I set foot in any of the buildings, I saw people I knew and liked. And those people liked me, too. They knew what I was good at. They valued me. I was important here.

The Alden School was my life, my world. All of my friends were Alden parents; most of my clients were Alden families. Many, many days the only time I spoke to another adult was at school.

But it was not my school. It was my children's school. They were my children, but this was their school.

How had I let this happen? But leave? I couldn't imagine it.

I almost never saw people from my old job anymore. We had all promised that we would have lunch and such, but we never did. Would it be like that with Mimi, Blair, and Annelise? Without the car pools, the parents' coffees, and the committee meetings, would we see each other less and less? I was sick at the thought. These were the closest friends I had ever had, the first time I had ever been so secure in friendships. I couldn't lose them. How would I manage without them?

I was home now, pulling into our driveway. Thomas's window was dark, but Erin's light was on. When we had redone her room over Spring Break, we had bought extra sheets and used them to make new curtains; they were a cheerful teenaged plaid of aqua, teal, and plum. The curtains looked fine from inside the room, but we hadn't lined them, so in the soft gray shadows of our beautiful tree-lined street, her window was a garish rectangle, an almost clownlike slab of aqua.

Chris had said that the deadline for answering Sidwell was tomorrow. I should call them, he had suggested, asking for more time.

Why would they give us any more time? The families on the waiting list would have been calling the Sidwell admissions office every day, desperate for places. And I never ask for extra time. I always meet deadlines.

I went to the kitchen desk and took out one of the big Sidwell envelopes. Maybe Chris was wrong. Maybe the deadline had already passed. I pulled out the papers and scanned the cover letter. The deadline was tomorrow.

I went up the back staircase and knocked on Erin's door.

When we had been taking everything out of her room so that we could paint, I had found the cotton-fleece drawstring skirt that she had worn on the first day of school. It had fallen off its hanger, but the drawstring had caught on the button of a dress that she no longer wore. She had seen me shake the skirt out and rehang it, but neither one of us had said anything.

She called for me to come in. Every other time I had come into her room this week I had been jarred by the strong colors, the teal of the walls, the plum of the trim—I had let her pick her own paint—but tonight all I saw was her face. She was pale and her eyes were tense and worried.

Usually when she read in bed, she lay on her side, often falling asleep with her hand still marking her place in the book. But tonight she had been sitting up, hunched forward.

I sat down next to her. I patted her on the leg, then noticed her bedside light. "Oh, you did the lampshade. It looks great."

After we had painted her room and made the curtains, we had used grosgrain ribbon to duplicate the plaid pattern across her bulletin board. We had intended to cover the shade of her lamp with more of the sheet fabric and attach a plum chenille fringe, but then we had gotten interested in the caramel corn. Apparently, after I had left this evening, she had gotten out the hot-glue gun and done it herself.

Good for her.

What would I have done, I wondered, if I had been in her

place, knowing that my work was going to disappoint my mother, knowing that in front of all her friends—no, her acquaintances, my mother didn't have friends, not like I do—my mother was going to have to see that I didn't measure up?

I couldn't imagine it. It wouldn't have happened. I know, I know with all my heart, that rather than have that happen, rather than disappoint my mother about the one thing she cared about, I would have cheated.

But what had my own daughter done? She had copied that hated essay—for I am sure she did hate it—in her absolute best handwriting, putting her best foot forward even though she knew that she had long since lost the race. And then in my absence she had taken out the hot-glue gun and tackled a new project.

I once joked about not wanting to send the kids to Sidwell for fear that they would be eaten alive by the other students, but this year, this year of not being invited, had made Erin strong. Chris had said that she was tough as nails; I would have never said that about her, but he had seen her in the hallways, in the lunchroom, on the playground.

"You saw the essays, didn't you?" she asked. "All of them?"

"Of course. Some of them were remarkable."

"Did you read Marissa's about the bird? I would have never thought of that, not in a hundred million years. Mine was awful, wasn't it?" The last words came out in a rush.

There was no point in lying to her. Nothing I could say would make her feel good about the essay. "Erin, you didn't quit. That's the important thing. The result wasn't what you would have wanted because you don't have the kind of imagination that some of those other kids do. But even when you knew that yours wasn't going to be among the best, you didn't quit. Maybe you aren't proud of the product, but you can be very proud of your process."

I thought that that was a pretty good thing to say, but it made no impression on her at all. "But the assignment was just too hard for me. I was awful. I could see that everyone else could do it, and I couldn't. Don't you think maybe I ought to transfer to Sidwell?"

I had to smile at that. "Erin, people don't transfer to Sidwell because Alden is too hard. In many subjects Sidwell is harder."

"Oh." She looked blank, then bewildered. If Alden was too hard for her and Sidwell even harder, what was she going to do? Where would she go? Who would have her?

"Erin, sweetie, but that's why Sidwell may be right for you because the math and the sciences are harder. Mr. Goddard talked to me about both you and Thomas this evening—"

"*He* saw my essay?" She was mortified.

"This isn't about your essay. It's about all the things that you are good at. You know that you are good at math, don't you?"

"Grandpa Tom says that I am."

Jamie's father was a high-school math teacher. "Has he said anything to you about Alden?"

"No, but I did show him how to log on to the Web site. Then he said that maybe we could work together in the summers sometime."

So he had seen the limitations in the curriculum. "How do you feel about going to Sidwell?" I asked.

"I don't know. The other day some of the big girls who have parking stickers"—those would have been seniors —"were getting in their car and it had a flat tire. At first they were a little upset, but after they called someone, I guess they decided that it was funny because they lined up and started to sing these silly, sad songs, all pretending to be heartbroken right there in the middle of the parking lot, throwing themselves across the hood of the car, and they were harmonizing without rehearsing, and they looked so cool and like they were having so much fun, and you could tell that everyone wanted to be like them when we are in high school, and then I realized that I couldn't ever be like them because I can't sing. I don't know, Mom, I'm starting to think that maybe I'm just a math nerd."

"Oh, Erin . . ." "Popular girl" to "math nerd" in six months? Why couldn't she just think of herself as Erin?

Because middle-school kids think in labels; that's how they start to figure out who they are. "You may be very good in math, but you aren't a 'math nerd.' Math nerds do not get the most playing time of any kid on their soccer teams. Math nerds do not care about their clothes anywhere near as much as you care about yours. You're a scholar-athlete." If my daughter had to have a label for herself, let it be that one. "And Sidwell does a better job of educating kids like you than Alden does."

"But it would be fun to be like those big girls; it would be fun to be able to sing with them."

Erin would always feel that way as long as she was at Alden.

She would always judge herself by the school's standards, thinking that it would be better if she could sing. I put my arm around her, pulling her close so that our foreheads touched.

"If I go to Sidwell," she asked, "will Rachel and Elise still invite me to their bat mitzvahs?"

"Yes." I had a feeling that now we were talking about the important stuff. "And Jacob and Suzanne will, too. And you'll probably get a lot of invitations from the Sidwell kids."

She liked the sound of that. "And will I be able to have a sweet-sixteen party? That's what everyone says. The girls who don't have bat mitzvahs have sweet sixteens."

"Of course, you can."

She pushed back so she could look at me. "No, Mom, I mean this. A nice party, not the usual thing here at the house, but with a DJ if I want."

"Yes, you can have a nice sweet-sixteen party."

"Then it will be okay."

I needed to reread my books on raising teenaged girls. We were supposed to be talking about the crew team and whatever-that-upper-level algebra was, and instead we were talking about a birthday party to be staged four years hence. But the thought of such a party comforted her, made her think that she would still have friends.

Maybe I needed to have my own sweet-sixteen birthday party.

"I still need to talk to Dad, but I would appreciate it if you didn't say anything at school tomorrow. If you tell Rachel, she will tell Gideon, and then Gideon will tell Thomas that Sidwell keeps live carp in their toilets."

"Okay." And then she smiled. "I want to be the one to tell him about the fish."

I rarely call Jamie. I let him call me. He has been sleeping so badly that I don't want to risk waking him up, but as soon as I was in our room, I called him.

He picked up immediately, and at the sound of his voice I suddenly sagged under all the pressure of the evening, the strain of trying not to mind too much about Erin's essay, the effort of trying to say just the right thing to her, and then the awful awfulness of leaving Alden. My eyes burned. I could feel myself starting to cry.

Why wasn't Jamie here? I needed him here. This was no way to be married, to be a family.

"Lydia, what's wrong? The kids . . . they're okay?"

The rising worry in his voice made me get control of myself. "They're fine. Nothing's wrong."

Except with me. I thought about all the wonderful things Chris had said about the kids, how smart they were, how athletic they were. I should have been thrilled—who wouldn't want to hear that?—but when I spoke again, my voice was leaden. "I did tell you that they got into Sidwell, didn't I?"

"Actually, you didn't. But I knew. Some of my partners send their kids there. One of them is on the board and saw Thomas's name on the list."

"Oh, Jamie . . ." I was mortified. How could I not have mentioned this to him? I had seen the envelopes when I had gotten home from Houston, and the next morning Faith had gone to Martha Shot. From then on, the school's problems had been all I had thought about. "Why didn't you say anything?"

"Because you already knew what I thought. I don't have anything new to say, and I don't fight losing battles. Lydia, what is this about?"

I told him what Chris had said although I knew so little about upper-level math that I couldn't remember the details of the curriculum. "And he talked about athletics, not just for Thomas, but Erin, too. He said she ought to try out for the crew team. They have a women's crew team at Sidwell. We don't." Jamie was athletic. He would want the children to try a variety of sports.

"That was very generous of Chris," he said slowly. "It can't be in his self-interest to have you leave the school."

If Jamie had been being careful about his words, he would have said "us" or "our family," but he was tired. He had said what he meant. "It isn't me leaving the school," I said stiffly. "It is Erin and Thomas."

He didn't say anything.

My eyes started to sting again. "Do you honestly think that I would have kept them at Alden because I have friends there, that I would have deliberately sacrificed them for me?"

"No, not deliberately. But it did seem that you didn't want to see the problems. How do the kids feel about it?"

I took a breath. This conversation should be about them, not about me. "Erin is more positive than I thought she would be. I think she sees more than we realize. I haven't talked to Thomas, but I think he will be okay. He's figured out that the best players on his soccer team are from Sidwell, and he already has play dates with those kids a fair amount."

"So do you want to call Sidwell," Jamie asked, "and see if they will give us more time? I think that they will understand."

I spoke slowly. "I don't think we need more time."

He was silent for a moment. He had never imagined that this would happen, that I would actually consent to sending Erin and Thomas to Sidwell.

"A couple of weeks ago," he said, "when I said that there wouldn't be any more trials like this, you didn't believe me, did you?"

"Jamie, let's not talk about that now."

I didn't want any empty promises. I wasn't making a deal with him—*if I do what you want with the kids' school, then you need to be home more.* I—we—were doing this because it was right for our children. That was all.

But as he does so often, Jamie surprised me. After all, he made a very good living knowing what convinces people and what doesn't. "I'm not leaving my firm."

"What?" That seemed to come from nowhere. "Is that even an issue?"

"My partners think it is. The feeling is that if I want to take on another criminal case like this, I should go to another firm or start my own. It's not personal. No one's in a snit about it, and I can take anyone who wants to leave. But this press conference at every lunch break, make your case in the media, that's not us. We do good, solid legal work. We're always prepared, better prepared than anyone. We don't fight our cases in the media. So either I leave the firm or I lie low for a while, working behind the scenes and not taking on cases that might come out of this one."

Jamie might be desperately weary, but his partners, back here in D.C. working on other cases, weren't. They were thinking clearly. If they had already declared that this was not the direction that the firm was going in, I could believe them. At a minimum, this meant that Jamie couldn't back into a career of criminal work. He would have to make a deliberate decision about whether to stay with the firm. He couldn't take "just one more case," and then just one more and one more.

So even if I did lose all my girlfriends, even if my phone never rang again, at least I would—if he decided to stay with his firm—have my boyfriend back.

That was something.

With the Spring Fair being only a day away, I had a million things to do on Friday, but as soon as I thought someone would answer the phone, I called the admissions office at Sidwell. The receptionist put me right through to the head of admissions. He knew who I was and professed to be delighted to hear from me. He said that with Jamie being in the middle of a high-profile trial, they would never have given our places away without speaking to us. The school was used to parents in public life.

I wouldn't have thought of us as having a public life, but I supposed this year Jamie had. I took a breath. "It isn't like us to leave things to the last minute, but we would like to submit the enrollment contracts."

"That's wonderful, and as long as we get the contracts sometime next week, that will be fine. Just put them in the mail when it's convenient."

But I wanted to have it done. I didn't want to tell people at Alden that we were planning on doing this next week. I wanted to say that it was done. So I filled in the contracts, wrote out the checks, and drove over to Sidwell, crossing over on Van Ness to Wisconsin Avenue.

I didn't know where to park. At Alden when you have to pop in the school for something quick like this, you park in the fire lane. I didn't know how Sidwell felt about its fire lanes . . . or even where the fire lanes were. Should I try to find visitor spaces in one of the lots? Or park in the neighborhood? But wasn't the campus fenced? If I parked in the neighborhood, would there be a back gate, or would I have to walk all the way around the school to the Wisconsin entrance?

This was all stuff I knew at Alden.

I did park in the neighborhood behind the school, and I did find a gate, but as I crossed the campus, I didn't see anyone that I knew. Not a soul. No one from the neighborhood, no one from Thomas's team or Jamie's firm, no one from church. That never happened to me at Alden.

I would be starting all over. People would ask me to bring the paper products to the school potlucks. That's what the or-ganizers do when the phone list has a name that they don't recognize. They ask that person to bring the paper products.

Walking into a potluck with the plastic cups is a sign that no one knows you, that no one can trust you yet.

Why me? I felt so sorry for myself as I walked along these unfamiliar sidewalks. Why was this happening to me? Faith should have been expelled. Martha Shot should be asked to retire. Chris wanted to leave. But who was leaving? The one who longed to stay—me.

I spent the rest of Friday listening to the silent auction committee members fuss about one another. When one member had been unable to get some of her donation forms signed in time for the catalog, the committee—because most of them liked her—had agreed to publish an addendum that they would put together Friday night. Most of the committee members had assumed that this would be a single sheet, but another member had used the additional time to fulfill her own vision of what the auction should be. She felt that everything in the auction was too expensive, that the event had become too elitist, that it should be a "fun" event for all families, not just the most wealthy. So without speaking to anyone else on the committee, she had solicited more than fifteen low-end donations: two McDonald's Happy Meals, a child's cut and shampoo at The Hair Cuttery, and the like.

The rest of the committee was furious. Each of these items would take up the same amount of table space as items worth hundreds of dollars.

But what about families who didn't want to spend hundreds of dollars? The populist committee member was now quite belligerent. There were scholarship families at this school. Shouldn't there be something for them? Wasn't it classist and racist not to?

The problems that the Alden School has with racial diversity are far beyond anything that the silent auction committee could fix.

You would think that I would be impossibly sick of these women, and maybe I was. But even if I didn't like them, I liked who I was when I was dealing with them. I knew all the players, I knew who was friends with whom, who had ideas that she really cared about and who was just running her mouth off, who did the work and who just wanted the attention. That made me able to find good solutions, and I liked being the sort of person who could find good solutions.

The nightmare would be dealing with these people if they were strangers. Who would I know at Sidwell? A few families from church, the parents of Thomas's teammates, but most of the moms would be strangers.

I told everyone that I agreed with the spirit of the populist member, but her ideas, however laudable, had come too late. The families she was concerned about would have already seen the catalog, and if they were even coming to the evening barbecue, they probably would not come into the library where the auction would be set up, much less pick up the addendum with all these fun items. So this year we would group all these donations into a single basket, and next year alternatives could be discussed.

"You remember that you said that, Lydia," the populist

snapped. "I want you to be sure and remember next year that you said you agreed with me."

Oh, I would remember, but what good would that do her? I wouldn't be here.

√

I got a long, gossipy e-mail from Blair. She told me about the various Spring Fair fires that she had been putting out and then concluded with news about Mary Paige Caudwell. Mary Paige's strategy for getting a big settlement in her divorce had been to depict herself as a perfect mother devoting herself to raising a perfect child. Faith's false accusation blew a big hole in that, and so Mary Paige was frantically trying to re-depict herself as a long-suffering saint devoted to raising a troubled child. Her lawyer said that the "long-suffering" would sell better if she had a job.

Apparently her credentials as an "interior-design professional" weren't as impressive as she had led us to believe. She had had one interview at a high-end, upscale boutique—the only kind of place in which she would ever consider working retail—and another at a public relations firm, but she had gone into those interviews with such a sense of entitlement that she had not gotten the jobs.

So a friend of her mother's was getting her a position as a bank teller. She was starting the training next week.

Working the counter at a bank is a safe, clean, responsible, white-collar job, but the work environment would be hierarchical. Mary Paige would be working under people who were younger and more able than she, people who were less well-dressed, less cultured, less likely to belong to a country club, less likely to have parents born in the United States. She would hate it.

And I found that I didn't care. I wasn't happy that she had to get a job that she would consider so beneath herself, but my heart didn't break for her, either. She was a part of the Alden School world, and I needed to stop caring.

14

Blair and I were scheduled to meet the custodian at school at six on Saturday morning. Her husband would bring her kids over when the fair started at nine, and mine would come with Mimi's husband and her kids.

But I arrived at five-thirty. I had awakened so many times in the night that I finally decided to get up. I checked Erin's alarm clock to be sure that it was set—how marvelous it was to know that I could count on her to get herself and her brother out of bed—and then I got myself ready.

Normally I love loading up the car to go to the kids' events. I love packing the orange slices for the soccer games and the craft projects for the Brownie meetings. I like antici-pating the event—sometimes I like that as much as the event itself—and I like the fact that I'm good at this kind of preparation, that I know what to take. I may not be a perfect mother, but I am one hell of a mom.

But this morning I felt disengaged, as if I were standing apart from myself, watching this mom gather up signs and clipboards, tablecloths and the cash box, her laptop computer and seven shoe boxes with slots cut into the tops. She didn't take any folding chairs—the school had plenty of chairs—and she didn't take any serving dishes—the bake-sale committee was taking care of that.

I had to stop feeling this way. This wasn't me.

Most of the parking lot was being used for fair activities, and, the setup committees having worked late into the night, the lot was full of pop-up canopy tents and tables. Along one edge, a few parking places had been left open. An orange traffic cone sat in the middle of each one, and each cone had a laminated placard affixed to it. One of the cones had my name on it. I got out of the station wagon, moved my cone, and pulled into my place. I was the first one to arrive.

I popped the tailgate and reached into the station wagon to get out the signs that had been dropped at our house last night.

Then I stopped and slammed the tailgate. I had the school to myself. I needed to say good-bye.

Living in a small town teaches you a lot, but one thing it doesn't teach you is how to say good-bye. Families don't move away as much as they do in D.C., and even when you yourself leave, you don't say good-bye because your parents are still there and you will be coming back.

My dad left without saying good-bye. He went back to his office one day after lunch, sat down at his desk, and had a massive stroke. And when I left my job, instead of saying good-bye, I promised I would come back and we would all go out to lunch, and then I had gone back only once.

This time I was going to say good-bye, bid farewell to the first place I had felt so completely a part of, so completely at home.

What precious, precious memories I had—the Halloween parades with the masses of little witches, Indians, and princesses; Erin and her friends wearing their Brownie uniforms for the first time; both Erin and Thomas being so excited about reading their first "chapter" book; and that funny, wonderful moment when Erin was in first grade and one of her classmates saw me and chirped, "Hi, Mrs. Erin's Mom."

Mrs. Erin's Mom. Shouldn't I have hated being called that? My mother would have. But I had loved it.

I wasn't just saying good-bye to the school; I was saying good-bye to my children being young.

Then I went up to the high school, that beautiful old white mansion that had always been our family's future, the real heart of the school that now we would never know.

It was hard.

When I came back down to the parking lot, I saw Blair's car and the custodian's truck. A green minivan was turning into the lot. It belonged to the chair of the games committee.

She would need the signs that were in my station wagon, but she would have a million other things to unload. I had time to go find Blair. I needed to see Blair, not because she was cochair of the fair, but because she was my friend. Seeing her would be like putting tired feet in a clear, cool running stream. She was reserved and serene, this dear friend of mine, and the strength of her coloring—her blue-black hair and her ivory skin—and the vividly feminine hues of her clothes would energize me, turn me back into myself again.

The lower-school office was to be the fair's command center for the day, and so I went there to find her. But she was not alone. With her, waiting for the coffee to finish brewing, were Annelise and Mimi.

My friend Annelise—my fellow midwesterner—the trees of Wisconsin had taught her the same lessons that the plowed fields of Indiana had taught me. And if Blair was water and Annelise the earth, then Mimi was the sun: bright, boldly honest, unrelenting.

I was *not* going to say good-bye to them.

"I saw you drive out this morning," Mimi said, "and I realized that I couldn't keep away. I wanted to be here in the thick of things so I called Blair—"

"Only to find out," Annelise added, "that I had done the same thing."

I was glad that they were all here. I touched Mimi on the arm, hugged Annelise.

They were looking at me curiously. "What's wrong?" Blair said quickly.

"It's not the fair," I assured her, "nothing with the fair."

It was such a beautiful morning. I wished that we could go outside. I didn't want to tell them in this cluttered office, I wanted to be outdoors where the air was fresh and the morning light still soft, but if we went outside, the games committee people would want to get the signs from me, and someone else would want something from Blair.

So standing here in front of the open door to the supply closet, next to three boxes of copy paper, I said it. "Jamie and I are sending Erin and Thomas to Sidwell next year."

Blair had been bending over to plug in her laptop. Annelise had been about to pour coffee. Mimi had been peeling printed computer labels off a pregummed sheet, sticking them temporarily along the side of the gray metal desk, her earrings swinging as she worked. They all stopped.

Mimi spoke first. "Lydia, no."

"You knew we were applying," I said.

"Yes, but . . ." This was Annelise.

"This isn't about Erin not being invited to the movies. You don't leave a school for that." I knew that each of them was flushed with guilt over everything that had happened this year. "And it isn't about Faith and Chris. It's about the school not being right for Erin and Thomas. This school is strong in music and arts; it is a wonderful place for smart, creative kids. My kids color between the lines, and they always will. They like coloring between the lines. They're good at math; they're good at sports."

"Not everyone here is musical," Annelise pleaded.

She and I were wearing the same cotton sweater. That happened once in a while. Our coloring was the same; our taste, incomes, and figures were similar.

"But the best kids are," I answered. "It's going to be hard for my kids to believe in themselves here."

"But haven't we always said we're not the type of people

who need our kids to be best at everything all the time?" Blair said.

"Of course, but this isn't—" I stopped. *I can't do this. Please don't make me do this. Don't make me defend myself.* I ran my hand over the top box of copy paper. It was a red-and-white box with a separate lid. My fingers caught on the plastic strap that encircled the box, holding the lid on. "You have to believe me, Jamie and I honestly think we are doing what is best for our children."

"I didn't mean to question you," Annelise said quickly. "It's just that I don't want it to happen. I can't imagine you not being here. I feel as if I can't breathe."

If Blair were water, Annelise earth, and Mimi the sun, was I their air?

Blair nodded more slowly. "Of course, you're doing what is right for your kids, but, Lydia, not have you here? It feels so completely wrong."

"It does to me, too," I said.

Mimi was fingering one of the adhesive labels. She spoke without looking at me, which wasn't like her. "Lydia, everything I know about being a friend I learned from you—"

"No, no," I interrupted. "We all learned together. And I'm not moving. I will still live across the street from you."

"But not from me," Annelise put in. "Not from me or Blair. When are we going to see you?"

We had never had to make arrangements to see one another. It had always been easy. I would go to a soccer game or to the musical at the high school, and my friends would be there. I would see them in the parking lots. I would talk to them when one of us dropped off the kids at the other's house. We would pick up the phone to make arrangements for driving and then start talking about something else. All that was going to change. It wasn't going to be so easy anymore.

"We will have to make an effort," I said with more confidence than I felt. "We'll have to make plans. Or set up a routine where we exercise together three times a week or something like that."

Blair looked at me curiously, her head tilting, her black hair dropping across her shoulder. "You're not worried?"

I looked at her and spoke more honestly. "I'm too overwhelmed to worry, too tired, too bewildered. I just know that I have to do what it is right for my children, even if it does feel wrong for me."

Mimi looked down at her computer labels, little white flags ready and waiting to be stuck somewhere. "Just because it will be different doesn't mean that it will be wrong," she said. "Sometimes we get together and all we do is talk about school and the kids and nothing else. Lydia's not going to want to obsess about Alden School politics every time we get together any more than we will care about Sidwell. And maybe that's healthy. Either we will have to talk about something else or we will discover that we aren't really friends, just mom associates."

She was right. Before Spring Break I had been caught in that sucking morass of unproductivity, unable to fold a basket of laundry without checking my e-mail for the latest Alden School gossip. With Jamie never home, with all my friends as involved in Alden as I was, it had been too easy to give myself over to those addictive dramas. It would be easier to be something more than just a mom if my friends' lives were a little different from mine.

But if our kids weren't at the same school, could they still be my lighthouse?

Maybe . . . maybe not . . .

The problem with my lighthouse image was that the boats never left sight of the lighthouse; they weren't going anywhere. They were simply struggling to make safe circles around the lighthouse. If I were to take my family's boat on a journey up the coastline, we would need different lighthouses.

And I'd probably be able to find them because I knew how to make friends. I might not have known how to do that when I was a girl, but as a woman I knew how to do it.

"Are you going to burst into tears," Blair asked, "the first time someone at Sidwell asks you to bring the paper products?"

"I certainly will."

"We could submit an affidavit," Annelise volunteered, "saying that you can be trusted to bring an entrée."

"I don't know . . . maybe bringing the paper products isn't so bad. It's certainly less work."

A sharp rap on the office's glass door made us look up. Three members of the auction committee were standing outside, looking flushed and urgent. "What do you think they want?" Annelise asked. The auction doesn't start for another twelve hours."

"I'll deal with it," Blair said. "Mimi, can you go check with the games people, see if they need anything?"

"Oh, no." I winced, remembering the signs that were in my car. "I need to go." I ducked around the auction people and hurried outside.

There were probably twenty volunteers in the parking lot, mostly women, but some men as well. More were arriving by the minute, backing their cars to the edge of the lot, unloading quickly, and then moving the cars out of the way. A woman from the development office was laying out the Alden School T-shirts and baseball caps that would be offered for sale. The cakes for the cake walk were being wheeled across the asphalt on rolling caterer's racks. At the soccer-kick booth, two men were assembling the frame for the net, and the face-painting people were stringing yellow police tape between folding chairs in hopes of managing the line that always developed at that booth.

I went around to the lawn and the circular drive in the front of the high school. The kids from the theater-tech construction crew were assembling their "Powder Puff" goalpost for this afternoon's football game between the girl's soccer teams. The ponies had arrived, and the popcorn truck was backing into place.

Everything looked beautiful. So many of the parents at this school were creative themselves. The bake-sale table had cloth-swaddled tiers at the top of which the homemade breads, seeded and braided, cascaded out of a rattan horn of plenty. Even the Rice Krispie treats, individually wrapped for the pre-K trade, were each tied with a little ribbon and displayed on footed silver platters.

At nine o'clock, the first shuttle from the church parking lot arrived, dropping off a load of fairgoers. Ten minutes later my kids checked in with me. Mimi and I had told Thomas and Gideon that they could go around by themselves if they stayed together every single minute. That was always a big step for the kids—being allowed to go around the fair by themselves. Second children always got to do it a year or two earlier than their older siblings had.

Clouds of whipped pink sugar spun out of the cotton-candy machine, drenching the air with a high-pitched, slightly burnt sweetness. The smells from the popcorn machine were deeper and saltier. Parents were already carrying cakes their children had won at the cake walk. Kids took off their jackets when they went into the moon bounce and then forgot to pick them up when their turn was over.

Had I loved this place too much? Again . . . maybe, but maybe not.

I'm sure that if there were a raising-moms book, it would have advised me to have a more balanced life, not to throw myself so passionately into one set of activities, and certainly not to let my children's activities become my own. I could probably write that book, calling it *Turning Moms into Mothers*.

It would be full of very good, very sensible advice, but I wasn't going to take it. I'm an all-or-nothing type. If I do something, then I'm going to overdo it. That's who I am. I know that a balanced life is supposed to be the ideal, but actually I love the frenetic imbalance of my life.

But when you choose to get so involved in your kids' activities, you need to be able to brake at high speeds. You need to stop when they're ready for you to stop even if that is long before you are ready to stop.

So I was going to say good-bye to the Alden School and find something else to be gloriously and deliciously obsessed about.

"Mom! Mom! Mommy!"

It was Thomas racing across the lawn, no longer wearing the sweatshirt he had had on when he had arrived. God might know where that sweatshirt was, but I was sure that Thomas did not. "Where's Gideon? You were supposed to stay with Gideon."

"I know, I know, but Dad's here."

"Dad? Your dad?"

Jamie wasn't coming home this weekend, and even if he were, he wouldn't come to the fair. I think he had only come once. He complained that I was always wildly busy and he didn't know anyone and so had to spend the day following Thomas around, keeping track of his tickets and his coat.

But indeed, following Thomas, holding his carry-on bag as he had apparently come straight from the airport, was my husband.

"What on earth are you doing here?"

"I have no idea," Jamie said pleasantly, handing his suitcase to Thomas. "It seemed like the right thing to do. Show up and be a supportive husband, although I admit I don't have a clue as to how to do that."

I remembered feeling this way when I had been on my way

to Houston, but showing up was certainly a good place to start. He had not needed to do this, I never expected it. But it said so much, his coming. It said that he got it, that he knew that today was going to be hard for me. I reached up and put my arms around his neck, and he put his around my waist, pulling me close. His body felt big, familiar, and warm.

He whispered into my hair. "I don't think I can compete with the way you greeted me in Houston."

I stepped back, a little embarrassed to be remembering, in the middle of this total-mom sort of day, my magnificent performance as a rock groupie.

"Oh, come on, Lydia," he teased, "you should be proud of that moment."

"I am, but right now I have a fair to run."

"It looks like you've done a great job. People seem to be having a really good time."

"Wait until they try to find their kids' coats." And then without waiting another moment, I said, "I took the contracts into Sidwell yesterday."

"I knew you would."

He knows me. He knows that I don't linger for second thoughts; if I am going to do something, I do it.

"Are you going to be okay?" he said.

"Of course." I did believe that now. It wasn't going to be easy, but this time next year I'd be fine. I would never love Sidwell as much as I had loved Alden, but that is because I would never take a nervous, silent four-year-old with her smiling puppy sneakers to Sidwell and pick her up three hours later, glowingly happy. I might never love Sidwell, but I could love our family being there. "It will be different, but I will be okay."

"I want it to be different, too," he said. "I want to change. I want my part to change. I've always thought of Alden as your world, and I've never really felt any connection with it since I don't have any desire to take off work to help a bunch of five-year-olds finger paint or use power tools. Everywhere I look, Alden seems to be about the women, the moms, and you know me, I do better if there are other guys around."

He wanted to change? That surprised me. "But, Jamie, as long as you are looking through my eyes, you will only see women. The investment committee and the buildings and ground committee are more than half men, but I'm always drawn more to the girl stuff."

"Oh." He stopped and thought. "I just assumed that the Alden volunteer community was dominated by women because it used to be a girls' school."

"Most schools' volunteer communities are dominated by women, but plenty of men do find their place."

"That's what I was going to say. Several of my partners send their kids to Sidwell, and some of them work just as hard as me and yet they don't seem to mind going to school events."

I smiled at him and patted his arm. "That's because—I'm willing to bet—they go and meet up with the other business-litigation attorneys and stand around and talk to each other, ignoring the consumer-advocate attorneys and the estate-planning attorneys. And I can get you four nice cotton-fleece drawstring skirts to wear so that everyone knows who is in your clique."

He drew back. "I'm sure that there is a joke in that, but I don't know what it is. I just hope that you're noticing I'm not saying that it will be nice to have Thomas play on teams that have a chance of winning."

Jamie was a guy; he couldn't help that, and when guys play sports, they don't mind if the activity builds character and teaches them about teamwork, but that's not what it's really all about. They want to win. "I do give you credit for not saying that, but only because you're going to like having Erin be on a winning team just as much as Thomas."

He smiled, obviously thinking of watching our daughter run down a soccer field. "You're right. I will." He put his arm around me again. "We're going to do this as a family, Lydia."

I pressed my cheek against his shoulder for a moment, then stepped back. I felt wonderful and light. "Well, getting more involved starts right now. You can help me with that trash can."

I pointed to the trash can closest to the cotton-candy machine. It was brimming. Jamie went over and started to gather up the edges of the heavy fifty-gallon sack.

Just then Erin raced up. "Hi, Dad! Thomas said you were here. Can I have more money? Please?"

Jamie let go of the bag. "I think this is what the future really holds, Erin saying 'hi' and asking for more money." But he reached into his pocket, handing her two bills.

She looked at them. "Wow, Dad! Thanks!"

"You need to give one of those to your brother."

"Okay, sure." And away she dashed.

"You didn't have to do that," I said. "Every time she wasn't invited somewhere this year she baby-sat, so she's loaded."

We watched Erin catch up with Thomas in line at the moon bounce. She handed him the money, and he looked up at her, startled and gratified. She rapped her knuckles on his head, apparently a gesture of extreme goodwill, and danced off to join her friends.

This was the one constant in my life, the one thing that would devastate me to say good-bye to. I would have other activities, other projects that would consume me; there would be other things I would get way too involved in, care way too much about. I might have other careers, even other friends, but—God willing—I would only ever have this husband and these children. They would give me all the balance I would need.

Jamie and I stood side by side for another moment watching Thomas crawl into the moon bounce. This was what was real in theme-park land, the way the four of us felt about one another.

Then Jamie dropped his arm, and we picked up the trash and headed for the Dumpster.

acknowledgments

My niece Erica Gilles read a draft of this book with insight and confidence. Peg Serenyi and Roger Vilsack contributed their expertise. Washington, D.C., photographer Leslie Cashen, who has taken great pictures of my kids over the years, unknowingly furnished the model for Lydia's work. Lydia herself was named in honor of the dear, late Lydia Lee, a woman much missed.

Every time I would stop working on this book to try something else, my agent, Damaris Rowland, would prompt me to come back to it. My editor, Jennifer Enderlin, with whom I have ascended to the heights of Mount Silliness, proved herself as talented at editing as she is at reading "Romance Jeopardy" questions.

Acknowledgments

My greatest debt is, of course, to my own mom-friends, most notably Mary Candace Fowler, aka Laura B.'s mom. Candy and I led a Girl Scout troop together; we owned a swing set together. She wrote the swim team newsletter, while I wrote the one for the dive team. She's my friend, my next-door neighbor, my volunteer editor . . . and, needless to say, an ex-lawyer.

A MOST UNCOMMON DEGREE OF POPULARITY

By Kathleen Gilles Seidel

In Her Own Words

- "Isn't It Time to Stop Blaming the Popular Girls?"—an original essay from Kathleen Gilles Seidel

About the Author

- A Conversation with Kathleen Gilles Seidel

Reading Group Questions

For more reading group suggestions
visit www.readinggroupgold.com

 ST. MARTIN'S GRIFFIN

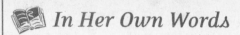 *In Her Own Words*

Isn't It Time to Stop Blaming
the Popular Girls?

An original essay from Kathleen Gilles Seidel

The woman's voice was shaking as she talked about going to pick up her daughter during a middle-school dance. The girl had called her from the school restroom in tears, wanting to come home because no one would talk to her. "It was those popular kids," the mother said angrily. "They just ignored her."

"I'm not a sociologist or a psychologist. I'm a mom and a novelist."

It makes a good story, doesn't it? Good stories need villains, and so the villain of the young adolescent years is the popular girl—the pretty one, the well-dressed one, the mean one, the one who won't be your friend. Parents are happy to blame her when their child is unhappy; researchers talk to her self-identified victims and assume that that is an accurate picture. But is the story really that simple?

I have two daughters. During middle school, the older one, Becca, had a very stable, very clearly defined group of friends. It was a great group of kids, and while they weren't unpopular, they certainly weren't "the" popular crowd. My younger daughter Abby went to a different middle school. She, too, had a very stable, very clearly defined group of friends. It was also a great group of kids, and they were the popular girls.

Suddenly I was a lot less willing to call the popular girls villains. My Abby was a happy, lively, confident kid. Why was it her fault if other kids weren't?

Popularity as a phenomenon peaks in middle school. During elementary school, parents make their children's social plans, and during high school, the influence of the popular group diffuses. But very often during the middle-school years, a single popular crowd dominates the social life of the environment.

I'm not a sociologist or a psychologist. I'm a mom and a novelist. I don't have data; I have observations and

insights. Of course there are exceptions to everything I'm about to say, but I do believe that much of what is said and written about popular girls is biased against them.

1. Everyone hates the popular girls.

This is an oxymoron; the definition of the word "popular" involves likeability and approval. Popular girls are, in fact, very likeable. They are lively, verbal, and poised. People may *envy* the popular girls more than hate them.

What makes adults uneasy about the popular kids is their power. A variety of students in middle school have power. The ones who beat you up and steal your lunch money have one kind of power. The kids who manage to get everyone to feel sorry for them have another kind of power. The popular kids have power because, for whatever reason, the other kids look to them for validation. If you are wearing what the popular kids are wearing, you aren't a dork. If you are sitting at their lunch table, you aren't a loser. As the vice principal of Abby's middle school repeatedly reminded parents, the other kids give the popular kids their power. They haven't necessarily asked for it.

2. The popular girls are mean.

This may be true, but if so, it's because all middle-school kids are mean to some degree or another. In fact, the meanest things I heard said while driving carpools were what Becca and her friends—the "other" kids—said about the popular kids. Probably suffering some degree of suppressed envy, they were very critical of the popular kids. But Abby and her popular friends never spoke about the other kids; they simply weren't thinking about the other kids. Although your child may be thinking about the popular girls all the time, they may not be thinking about her much at all.

This may result in errors of omission. If one girl says to another, "you can't sign my yearbook," that's mean. If she hands her yearbook to one girl, but then not to a second girl standing right next to the first one, that's objectionable as well. But when she doesn't cross the lunchroom to get a signature from a kid she never socializes with, if that is a sin at all, it is one of omission.

The kid on the other side of the lunchroom, however, might interpret that omission as either direct rejection or at least as something that diminishes her own status. I doubt that popular girls are meaner than other kids, but what they do is more visible, and sometimes their sins of omission are perceived as meanness.

3. Popular girls only care about being popular.

Abby, now safely in college, added this. Through most of middle school she says that she never thought about whether or not she was popular. She just really liked her friends. Popularity matters the most to the girls who don't quite have it.

A director at a private girls' school agrees. She told me that if you want to know who the truly popular girls are, ask all the girls to map the social hierarchy. The truly popular girls—the innermost circle—will be the ones who don't believe that there is one.

Abby now says that being popular is a label, and some kids simply want that label. They want the status, the power, of being popular far more than they want to associate with the specific individuals who are popular. "They would want to hang out with us," Abby now says about the kids who cared so much about popularity, "but it never seemed that they liked us."

4. Popular girls are obligated to act with the graciousness appropriate to their high social status.

Once it is formulated with such precision, I don't suppose that anyone would admit to believing this, but when you listen to parents talking about what the popular kids "should" have done, they do seem to believe that the popular girls are obligated—and have the skills—to make their children feel comfortable and validated.

"For almost everyone in American life, social status varies with the situation."

For almost everyone in American life, social status varies with the situation, and as adults we've learned to modify our behavior accordingly. If you go to a dinner as the boss—or worse—the boss's wife, you know that some of the younger people aren't going to be entirely comfortable with you so if you want there to be any conversation at all, you will need to put them at ease. Similarly, if I am the only published author at a dinner with people who haven't sold their first book, I am going to act differently than when I'm the only author who hasn't been on the *New York Times* bestseller list.

But that kind of ability to understand social situations and read social cues requires the knowledge and confidence that comes with experience. Twelve-year-old girls don't have those social skills.

Think about that girl who called her mother from the school dance because none of the popular kids had talked to her. Probably anxious when she came into the gym, she would have made little eye contact; at most she would have murmured a greeting. How were the popular girls to know what she wanted from them?

5. Popular girls are growing up too fast; they are boy-crazy clotheshorses.

I wish a sociologist would take the following as a hypothesis and see if it can be proven. I suggest that popular girls are, very often, not the oldest child in their family.

This goes against the common wisdom about leaders, that leaders are usually oldest children, but when we are talking about middle-school popularity, we are less talking about leadership than we are talking about group behavior, about fitting into a group, and second and third children may be a lot better at that than first children.

So if this is true, popular girls may seem, to parents of firstborns, like boy-crazy clotheshorses, because younger siblings have more information about popular culture than do first children. When Abby started middle school, she had been observing middle-school life for two years already, she had been listening to her sister's music, looking through her sister's preteen magazines, watching what her sister wore. She heard her sister and friends giggle about boys. So she simply knew more about how to be a cool middle-schooler than a first child can know. To a first-time parent she may have seemed too sophisticated.

I got this wrong in *A Most Uncommon Degree of Popularity*. Because I was interested in how involved mothers get in their children's lives, I made all the girls firstborns. But I think that the incident with the matching skirts would have required at least one of the girls to have had an older sister.

"When most people think about Austen, they think of her courtship plots. But there is so much else going on in her books."

6 Popular girls are having more fun than you and me.

This is probably true.

But that doesn't mean that if your child were invited to all the popular kids' parties, she would be having as much fun. Some people are simply livelier than others, some people adore the noise and confusion of a group. They are the ones who do seem to be having the most fun.

Fun-filled vivacious gatherings aren't for everyone. Other children are happiest with one close friend. They are satisfied with quiet and intimacy. They might or might not want the label "popular," but they don't want the social life of a popular kid which almost always involves a group.

But just because they are having "fun" doesn't mean that the popular kids are happy all the time. They are middle-schoolers, and that is a difficult age for anyone. Popular girls have a great many relationships, and managing them can be exhausting. Used to success, many of these kids are very afraid of failure. The principal of a large public middle school told me that if a popular girl comes into his office and starts to cry, she can't stop.

 # A Conversation with the Author

What got you started on this book?

Toward the end of my younger daughter's eighth-grade year, another woman invited me to tea at the Four Seasons and dropped $50 on food to find out who my thirteen-year-old had been inviting to the movies. At that point, I knew that there had to be a book in the middle-school drama we had been living through.

So the whole thing is true?

Actually not. The Alden School is entirely fictional, and the particular story line and characters of the book are fictional as well.

Two elements are "true." Some of the incidents of over-involved parenting are pretty close to things I have observed. I also hope that the socioeconomic detail is an accurate reflection of the way some people live.

Why did you title the book with a quote from Jane Austen . . . and then not give us Mr. Darcy?

Jane Austen didn't give you Mr. Darcy, at least not Colin Firth's gorgeous sexy version.

When most people think about Austen, they think of her courtship plots. But there is so much else going on in her books. For example, I've always loved her interest in the nuances of social status and manners, and if you're looking for people in contemporary American society who are obsessing about social status with every breath, middle-school girls are a good place to start.

In Austen's books, marriage is the most important choice a woman makes. In *Pride and Prejudice,* if Mr. Darcy does not come back to Longbourn, Elizabeth faces not only a loveless life, but one of poverty as well.

There's not much of a second act for her. But today's woman has a life after the first act. If she is disappointed in love at twenty-two—or even at forty-two or sixty-two—she can get out there and try to meet someone else in way that Elizabeth Bennet could not have. Furthermore, any heroine whom I like and respect is also going to be capable of supporting herself.

I believe that the relationship with the highest stakes is not the one you have with Mr. Darcy (or his real-life equivalent), but the one you have with your kids. If the parent-child relationship fractures, it's going to be pretty hard to come back after intermission and find a script for act two.

What was the hardest part about writing this book?

I had trouble with Lydia's trip to Houston. I had initially intended it to be a positive experience for her, but as my editor pointed out, the book needed a "make it worse" episode at that point, not a "feel good" moment.

So there were multiple rewrites. The scene in which Lydia's husband kicks her under the dinner table was the last piece of the book to be written. But I never rewrote the opening of her Houston visit, how Lydia greets Jamie in the hotel room. I have mixed feelings about the passage. Is it too strong and confident a gesture? Or does it provide a complex, interesting contrast with her getting kicked under the table? I'm not sure.

You have daughters. What about boys? Are popular boys as powerful as popular girls?

Certainly a book about mothers of sons would be different. While boys' mothers, of course, care deeply about their sons' happiness, they may identify less strongly with the ups and downs of the boys' emotional lives.

As for the boys themselves, many middle-school boys are not very interested in relationships yet; they don't

"Today's woman has a life after the first act."

look to other kids for social validation. But to the boy who does care, the popular boys may be even more powerful than the popular girls. Popular boys are budding alpha males—athletic, confident, with good organizational/leadership skills—budding Colin Firths. When a boy feels rejected by them, he may be devastated for all kinds of anthropological reasons that I don't know enough to talk about. And we give girls permission to be upset when they feel rejected; boys aren't supposed to mind, which must make it even harder for them.

*About the
Author*

Mary Noble Ourso

Read more about Kathy at
www.kathleengillesseidel.com

Look out for Kathy's next novel
Keep Your Mouth Shut and Wear Beige
Coming soon in hardcover from St. Martin's Press

Reading Group Questions

1. Jane Austen, speaking of perfect novels and heroines, said, "pictures of perfection make me sick and wicked." How might she view *A Most Uncommon Degree of Popularity*? Does it avoid "pictures of perfection"?

2. What do the four friends—Lydia, Mimi, Blair, and Annelise—have in common? Is it a good basis for a friendship?

3. Lydia had always thought of popular girls as "manipulative little blonde bitch-goddesses" only to discover that her daughter was one. What issues confront the mothers of popular girls? To what extent do you sympathize?

4. Lydia stops practicing law to stay at home. "I was afraid I would disappear if I quit work," she tells us. Does she disappear?

5. What challenges face professional women who decide to become stay-at-home moms? Would more women stay at home if they could afford to?

6. Lydia travels to Houston to visit Jamie.
Does the novel's depiction of marriage
seem too pessimistic? Too optimistic?

7. The novel is set in a "theme-park version of
a small town." Does this setting reflect a
trend in American culture that transcends
this affluent section of Washington, D.C.?
What is appealing about life in a small
town?

8. How valid are the meritocrat/aristocrat
class distinctions that Lydia makes?

9. We see the events of the novel through
Lydia's eyes. How would Mary Paige tell
this story? How would Chris Goddard?